TREACHEROUS WATERS

DAN WALSH

BAINBRIDGE PRESS

COPYRIGHT INFO

Treacherous Water

Joe Boyd Suspense Series – Book 4

Bainbridge Press

Editor - Cindi Walsh

ISBN: 978-1-7341417-7-1

Copyright © 2022 Dan Walsh

PROLOGUE

March 18, 1977
Just Outside of Culpepper, GA

TREVOR'S LEGS WERE KILLING HIM, RIDING UPHILL FOREVER ON this bike. "Guys, I don't know how much further I can go."

"Don't be such a wimp, Trev. We're almost there," said Davey Bogart, unelected leader, out in front.

"I don't know, Davey. I'm kinda with Trevor." Vic Waters, one bike behind Trevor. "You sure we didn't miss the curve that black fella was talking about? We passed three of 'em already."

"Would you guys stop?" Davey yelling over his shoulder. "Like riding with a bunch of old men. We're young. We can do this. And we ain't missed the curve yet. The man said it was at the top of the hill. Look like we reached the top yet? Not to me. But I see it just up ahead."

Trevor rode into the street a few feet to see past Davey's bike. The hill did end just up aways. A car appeared. Just crested the hill, coming right at them. Trevor whipped his bike back to the edge just in time. A blue Dodge, sailing past, horn blaring, Vic gave him the finger.

"What's that guy's problem?" Davey said, not seeing what happened.

Vic smiled at Trevor, neither answered back.

Trevor thought about that nice black guy at Hamptons' Quik-Stop. Saw their fishing poles. *You don't wanna fish at Lake Samson*, he'd said. *Everybody do that. You wanna fish at my secret hideout. Best fishing hole in all of Culpepper. But nobody knows it. Catch more trout than you boys can carry home. Big ones, too. Way bigger than folks pull out of the lake these days.*

Davey asked him if it was so good, why wasn't he out there himself?

Can't get to it no more. Need young legs to get down there.

They did some more talking. Convinced all three of them it was worth the extra thirty-minute bike ride into the winding hills outside of town.

So, here they were.

A few more agonizing minutes of pedaling, and they finally arrived. Like the man said, a curve at the top of a hill. Trevor looked around. The whole ride here, like this whole area west of town, tall trees everywhere. Not just evergreens neither. It's March. Spring break. That's why they were able to make this fishing trip on a weekday morning. Vowed last week they'd be out fishing every day.

"Okay," Davey said, walking his bike away from the road. "This is more like it."

Trevor and Vic followed. Also like the man said, right at the curve there'd be a clearing, nice grassy area. After about fifty feet, it blended into another area of thick shrubs.

"There's that big boulder the man talked about," said Vic. He put his kickstand down and headed over to it. "But I ain't seeing no path."

Davey came over. "Well, that old man said he ain't been here since he was younger. Maybe no one else has, either." Brushed the bushes and shrubs away, kicking at them with his feet. "Look, you can see it underneath all this."

Trevor and Vic hurried over. Sure enough, the more Davey pushed back, the more path could be seen. Not wide, but enough they could make it through single file.

"Well, I'll be." Vic smiling again.

Even Trevor joined in. Wasn't quite like following a treasure map, since they were only talking about fish. But still, having the best fishing hole in all of Culpepper to themselves? For every day of spring break?

"Should we yank out all these bushes for good?" Vic said. "Make the path clear for next time?"

"No, dummy," said Davey. "Want the whole world to know? I say we leave it be. Ain't that hard to push through." Looking to the bikes. "In fact, we should hide them in the bushes every time we come, so they can't be seen from the road."

After doing that, they headed down the path.

IT TOOK about fifteen minutes to make their way down the hillside to the water. Tricky business, with how steep it was and not losing the fishing poles and gear. But they got it done. Man, Trevor thought, the old man wasn't lying. Place was as private as it could be. They could still hear the occasional car driving by way over their heads. Down here, it was nothing but woods.

"Whoa," Vic said, "hope there ain't no bears 'round here. There is, we're done for."

"You ain't gotta worry about bears," Davey said. "Mountain lions. You wanna worry about something, worry about that."

"Really?" Dread on Vic's face.

"No, not really. Ain't no bears, and there ain't no mountain lions. Think that old man would-a kept coming back to this place if it were dangerous?"

"Guess not."

"No, he wouldn't. Now let's get to that pond and do some serious fishing."

Where they came down was more like a creek, the kind you'd see in any woods. Maybe eight to ten feet across. But he'd said you head north about fifty yards and it opens up into this great big pond. That's where they'd find all the fish. Davey led the way, then Trevor, then Vic. If they ever walked in a line anywhere, that's how they walked.

"Well, would you look at that?" Davey said. "It's all coming true."

Sure enough, they came to a pond that was easily fifty feet across and about the same distance long. Trevor was pretty happy now. How could everything else be true, and there not be any fish?

"And look at these flat rocks by the edge of the water," Vic said. "Like perfect little seats. Big enough for our butts and our gear."

In no time at all, they had their poles loaded up with worms. Davey was the first to cast. No surprise he took the center. Trevor and Vic cast out on either side of him. Those worms weren't in the water more than two minutes before — BANG! Trevor got hit. Biggest hit he ever got. He yanked back on the rod and set the hook like a pro.

Moments later, Davey and Vic got big hits, too. All three of them, reeling in like mad, poles arced over like they were about to snap. But all three boys landed their fish, biggest trout any of them had ever seen.

Trevor held his up, face beaming. "This baby's gotta be three pounds. At least."

"I bet mine's four," Davey said.

Course, that's what he'd say. If anything, his fish looked a little smaller than Trevor's. So what? They put all three fish in their baskets, re-baited the hooks, and cast out again. And again, in no time at all, they pulled in three more fish. This went on for about thirty minutes. Their arms were actually sore from fighting and reeling in fish.

Finally, Trevor realized a problem. He looked up at the hillside. "Hey, guys. Maybe we need to stop."

"Stop? Why would we ever do that?" Vic hooking another one.

Davey looked. Trevor pointed up. He got the message. "Hold on, Vic. Trevor's right."

"What?"

"We gotta carry all the fish we catch back up that hill," Trevor said. "Then ride 'em home on our bikes."

"Well, that part's not a problem," Davey said. "It'll be mostly downhill. But yeah, climbing up that hill with all these fish...and our gear?"

"Oh, yeah. I get it." Vic pulled in the fish he'd just caught, sighed. "Man, this has been amazing. Almost like a dream. Why do you figure the fishing's so good here? And why they're so big?"

Davey looked at the pond. Looked around. "I bet that water's deep. And because of this creek flowing in and out, it stays fresh. With all this tree cover, they don't gotta worry about eagles or hawks."

"And nobody fishes here," Trevor said. "Ever. With no fishermen and no predators, they can just grow and grow."

Vic looked down at their fish baskets. "I think we got more here than we can even eat. Maybe we can sell some of 'em."

"We could give some to the old man who told us about this place," said Trevor.

"Well," Davey said, "let's talk about that later. Right now, I think I want to take a swim. Cool off before we start that hike back up the hillside."

"Sounds like a plan," Trevor said.

Shirts and shoes off, all three dove in. Swam around about a half-hour.

Then Davey said, "You know, except right there at the shore, my feet have never touched bottom."

"Mine, neither," Trevor said.

"Wonder how deep it really is," said Davey.

"I'm the best swimmer," Vic said. "I'll go see."

He took a deep breath and, just like that, went under. Trevor and Davey swam over to the flat rocks, stood, and looked down. Just dark water and bubbles.

For the longest time.

"Shouldn't he be coming up?" Trevor said.

Davey, waiting to respond, felt like forever. "Yeah, he should be. Something ain't right."

1

Lake Samson,
Culpepper GA

As he stood at the edge of the lake, Trevor marveled that this day had finally come. Retirement. And like he'd always planned...early.

And he was getting to spend his first day exactly how he'd imagined it at least a thousand times over the last year while counting down the days — when he was bored out of his mind running the forklift at Madison's Furniture Warehouse. He had just launched his pride and joy, a little fifteen-foot fishing boat, named Lady Marie. He didn't care that most folks didn't name boats this small. The Lady Marie was named after his late wife, the love of his life, who passed away three years ago. How he wished she were going out with him today. Instead, he'd have to settle for an old friend he'd known since grade school.

But hey, it was still better than fishing alone.

The sun had just cleared the trees on the Eastern shore. Barely a cloud in the sky. Lots of boats of various sizes already out on the lake, although a fraction of what it could be if this was the weekend. But retired guys don't have to fish on the weekends, fighting the crowds. They could come out on a Tuesday, like today, or a Thursday, or any other day they pleased.

Being early September, there was a slight nip in the air. But that was good. Felt refreshing. The high today was supposed to be in the low 70s, so things would only get better from here.

He looked at his watch, glanced around the boat launch area. Where was he? A beep in his pocket. Pulled out his phone. It was him, texting.

Just around the corner. Don't leave without me.

As if he would. Trevor decided maybe he should hit the john one last time. Would be just like him to get the urge halfway out on the lake. He quickly tied Lady Marie to the dock, then pulled his truck and trailer into the closest parking spot. After taking care of business, he was happy to see his friend's blue Audi SUV pulling into the launch area.

Vic Waters saw him, waved as he pulled into the spot next to Trevor's truck. They had been friends through middle school but parted when Vic headed off to an upscale private high school, then onto Culpepper University, all made possible by Daddy's money. Whereas after high school, Trevor blended into the blue-collar world, where he'd stayed in one form or another until last week.

They'd reconnected about a year ago when Vic had visited the warehouse to replace a defective leather sofa. Apparently, damaged by the delivery crew. Trevor had been the one to fetch the new sofa and bring it out for the customer to inspect. Turned out, that customer was Vic.

Getting out of the car, dressed like a guy who's just paid a bundle at Bass Pro. "Sorry, I'm late. Hope the fish are still hungry."

"No problem, Vic. I'm sure they are. Boat's all ready to go, if you are."

"You did say you have fishing gear I could borrow?"

"Already in the boat."

"I'll get my own we start doing this more often."

Trevor made his way to the dock, Vic following.

"I hope that's how it goes," Trevor said. "I plan to be out here as much as possible, now that I've got the time."

"Yeah, congratulations on retiring. I know you've been wanting to do that for quite a while."

"Thanks. Would've liked to do it sooner but still got it done before I hit sixty. How'd you manage to get there before me?" Trevor knew Vic used to run a big pawnshop downtown.

"You'd be surprised how much money you can make in the pawn business," he said, "you play the game right. Ain't you ever seen that show *Pawn Stars*?"

Trevor motioned for Vic to get in the boat. He knew to get in the front. "Oh, I have. Fun show to watch. But I figured, they're in Vegas. This is...Culpepper." Trevor untied the rope, sat in his spot.

"True," Vic said. "But there's a surprising bunch of folks here with plenty of money to buy and sell things. We definitely did all right. And, let's just say, I invested well."

Trevor started the motor, and they headed out toward the first spot he had in mind. He'd heard rumors that Vic's pawnshop was also mixed up in the drug trade, as well as money laundering. But he'd never bring up something like that. "So, why'd you sell it?"

"Like anything, it gets boring. And it wasn't like I needed the money. Besides that, my oldest son was itching for me to get out of the way and let him take over."

"So, what've you been doing with your time? Since you haven't been fishing?"

"Yeah, this may be the first time I've fished since the days you, me, and Davey used to go. Mainly, I been golfing. And doing some traveling, you know, see the world."

Trevor and Marie had always wanted to travel. Didn't get too far. One road trip out West. Got to see the Grand Canyon, Carlsbad Caverns. Never made it to Yellowstone.

"Really nice out here," Vic said. "You usually catch fish when you come?"

"Almost always. Of course, hope to do even better now with this boat. And this nice little gizmo here." He tapped his digital fish-finder.

"Shows you where the fish are, right?"

"That's the idea."

"Course," Vic said, "I don't imagine — even with that thing — we'll ever do as good as that old fishing hole. That place was a gold mine."

Trevor smiled, nodded, memories came to mind. "I'm sure you're right about that. That old fella was right. Best fishing spot in Culpepper. Remember that first day? We hauled in so many, could barely get them up that hill."

"Yeah," Vic said, smiled. "I remember that first day how I scared you guys half to death when I went diving for the bottom."

Trevor shook his head. "We were both sure you were a goner. I'd never seen anyone stay underwater that long."

"Yeah, I could hold my breath for, like, two minutes I think. Back then anyway. But that's how deep that place was. I never did touch bottom."

They reached a place in the lake where Trevor had to redirect the boat to stay on course. He looked at the meter. "Not too deep right here. Maybe fifteen feet."

"I was way deeper than that. The creepiest thing was bumping into a couple of those big trout on my way up."

Ten minutes later, they reached the spot Trevor had picked. Although they couldn't see more than two feet below the surface, the fish-finder showed plenty of fish below and off to the right.

For the next three hours, Trevor and Vic stayed pretty busy hauling in more than their share of trout. The only problem was finding ones big enough to keep. The current regs said any less than sixteen inches had to be thrown back. It was fun catching them but both had their hearts set on a nice fish fry. Trout were real good eating fish. Trevor had moved to three different spots, pretty much the same story.

"How many keepers we got in the live well?" Vic said.

Let me check." Trevor opened the lid and counted. "Seven. Everybody seems nice and healthy."

"Seven," Vic repeated. "Between us, we must've caught a

dozen more than that. You sure we gotta, you know, follow the rules to a T?"

Trevor shrugged. "It's a pretty stiff fine you get caught with any under-sized fish. Don't want to take a chance. These guys are good-sized, should make a couple good meals for each of us. That last one you caught was a big boy. Reminded me of the fish we used to catch at the hillside fishing hole."

"Yeah, I don't think we ever caught any smaller than sixteen inches," Vic said. "Course, back then we didn't have to worry about rules."

Trevor sighed, remembering. This was a pretty fun experience overall. But he had to admit, didn't even come close to the joy of fishing that hole. "All the fish we could ever hope to eat, and made some nice money selling the extras to the River Bend Restaurant."

Vic smiled, cast out again. "Way more fun making money that way than mowing lawns."

Trevor held onto his pole a few minutes, remembering. "I wonder what that place is like now."

"The fishing hole?"

"Yeah," Trevor said. "Maybe we should go back there tomorrow, give it a try. I doubt anyone's fished there since we did as kids."

Vic shot a look, reeled in for another cast. "You're kidding, right? Tell me you're kidding."

"No, why would I be kidding? Aren't you curious what it would be like? I bet the fish are just as big and there's just as many as the last time we were there."

"Trevor, we're both getting up there. You forgetting the

path down to that spot? You'll break your neck you try going back there."

"What? Nah, it wasn't that steep. And I'm not in that bad a shape for an old guy. You're the one who got all squishy around the middle."

"Hey."

"I'm just saying. I think I could make it down that hillside path, no sweat."

"Well, I think you'd be making a big mistake. If you go, you'll have to make the trip without me. But I really think you should forget about it. This ain't so bad here. Beautiful day, great scenery, good company. So, we gotta throw back most of the fish. We still got plenty." He cast out again.

"Yeah," Trevor said. But for the next hour, he couldn't stop thinking about it.

2

Same Day
Culpepper Police Department

WITH THEIR FIVE-MONTH-OLD SURPRISE BABY, SAM, BREAKING up his sleep every night, Lieutenant Joe Boyd made the executive decision to switch his coffee back to high-octane. Kate had him drinking decaf the last few years, but that just wasn't cutting it anymore. He loved that little guy, but man, he'd forgotten how hard it was with babies at this age. He was freshly amazed that the expression *sleeping like a baby* had ever become a thing. Unless one meant by it waking up every two hours for a snack or because you pooped your pants.

The office door behind him opened. He knew it was his partner, Hank, by the way his new shoes clicked on the floor.

"Thought I'd head downstairs and get this before coming

in this morning." Hank dropped a big cardboard box on the worktable between their two desks. Still sharing the same office.

Joe swiveled in his chair, recognized it instantly. The Cold Case Box. "Good idea. We need to pick out another one pretty quick. Before the Captain assigns us one of his new community relations gigs."

"What I was thinking, too," Hank said. "After the way that meth case went down last week." He sat, took off the box lid.

Yeah, Joe thought, that didn't turn out too good. The department's reputation took a hit in the local news and social media. Seemed like the wider audience failed to grasp the big picture. The meth lab was completely shut down and the perps spared the taxpayers the high cost of a lengthy trial and imprisonment when they blew themselves up, along with their equipment, and the balance of their stash.

No way to know if it was an accident or one of them deciding no way were they going back to prison. Problem was, the explosion was so powerful it destroyed the homes on either side. Innocent civilians. Hard-working people. One young couple, their first house. Their dream house. They'd spent years saving for it. Another year remodeling it after moving in. In a moment, in a flash, it got leveled. A sad story, for sure. But hey, the upside was, none of these innocents were home at the time. Only the perps died.

That part of the story wasn't emphasized.

Joe took a sip, watched Hank thumbing through the folders. "Should be a list in the front of the box, citing all the different cases with a little summary for each. Unless you enjoy doing it the hard way."

Hank stopped, found the list. "When did you do this?"

"I didn't. Remember that intern we had over this summer? She needed a project. Should be a couple copies. Why don't you hand me one?"

Hank did, started reading it over. "These in any special order? Certainly aren't by date. Order of importance maybe?"

"No," Joe said. "That would make too much sense. Apparently, I failed to give the intern sufficient instructions. So, she just listed them in the order they were in the box."

Joe started reading through the first one on the list. Before he finished, Hank looked up.

"Talking about cold cases, how's Sam doing? I don't mean your Sam, I mean the Sam you named him after?"

Joe smiled. "Glad you cleared that up. Didn't think we had a cold case file on my Sam. But the other Sam's doing great. More than great, I think. Know where he is right now? Spending some of that settlement money. He's on a ten-day Caribbean cruise. Kate helped him set it up. It's the same one we took on our twentieth." Joe looked at the calendar. "Right now, he should be out on his balcony heading toward the island of Dominica."

Hank shook his head. "That's so good to hear. Not every day we get cases turn out that way." Looked back at the list. "So, should we just go eeny-meany-miny-mo?"

"Well, we gotta start somewhere. Maybe we should just take turns reading them out loud, see if any of them start talking to us."

Hank, eyes still down at the list, "You know what would have been really nice? If the intern could've given us a little more info on each case. Maybe take out the file for each one, make a list of the evidence we still have."

"That would've been nice," Joe said. "Too bad you weren't here when I gave her this project."

"Because really," Hank said, "that's probably the thing that's gonna matter most, picking which one to start next. We have enough evidence to make a difference? Enough to even make a start?"

Joe knew instantly he was right. Some of these cases probably didn't have a prayer of ever getting solved this side of heaven. "Tell you what, while I refresh my coffee, why don't you take out the files for the first three or four of these? Spread them out on the table. We really are gonna need that info to make this work." Joe stood. "Be right back. Want some coffee?"

"No, I'm good."

Joe came back, set his mug down. Hank had the box shoved off to one side, and three files laid out on the table. He was reading a fourth. "That the first one in the box?"

Eyes looking up, Hank said, "Yeah. Can pretty much tell already this one'll wind up in the hopeless pile."

Joe sat, put his legs up on the corner of the table. "Why's that?"

"Eddie Simmons, age 12," Hank reading aloud. "Killed by a hit-and-run driver, eleven o'clock. January 31st, 1986. A Friday night. No witnesses, even though it happened on a busy street. South end of Haley Road. No skid marks."

"So," Joe said, "the driver hits him at full speed. Probably killed him right away. Speed limit on Haley is thirty-five."

"Could've been going faster than that," Hank said. "A kid

from the University out drinking on a Friday night. Racing down the road without a care."

"That could be." Joe took a sip. "If he was drunk, that'd be plenty of motivation not to stop.

"Wonder if he even stopped long enough to check on the kid?"

Joe got to thinking. "If this was a kid out drinking on a Friday, seems likely he had friends in the car. Eleven PM's way too early for a college kid to head home by themselves on a Friday night."

Hank looked at the file again. "Nope, no witnesses. If there were any in the car, they never spoke up."

Seemed hard to fathom. Keeping your mouth shut all this time about something like that. "That's over thirty-five years ago. I can see friendship and loyalty counting for something. At least in the beginning. You kept in touch with any of your college buddies?"

"Joe, come on. You think I was a Culpepper graduate? I barely made it through the Academy. Made some good friends, though, some guys I hung around with a lot. But after I started working at the department, we saw each other a few times in the beginning, but then pretty much went our separate ways. Most of them went on to bigger opportunities than they could get here in Culpepper."

"Even still," Joe said, "you're kinda making my point. That was only what, ten, twelve years ago, right? Not thirty-five. Would you keep a secret like this — if one of those buddies killed a kid – with you in the car? For over thirty-five years?"

"Not a chance," Hank said. "Course, seeing as I was in the Academy, I would have them arrested on the spot. But I do get your point."

"That could be one place to start," Joe said. "If we could find who the driver's friends were."

"That's a big IF, Joe." He looked back at the file. "There's absolutely nothing here. Can't find the driver's friends if we don't know who the driver was. Not a single person we can talk to."

Joe took another few sips. No one spoke. Then Joe said, "Yeah, close it up. Let's look at the next one."

3

THE FOLLOWING MORNING, TREVOR DECIDED TO FOLLOW
through on the "crazy idea" he'd talked to Vic about
yesterday out on the lake. He didn't know why Vic was so
opposed to even trying it, unless maybe he was just so
embarrassed about how he'd let himself go. Now that he'd
driven to the hill that overlooked their hidden fishing hole, it
was clear Vic — in his present state — could never make the
hike down. But Trevor didn't mind. Jury was still out on
whether he wanted to make Vic his new fishing buddy.

He wasn't that hard to be with, but Trevor wasn't sure
they really clicked. "He certainly doesn't hold a candle to
you, boy." Trevor reached over in the passenger seat and
scratched Seymour, his three-year-old black lab, behind the
ears. "You're going to be my fishing buddy today."

Seymour just smiled back, thumped his tail on the seat.
Trevor could tell he was eager to get out. "Just gimme a
minute to get my stuff together, then I'll come get you."

It wasn't that hard finding the place. He'd been here so

many times back in the day. But now the pull-off spot was blocked by a guard rail, hardly any clearing left at all. He'd better keep Seymour on a leash till they got well down the hillside path. He pulled his fishing pole and backpack out of the bed of his truck. Figured going downhill, better to stick his tackle box in a backpack. A red sedan came whipping around the curve and then headed down the other way. Trevor's eyes tracked an imaginary line between the curve of the road and the edge of the hill, knowing that just on the other side of those shrubs was a sheer drop off — maybe a hundred feet — straight down to the fishing hole.

Figured probably a good thing they added that guard rail around the curve. Wasn't there when they were kids. "Okay, boy. You can come out now." Trevor opened the truck door. "But you got to stay on the leash...for now."

Seymour jumped down and quickly headed for the nearest bush. He minded well ever since Trevor hired a dog trainer, about two years ago. Prior to that, he'd all but yank Trevor's shoulder out of its socket whenever they'd go for a walk. He bought him as a pup shortly after Marie had passed on the advice of his son, Rob. Trevor was so glad he listened, because Seymour and he were best buds at the house. And he hardly ever felt lonely anymore.

"Over this way, Seymour." Trevor found that big rock they used as a marker for the path. Took more effort than he'd imagined to relocate the actual path under all the over-growth. Guess it was fair to say, no one else had used it in decades. The thought made him smile, all the trout just down there breeding and getting fatter. He held the bushes back as best he could to let Seymour through.

A flash memory. Davey yelling at Vic the first time they

came here, Vic asking if they should pull out all the bushes to make the entrance easier to see. Davey was so concerned someone else would discover their special spot. Davey Bogart. He'd moved away before tenth grade. Somewhere out west. Hadn't heard anything about them since.

Well, regardless of Davey's decree to leave the entrance all covered up, Trevor decided he ever came back here again, he'd be bringing his big branch loppers, make that path nice and wide.

It took Trevor at least thirty minutes to get down to the creek level. Poor Seymour, left to himself, probably could've made it down in three. But he had to keep stopping every few steps for Trevor to secure his footing. He had no idea if he was following the original path. That wasn't a priority. Not breaking his neck was. He did have his cell phone in his pocket and confirmed there was a signal before making the hike. Something did happen, he doubted Seymour would do anything but run away.

Another memory. Watching black and white episodes of Lassie as a kid. Could always count on Lassie to run and get help if ever little Timmy was in trouble. Course, as an adult Trevor read an article about the collie he'd adored in his youth. Turns out, Lassie wasn't actually Lassie. Or at least nothing like the Lassie depicted on the show. There were, in fact, nine different collies that played Lassie, and all of them male. And Timmy never really was in danger, and Lassie never really did go for help.

If Trevor slipped and fell, he'd rely on good *old-fashioned* digital technology.

As he carefully made his way along the creek's edge, he

could see the pond up ahead. Getting closer, he realized something he hadn't noticed back then. The pond was actually created by a wide, multi-layered beaver dam, abandoned by the little critters ages ago. Whatever the cause, he was grateful that dam had held all these years. When he got to the row of flat rocks, he just stood there and smiled. So many fun memories in this very spot. Seymour, who had been exploring a bit, came up and sat behind him.

Trevor took advantage of the moment and re-clipped his leash to his collar. "Sorry, boy. Now that we're down here, I'm just not comfortable with you being loose." He wrapped the handle-side around a small pine tree. Seymour didn't seem too bothered. He took a long drink from the pond and lay down.

Trevor set his backpack down, pulled out the tackle box. These days he didn't have to resort to finding worms, had a whole array of fishing lures. Pulled out the one that worked best with trout and attached it to his line. Looked into the deep, dark water remembering the moment Vic finally appeared after diving underwater, trying to reach the bottom. Then he glanced around at the scene, grateful to be here, at this age.

Retired, fishing, here with his buddy Seymour.

This was going to be a fine day.

It was nice casting out without worrying about tangling on someone else's line. This was the first time he'd fished here alone. He'd barely got the lure in the water and had just started the little jigging motion he'd practiced when — WHAM! A bigger hit than he'd gotten all day yesterday with Vic. Quickly, he set the hook and began reeling in. Seymour stood up and started barking. Trevor was just about to quiet him, when he figured why? He was fishing, not hunting. The fish fought hard for about thirty seconds, but soon Trevor had him up on the rocks.

Seymour came over to inspect the situation. "What do you think, buddy? Ain't he something?" Seymour lunged at the fish. Trevor scolded him gently. "You lay back down now. Can't be attacking my fish." Trevor had already set up a stringer, added this fish to the first slot, and dropped it in the water.

He laughed out loud. Just as good as he remembered. He cast out again. Took a tad longer this time, but sure enough, another big hit. Two minutes later, another big trout on his stringer. Seymour got up again but behaved. Trevor cast out again...three more times. And hauled in three more fish.

At that point, he had a thought. He was catching these trout no deeper than two or three feet beneath the surface. Vic had dived down and never reached the bottom. How big must the fish be hanging out down there? Quickly, he switched rigs for one meant to be used in bottom fishing. Seymour watched intently. "Let's see how this works, boy."

Trevor cast it out right in the middle. Heard a ker-plunk, saw the big splash. He let the line run out a good ways until it finally stopped on the bottom. He started reeling it in, slowly. Finger on the line, trying to sense the first sign of a hit.

Then it came. He hauled back on the pole and set the hook. "Oh. My. Goodness." This fish had to be huge. The pole was bent over so far he thought it might break. He stopped a couple of times to make sure he wasn't snagged on the bottom, but he felt whatever it was still moving, so he kept at it. Looked over at Seymour, now standing beside him. "This thing's gotta weigh ten-fifteen pounds."

He kept reeling it in, praying the line wouldn't break. Finally, he saw a glimmer about three feet down. Something was wrong. He expected it to be at least two to three feet long. It was only eight to ten inches, at best. "What the heck?" Finally, it broke the surface. He couldn't believe his eyes.

Seymour walked over to the edge, sniffing, as Trevor finished reeling. Afraid the line might break after all this, he grabbed his net and lifted it out of the water. "Well, I'll be."

He pulled it out of the net and held it up to eye level. It was an old, rusty sideview mirror. What a disappointment. Just an old piece of car junk. Carefully, he freed his lure from the mirror, set the pole down against the rocks, and turned the mirror around in his hands. Didn't seem right just to throw it back, be like littering. "How in the world did you get down there?"

Really, why would someone throw an old car mirror into the pond? As soon as he thought this, he realized...they wouldn't. Then another thought. Maybe no one had thrown it into the pond. Maybe it had just detached from the car it had been attached to. He looked back into the deep, dark water.

And maybe that car was still down there.

Slowly, his eyes traced the line from the center of the pond upward to the top of the hill. Then it hit him. This car mirror was old. Very old. What if — back up there on the hill by the road...before they'd put in that guard rail — a car came whipping around that curve, missed the turn, and went straight instead? It could've sailed right off the edge—straight down into this fishing hole.

He sighed. Nobody knows about this place. Nobody ever comes here.

Which meant...he looked back toward the murky water.

4

AFTER SPENDING ALL DAY YESTERDAY AND MOST OF THE morning reading through the cold case files, Joe was really glad most of this job did *not* involve sitting behind a desk. They had worked through almost a dozen. Maybe half were in the stack unofficially called "Unsolvable." It didn't mean they would never get solved. Just meant there was absolutely nothing to go on, not one shred of evidence to revisit, no DNA specimens to process.

Just nothing.

Really, for those cases, something would have to come in from out of the blue. Some witness coming forward who saw what happened but was afraid to talk back then— maybe now on their deathbed — they want to come clean. Something like that. Joe had just asked Hank to put the unsolvable files back in the box. They decided to spend what was left of the morning and the rest of the day narrowing down the remaining files till they had made their choice. Something they could take to Captain Pendleton, and say definitively: "This is what we're working on next."

Hank spread them out on the table. "Okay, we got five left."

"Any of these stand out to you?" Joe said. "Like, if you were making the call, you know which one you'd pick?"

Hank shook his head no. "I think that hit-and-run case is still in the running. You know, the twelve-year-old kid that got run over on his bike." On a hunch, they'd decided this one deserved another look. "And I like that used car lot owner who got killed in a so-called robbery-gone-bad."

"Yeah, I got my eye on that one, too. Feels like the detectives who ran that one just weren't that interested. The guy was a total jerk, did lots of people wrong with rip-off deals. All the guys who worked for him hated him. And we're supposed to believe some nameless punk killed him over the money he had in his wallet?"

"I know," Hank said. "Doesn't add up. And the nice part about this one, did a quick check...all the folks listed in the report are still alive, and most still live here in Culpepper."

"Okay," Joe said. "That one goes to the top of the pile. But let's give these other three a once-over before we decide."

TREVOR GOT out of his car at the Culpepper PD parking lot, feeling a little stupid. That morning, after catching as many trout as he could haul up that hill, he'd made his way back to his car with that rusty sideview mirror in his backpack. The whole time he was filleting those beautiful fish, he was wrestling with whether he should do what he was doing right now. After putting the trout fillets in the freezer, he decided to just do it. It's not like they'd make fun of him in there, some stupid old man coming in with some cockamamie theory. He was sure they'd be polite, listen to what he said, then talk about him behind his back once he got back in his car.

He could live with that.

What he couldn't live with was doing nothing, then wondering if some car was sitting at the bottom of the fishing hole with some dead body in it. He walked up the steps, opened the glass door, and stepped inside. There was a counter with a nice young lady behind it looking at a screen, talking on a headset. Their eyes met, she smiled, waved him forward. Gave him a one-minute signal with her finger. He nodded, set his canvas bag on the counter.

She finished taking some complaint from some fine citizen. Sounded like they were mad about that ridiculous traffic light on Madeleine and Vine. Stupid left turn signal only stayed green long enough to let four cars through. Then you had to wait ten minutes for your turn to come around again, even after hours when no one else but you was sitting at the light.

She pushed a button, apparently hanging up, and looked up at him. "Can I help you?"

"Uh, yeah. Maybe you can. But before I tell you what I got in this here bag, can I add my Amen to that caller ranting about the light at Madeleine and Vine? I thought about calling somebody on that thing a half-dozen times."

She laughed. "Yeah, I know. I'll pass it on, but I don't think anyone cares. The ones that could do something about it anyway. So, what did you bring me today?"

"I'm going to take a wild guess," he said, "that no one has

ever brought you anything like what I'm about to give you right now."

She sat up. "Sounds exciting."

"Naw, don't want to get your hopes up. More like weird, or at least peculiar." He unzipped the bag, pulled out the sideview mirror, which he had cleaned up as best he could.

"Oh, my. That looks like..."

"A sideview mirror?"

"Something like that."

"Well, believe it or not, I was fishing this morning and thought I had landed at least a ten-pound whopper." He went on to tell her the rest of the story and why he had decided to come there with this thing.

HANK AND JOE were discussing one of the three remaining cold case files when the phone rang. Hank could see it was the front desk and picked up. "Hey Eileen, Hank here. You wanting to talk to me or Joe?"

"You'll do just fine, Hank. I got this fellow out here named Trevor Burbank. He came in with a fairly odd...artifact, I guess you'd call it. Something he literally fished out of a pond."

"That's interesting, Eileen. Joe and I are kind of in the middle of something. You sure this is something you should be sending our way? We're homicide detectives, you know."

"I did know that, Hank. After hearing him explain what it was, and what he thought about it...well, I think you should hear him out, see what you think."

"Okay, I'll be there in a couple."

"What's that about?" Joe said.

Hank explained, said he'd be back in a few minutes.

Joe stood. "That's okay. I need a bathroom break anyway."

Hank followed him out of the office, turned the opposite way in the hall toward the front desk. When he got there, he saw Eileen sitting at her reception counter having a nice chat with an older man, looked to be mid-sixties. He'd already forgotten his name. Walking up, he held out his hand. "Hi, I'm Sergeant Hank Jensen. Eileen says you brought in something I should have a look at."

As they shook, the man said, "My name's, Trevor. Just convinced this young lady to stop calling me Mr. Burbank."

"Okay, Trevor. So, what...? Hank didn't need to finish. He slid what he had brought across the counter. An old rusty car part resting on a canvas bag. "Is that a—"

"Sidemirror?" Trevor said. "Yes, it is. I was fishing this morning at a fairly hidden and unknown spot out there on Route 40. Probably have to take you there since there's nothing on either side of it—"

"That's a fascinating story, Trevor. But I don't see how—"

"Give him a second, Hank," Eileen said.

"Go on."

"Anyway, if you could see this spot, you'd immediately know, there's no way someone tossed this old sideview mirror in that pond. It makes no sense at all. Oddly enough, what makes way more sense to me, is that it rusted off the car it was formally attached to. And I believe that car is sitting at the bottom of this fishing hole."

"Okay," Hank said. "And what makes you think a car is sitting at the bottom of your fishing hole? How would it have gotten there?"

"In a very tragic way I'm afraid," Trevor said. "Probably be better if I could show you what I mean."

5

AT FIRST, JOE THOUGHT ABOUT JUST SENDING HANK TO CHECK out this fishing hole with Trevor. Then he thought, why do that? He needed to get out and away from this desk for a while. When they got out of the parking lot, Hank suggested they follow him to the spot, but Trevor said he wasn't sure there was room for two cars by the side of the road. So, they told Trevor to hop in their back seat and give directions.

It was a familiar route for everyone involved, the main road anyone took from this side of town if you were heading toward Lake Samson. They started climbing one of the many hills along the way when Trevor said, "It's right up ahead, at the top of this hill. You get a little closer, you'll see the guardrail on the curve. Just before that, there's room to pull over. Though not much. When we were kids, that guardrail wasn't there. But now it's blocking a nice little clearing. Without it, probably could get two or three cars in there easy."

"I remember when they put that guardrail in," Hank said.

"First year I was in the department. One night some guy took the turn too fast and went sailing into that clearing you're talking about. Would have kept going except he smashed into this big rock."

"Yeah, I know that rock well. We used it to mark the path that leads down to the creek."

"I know after they looked into it more," Hank said, "a decision was made to put in that guardrail." Thought a moment. "Didn't ring a bell at the time but I remember one of the city councilman saying they had better, cause if that guy drove a few feet to the right, he would've missed that rock and gone sailing over that cliff."

"If Trevor's right," Joe said, "they were too late. Somebody already had."

Trevor pulled the car mirror out of his canvas bag. "Wonder what make and model this thing belongs to? And what year?"

"We got a mechanic takes care of all our department vehicles," Hank said. "He's like an encyclopedia of car parts. We'll get him to look at it. Might know it off the top of his head."

When Joe got to the top of the hill, he found things just as Trevor said. There was room to pull over, but just enough. They pulled the orange cones out of the trunk and set them on both ends of the car, just to make sure. They stepped over the guardrail and into the clearing. Trevor pointed to the big rock, as if that was necessary.

"I was planning to come back with my loppers to clear all the brush away from the path," he said. "But now that you folks are involved, not sure if you want me to stay away for a little while. It's just right here to left of this rock."

"Don't worry about it now," Joe said. "Not really dressed to take a hike. Just want to get a sense of the situation, decide where we go from here."

"Uh, okay. That's fine."

"Although, if you do think there's merit for it," Hank said, "we're probably going to need to get down there to the water's edge at some point."

"I agree," Joe said. "Likely going to need to get some divers to go down there, verify that there is a car that goes with this mirror." Looking at Trevor. "So, if you're willing, we would definitely like your help showing our guys the best way down."

Big smile on Trevor's face. "Be my pleasure." Walked from the rock further into the clearing, away from the road. "See all these bushes and shrubs here. If I were to push my way through, maybe five to ten feet, I'd come to the edge of the cliff. Drops straight off, goes down about a hundred feet. When I was down there by the water, just after I pulled up this mirror, I looked straight up, right to this point here. I'm thinking some poor soul, years back, missed that turn but wasn't lucky enough to hit that rock. He just kept speeding right on past, through these shrubs and straight down into the drink."

"Shrubs might not have even been there back then," Hank said.

"Could be right," Trevor said.

Joe looked the whole thing over a few minutes. Walked back to the trunk, pulled out a machete.

"What are you doing, Joe?" Hank said.

Looking at Trevor, said, "Not that I don't believe you. Because I do. But I'm thinking we need to hack away some of these shrubs, maybe four or five feet wide, right to the edge of the cliff. And take some pictures. It's gonna cost some decent money to get the dive team down there. And if they do find a car, it's gonna cost a whole lot more money to get a crane up here to haul it out."

"Not to mention having to take out the guardrail to get the crane in here," Hank said. "Judging by the size of this clearing, may even need to shut down one of the lanes out there." Pointing to the road.

"Yep, all that," Joe said. "Why we're gonna need to take some decent pictures, show all this to our captain."

Hank came up, reached for the machete. "Here, let me do that." Joe gave him a look. "I'll be careful," Hank said.

"Just the same, I want to tie a safety rope around your waist. Those shrubs are pretty thick. You get too close to that edge while you're hacking away...anyway, humor me."

TEN MINUTES LATER, Hank had done a good job opening up a wide swath through the bushes and shrubs. Sure enough, they ended right at the cliff's edge. Funny thing was, every time he got close, he yelled back at Joe, "You got a hold of that rope?" After a few times, Joe tied his end to a sturdy oak and assured Hank that even if he couldn't hold on, Hank wouldn't fall more than ten or fifteen feet before the slack in the rope gave out and the oak tree took hold.

When he was done, he carefully glanced down. "Joe, you need to come see this. Bring your phone to get some pics."

They tied a rope around Joe, and he made his way slowly to the edge. Soon as he looked down, he knew. "Yeah, very easy for me to believe a car going the right speed would drop right into that water below." He took several pics, then backed out and took some more of the whole trail between the road and the opening Hank had cut through the shrubs.

"Mr. Burbank," he said, "Trevor, think you might be onto something here. No way to know for sure until we get a dive team down there. But I don't think it'll be hard to make a case to get that done."

"Know when that'll happen?"

"Maybe a couple of days. Do we have your phone number?"

Hank suggested he give it to him out loud, then called his number right then. "We got it now."

"We'll definitely be in touch, sir," Joe said, extending his hand. "Appreciate you being such a good citizen. Somebody else might've just thrown that car mirror back in the water."

"Not the way I was raised," Trevor said. "Although, I'm being honest, hope I'm wrong about all this. Because that means some poor driver's been down the bottom of that pond, inside that car, for who knows how many years?"

"I have a feeling you're not wrong," Joe said.

"Okay if I still fish down there till your dive team's ready?"

"I don't see why not. Although, might steer clear of any bottom fishing for now."

Trevor made a face. "On second thought, might be too creepy fishing down there, knowing there's a dead body so close."

"Up to you, Trevor," Hank said. "Although, I doubt there's much of a body. If it's been down there all these years—long enough for that mirror to rust off—fish probably picked it clean."

He made an even worse face. "Kinda makes a man want to think twice about eating them trout I caught. They got dead body parts in their belly."

"You should be okay," Joe said. "Could've been decades ago. Don't think trout live anywhere near that long."

"Your probably right," Trevor said. "Even so, I'll have to give it some thought."

6

JOE HAD TO WAIT TILL THE FOLLOWING DAY TO BRIEF CAPTAIN
Pendleton on the situation with the fishing hole. He was on
his way to Pendleton's office now. Hank was bringing the car
mirror to the department's mechanic, see if he could get a
bead on the make and model of the car it came from, hopefully also the year.

Joe opened the outer door, smiled at Marsha, his secretary. "The big man in? Supposed to be expecting me."

"He is...to both questions. Go on in."

Joe found Pendleton on the phone, sounded like a
conversation with his wife, so Joe stood off at a distance.
Pendleton swung around in his chair, saw him, waved him
over to one of the chairs in front of his desk.

"Joe's here, gotta go, my dear. Love you. Bye." He hung up.
Looked up at Joe. "Saved me. She was just about to read off a
list of things she wanted me to pick up on the way home." He
leaned back in his chair. "So, what's this I hear about some
car at the bottom of a pond?"

"So, you read the email. Did you see the pictures I attached?"

"There were pictures?"

Geez. Joe took a whole paragraph to describe them. "Yeah, they were the attachments to the email." Pendleton hated emails. This was a guy who really needed to retire soon. Joe wanted to say, how about I go out get some coffee while you look at the emails I sent, like you should've done yesterday? Wanted to. He doubted Pendleton would approve the expense of the dive team without them. What Joe did was stare at Pendleton long enough for him to feel what Joe was thinking.

He opened his laptop. "Let me dig up that email, see if I can figure out how to see these pictures. While I do, tell me again what you think this is."

"Of course, we won't know for sure till we get the dive team down there, but we are pretty convinced —Hank and me— that at some point years ago out on 40, way before they put up the guardrail that's out there now, a car missed a sharp turn and went sailing off this cliff. Dropped straight down into this deep fishing hole with the driver still inside, obviously. And who knows, maybe some passengers, too."

"Okay, here they are." Pendleton, staring at the screen. "How is it possible something like this could've happened and no one has known about it till now?"

"Because, nobody knew. I mentioned in my email how remote this place is. You can see from the pics, nothing but woods all around. Hank and me didn't go down the path to where the pond was, the fishing hole. But from listening to this fella who found the car mirror, he and his friends been fishing at the spot since he was a kid. They've never seen anyone down there but them. We wouldn't have even known there was a path down the hill if he didn't pull back a bunch of bushes and show us. And you know how it is out there along route 40. Curvy roads, winding hills, not a lot of traffic. This could've happened at night. Nobody saw it go over. No one out there to hear the sound of the crash when it hit the water." The whole time, Pendleton looking at the pics.

"What year did they put that guardrail in?"

"Not sure. I'll find out. Hank says he remembers when it happened, shortly after he joined the department."

"So longer than ten years," Pendleton said.

"Yeah."

"You checked for any missing persons reports?"

"Not yet. Of course, would be a lot easier if we knew when this happened. Otherwise, we'll be digging through boxes of files. That's why I'd like to get the dive team right on it. They confirm there's a car, it'll really help narrow down the search."

He looked up. "Think I know the curve where this happened. You guys do confirm the car's down there, we're going to have one heck of a time yanking it out."

Joe nodded. "It's at least a hundred-foot drop."

Pendleton sighed. "Yeah. Then we're talking a crane, a whole union crew, blocking off the road..." Staring at the screen again. Without looking up, "Well, guess we got no choice then. Go ahead and get it going."

Mission accomplished. Joe stood, restrained a smile.

Pendleton sat back in his chair. "How you guys coming with your next cold case? Saw Hank in the hall yesterday morning, said you guys were narrowing down the list."

"That's accurate. Think we're looking at three. We'll

choose one of them in a day or two. Could've had it done today, but you know...this thing here."

"Right. Well, let me know which one you pick. People ask me about it in town. Gotta keep this squad's good reputation going. You know we took a dip with that meth lab blowing to smithereens."

"I know, Cap. I know." He headed back to his office.

BEFORE HE GOT THERE, he met Hank coming in the side door carrying that little canvas bag with the car mirror in it. His face all smiles. "Let me guess, we know what kind of car that mirror belongs to?"

"You got that right," Hank said. "The make, the model, and well, almost the year. Mechanic knew without even looking it up. A Chevy Camaro Z28, probably mid-8os."

"Is that right?" They got to their office, Joe opened it and let Hank in first. "A beautiful car to be sitting at the bottom of a fishing pond all these years."

Hank sat at his desk, set the bag down on the table, pulled out the mirror. "Actually, I can't agree. Those mid-80's models had ugly grills. The earlier ones from the late 60s and 70s were way cooler. Even the ones they got now. To me, a car like that, gotta have a hot looking grill."

"Really? I didn't know you were such a vintage car aficionado."

"I'm not. Not really. Mechanic showed me a book he had. Showed all these high-performance cars like the Z28, Mustang GT, and the Corvette. Bunch of others, and how they changed through the years. Way before my time. But they took an ugly stick to the Z28 in the mid-80s. Mustang, too."

"Well," Joe said, "my guess is, whichever year in the mid-80s this car turns out to be, when we pull this thing out of the pond, it's going to be ugly from top to bottom."

"So, Pendleton approved the dive team?"

"He did, reluctantly. You'd think he was paying for this out of his kids' college fund. You want to get on that, set it up? I'll keep trying to narrow down our next cold case file."

"Already on it," Hank said. "Anticipating a yes from your pitch to Pendleton, I called a diving outfit that works on the north end of Lake Samson. You know, by those caves. He said they'd definitely be up for a project like that."

"How soon could they do it?"

"They could be out there tomorrow morning."

"Really? Well, let's do it. Call him back. Guess I better call Trevor, give him a little heads up, case he had plans to go fishing there tomorrow."

7

THE NEXT MORNING, JOE WAS TAKING IT A LITTLE EASY, drinking his second cup of coffee at the dinette table. Usually, he drank it at his desk. But he and Hank had discussed it, thought Joe should be there when the dive team went in the water. They were showing up at 9 AM, about thirty minutes from now. With the drive there, gave him about another ten minutes till he had to leave.

Heard the car pull up in the driveway, Kate home from dropping the kids off at school. Hadn't mentioned to her his first task of the day. Debating about whether he should.

She came in from the garage entrance to the kitchen. "You still here? Telecommuting today?" Laughed at her own joke, as if a cop could work remotely.

"Wish I could do something like that today."

She set her purse down on the counter, refilled her coffee. "What they got you doing? I thought you were in between cases."

"Technically, we are. Supposed to tell Pendleton which cold case we're working on by the end of the day. But something kinda creepy fell into our laps." He told her all about Trevor, the fishing hole, the car mirror, the meeting with Pendleton.

"That's interesting. Never a dull moment around this town. Well, that's obviously overstated. Lots of dull moments in this town. But when things happen, they sure aren't ordinary. So, you guys think there's a car at the bottom of that fishing hole...with a body in it. Any idea who?" She sat at the table with him.

"None. That's why the dive team's coming out, help us get some answers. We don't know if there's one victim or several. Don't know if they're local or from out of town. You know, out there on route 40 you can have all kinds of folks from somewheres else taking that road to bypass the city. We know whoever's down there been in that water for at least a decade." Told her about the guardrail.

"So, that's where you're headed after this?"

Looked at his watch. "In about five more minutes."

She looked down at his feet. "Your metal detecting boots. Interesting combo with your shirt and tie."

He laughed. "Got my office shoes by the front door. I'll be changing into them after this little field trip. Need to take a hike down this hillside to get to where the car is. Or, is supposed to be."

She stood up. "Well sweetie, you at least gotta admit... who else do you know gets to supervise a dive team searching for a dead body in a car, as a part of their job."

"You're right about that. I should be grateful." He smiled. "Why you standing?"

"You don't hear the baby crying? Must've finally woken up. I'm telling you, you need to get those ears checked."

"My ears are fine. You got the ears of a border collie. Give me a kiss before you head upstairs. I'll be leaving in a minute."

She set her coffee down. "Hope I get to finish this someday soon." She leaned over, gave him a kiss, and headed for the stairs.

"Give Sammy a kiss for me, too." He took a swig of his coffee and got up. Might as well head out there now.

JOE REACHED the spot at least five minutes early but — judging by all the activity — felt like he'd gotten there thirty minutes late. His included, at the top of the hill, there were four cars pulled off to the side of the road, where there was only room for one. So, Hank had gotten the city to set up a little road crew. They had coned-off the area, had two guys in orange vests on either end handling traffic with stop/slow signs.

When Joe got to the guardrail he was relieved to see Hank still there, along with Trevor, and two guys with dive gear. He was afraid they had already gone down, and he'd have to navigate his own way down the hillside.

"Hey, Hank, Trevor. And I'm guessing you guys are the divers."

"This is Emmett and Phil," Hank said. Everyone shook hands.

"Did I get the wrong time?" Joe said.

"No, I came out early. Needed to because of the city guys

out by the street. Trevor and the divers just got here about five minutes ago."

Looking at Trevor, Phil the diver said, "Is there any space down there for us to change into our wet suits, or should we do that now?"

"No, there's some decent flat areas by the pond. Should be fine to do it down there." He looked around. "Everyone ready to go?"

"You lead the way, Trevor," Joe said.

IT HAD BEEN tricky business getting down that hill to the water level. A few times, Joe thought he might just take a tumble. It was either the mercy of God or sheer force of will that kept it from happening. Besides likely sustaining serious injury, he'd never live it down. Because for everyone else — including the divers with all their gear...and sixty-something Trevor — it appeared to be a piece of cake. Of course, when they did reach the creek, Hank asked if he was all right. And of course, he said he was just fine, hoping his insides would catch up with his words before long.

With Trevor in the lead, they walked along the creek's edge for about fifty yards until they reached a very obvious change in scenery. There was the wide, former beaver dam with the big pond area behind it.

"There's a nice ledge over here," Trevor said. "Right in the middle. We used to just sit on these flat rocks with our ankles wading in the water, cast right out. See, there's all kinds of space right here to change into your wetsuits."

Phil came up behind Trevor, set his gear down. "Any idea how deep the car is?"

"Remember guys," Joe said, "all we got so far is a car mirror. You're here to tell us if there's a car down there that goes with it."

"Don't rightly know the depth," Trevor said. "I don't know anyone that's ever made it down. Friend of mine tried, never reached the bottom. He guessed he had gone down at least twenty feet."

"Okay, thanks. Just give us a few minutes and we'll be in the water." Looking to Joe. "We do find this car, what kind of info you want us to get. We've never done a dive that involved the police before."

"You guys have an underwater camera in that bag?" Hank asked.

"We do. Can take stills or video."

"Well, videotape everything then," Joe said. "Unless the water's too murky to get a good picture. If that's the case, we obviously want the make and model of car, license plate info, how many people are in the car." He thought a moment. "Forgetting anything Hank?"

"No. That should do it for now."

As promised, Phil and Emmett were in the water in a couple of minutes, along with their scuba gear, cameras, and lights. The other three men stood on the flat stones, looking down. Watching the unending stream of bubbles rising from below.

Finally, about fifteen minutes later, both men surfaced. They made their way over to the flat rocks, carefully set down their camera gear and lights. Phil took off his diving mask first, looked up at Joe then the others. "Well, that's a first for me. I'm sure for Everett here, too. You definitely got a car down there. We reached the tail section at about twenty-six feet. Car's sticking straight down. The front end's wedged in there pretty good, and pretty smashed up."

"Yeah," Emmett said, "kinda wished I hadn't seen the next part. Go on, Phil, tell 'em."

Phil sighed. "Yeah, not sure I'll ever get that out of my head. There's just the one body down there. Mostly a skeleton with bits of clothing still attached. The thing is, it's half-hanging out the front windshield, and halfway in the car. Just floating, kinda stuck there. Windshield's totally broken out. Pretty sure he wasn't wearing a seatbelt."

"Could you tell what kind of car it was?" Hank said.

"Not at first. It was covered in scum. But we brushed enough of it away by the backend. It's a blue Camaro, Z28. And the driver-side mirror is missing. The other side is barely hanging on. I'm hoping the video came out okay. I wiped off the license plate, got a good shot of it. A Georgia plate. Maybe we should look at that part now before we get out of the water. If you can't make out the plate number on the video, I'll dive back down and try to memorize it."

Hank walked over, picked up the camera. Emmett explained how to use it. With Hank holding it, and Joe and Trevor looking over his shoulder, they watched the video. The screen wasn't that big, but the picture seemed clear enough. After a few moments of dark water and bubbles, the shape of the backend of the Camaro suddenly appeared. They watched for several minutes as Phil and Emmett swam around the vehicle, one holding the camera, the other the light, as well as wiping crap off the car.

Trevor gasped and turned away when the skeleton came into view. It looked just like Phil described it, something from a horror show.

"Definitely don't want the guy's family seeing this," Joe said. "You guys did good. Earned your keep today, that's for sure."

"There's the plates," Hank said. "Nice and clear."

"Okay, guys," Joe said. "You can get out of the water." As they did, he said, "You okay earning some more money in a day or two? When we can get a crane out here to haul it up? We'll need some divers to hook the car up right."

Phil looked at Emmett, back at Joe. "If the money's good, we'll do it. Might need to charge a little extra though, this time. Pay for each of us to see a shrink."

Joe smiled. "There's just one catch. We really need the both of you to treat this like a state secret. Can you do that for me? Word about something like this gets out, we could have all kinds of curiosity hounds coming down here to check this thing out. Could be the victim's local. Sure would hate it if his family found out something like this through the grapevine, instead of from us."

"No, we hear you, Lieutenant," Phil said. "We're good with that. When can we talk about it?"

"We'll let you know."

8

WELL, ONE THING WAS FOR SURE, HAVING THAT UNDERWATER video of the car turned out to be a big deal. Pendleton's reaction when the car first appeared was like the Titanic team's reaction when they'd first glimpsed the bow of that legendary ship emerge from the murky depths. Without hesitation, Pendleton authorized getting a crane out there on Route 40 to bring the car up to street level.

That took some doing. More than anyone anticipated.

Starting with, Joe had no idea all the people in government he had to talk with to get that guardrail removed temporarily, so the crane could even get situated on top of that hill. Eventually, Pendleton himself had to get on the line and lay into some bureaucrat who was talking like they *might* be able to get it on the schedule sometime next month. Joe smiled as he listened, never heard Pendleton so colorful. Reminded him of one of his favorite quotes from the movie *Christmas Story* about Ralphie's dad: *In the heat of battle, my*

*father wove a tapestry of obscenities, that as far as we know is still
hanging in space over Lake Michigan.*

But it did the trick.

All this had happened yesterday. The guardrail was
being removed today. The crane would be showing up
tomorrow morning.

Of course, for safety reasons, the city had to agree to put
temporary concrete barriers in place until the crane showed
up, but that wasn't too hard to pull off. Hank was taking care
of that, as well as nailing down the dive team for tomorrow
morning. Joe was back at his desk, trying to finalize which
cold case they'd be working on next. Pendleton wanted that
by the end of the day.

But first, he wanted to take a stab at identifying the John
Doe lying half-in the car at the bottom of the fishing hole.
They knew it was a blue Z28 from the mid-80s, and that it
had Georgia plates. Could be local, or could be someone
from another part of the state. The state didn't keep tag info
on cars going back to the eighties on their computers. No
one even used computers back in the eighties.

It seemed highly unlikely, though, that an individual
with a car that nice would *not* have any friends or family
who cared about them. There had to be a Missing Persons
report somewhere. But again, it also would be from the mid-
80s, which meant it wasn't on any computer database. No,
it'd be in a box, on a shelf, in a storeroom of some local PD
or Sheriff's office, somewhere in Georgia. Maybe it was time
to look up the name of that intern they'd hired last summer,
see if she'd like to earn some extra money making phone
calls all over the state.

Well, the least he could do was rule in or out whether

this John Doe had come from Culpepper. How much time could that take?

JOE WAS JUST FINISHING up his meatloaf sandwich. Kate had packed it this morning for him to take into work. He'd asked her to include a bag of Doritos, like she'd put in the kids' lunch bags, but his request had been denied. Too many carbs. You can have either the Doritos or the bread in your sandwich, not both. He opted for the sandwich. Kate made the best meatloaf, which in turn, became the best meatloaf sandwiches the next day.

The sandwich almost made up for the total waste of time he'd spent that morning, downstairs, rummaging through the Missing Persons files from the mid-80s. He gave up when he got to 1995. At least, he didn't have to read through the entirety of each report. All he had to look for was whether the missing person went missing with their car, and if so, was it a blue Camaro Z28?

None of them were.

He decided he'd better set this task aside for now and try to finish up picking their next cold case. He pulled out that short stack of three files he and Hank had settled on as the best prospects. The first was the hit-and-run with the twelve-year-old kid. The second was the used car dealer nobody liked. Joe wasn't even sure what the third one was. Hank had been looking at it himself when Joe had to leave and go meet with Pendleton. When he'd gotten back to the office Hank just said, "I think this one needs to be on the pile." They didn't get a chance to talk about why.

Joe picked it up and opened it.

The first thing that caught his eye was that it was a Missing Persons report, and not about a murder. By itself, that wasn't too unusual. When missing person cases extended out for years, they often turned out to be murders. He and Hank had handled such a case themselves a couple years back. That poor kid, Myron-something, who went missing from a convenience store in 1988. Joe smiled as he remembered the odd circumstances when Myron's body was discovered. They were on a family camping trip when their beagle, Chance, just a pup then, ran off in the woods. They'd found him after he'd just uncovered the boy's skeletal hand.

Joe lifted the report from the file folder and began to read. His eyes popped out of his head after drifting down the page looking for any information about a missing car being part of the story. "Oh. My. Gosh. I don't believe it." He reread the line three times:

The young man was last seen driving a new 1985 blue Chevy Camaro Z28.

9

'

JOE SPENT THE NEXT FORTY-FIVE MINUTES READING OVER THE file and could easily see why Hank thought this Missing Persons report belonged in the cold case murder pile. A guy with a situation like this doesn't just go missing. Not for more than a few days. Certainly not for months, years, or decades.

Of course, now they know what happened to Brewster McFarland. And to his beautiful new car.

It gave Joe an odd feeling reading all these things gathered and written down by other detectives and officers when he was just a kid living in Pittsburgh. A world away, an entirely different time. Reagan was president. The Soviet Union was the bad guy in all the movies. And this guy disappeared right after the space shuttle *Challenger* disaster. That was probably the first big news event Joe remembered as a kid. It was kind of like how his dad used to talk about the JFK assassination.

One of those things where everyone living could say,

"Remember what you were doing when the *Challenger* blew up?" And everyone did. Even if they could remember almost nothing else that happened that year. The whole country was grieving big time. Especially schoolkids because of all the publicity surrounding Christa McAuliffe, that teacher who was part of the crew.

Even just sitting there holding the file, Joe relived some of the memories from that time. Then he thought about this guy's family. How sad for them. This national tragedy happens the same week their college-aged son disappears. Just vanishes without a trace. Him and his car. They'd have to wait until the ME made a positive identification, but either he or Hank would have to go out there and notify the McFarland family that they had been right all along. Their son hadn't *probably run away*, which is what they'd been told. Looked like even by the Culpepper PD.

The door opened, Hank walked in. Joe looked up.

"Joe, I just realized something on the drive back from the fishing hole." He noticed Joe holding the McFarland file. "Actually, it's about that." He walked around the table, sat at his desk. "I can't believe I didn't make the connection sooner, when the divers told us what kind of car was in the water."

"The blue Z28," Joe said. "Yeah, isn't that crazy?"

"It's like you say," Hank said, "ain't no coincidences in this business. When I was reading the file before, the car wasn't the thing that really stood out to me. Why I thought it should be in the running for our next case. It's just how this kid—what's his name again?"

Joe looked down. "Brewster McFarland."

"Right. How this kid didn't fit the bill for a runaway. There was nothing about him that suggested he had any reason to take off. I remember how it bothered me that the idiots who were our counterparts back then couldn't see this. Other than interviewing his family and listing the comments from some of his college friends, it seemed like they didn't do anything else. Just filed it away."

Joe glanced down at the names of the officers who contributed reports to the file. Good. None were Pendleton. "You remember Cap was on the force then."

"No, I didn't. Guess I'll have to be careful how I talk about this case around him."

"Not all of it," Joe said. "Just the part about the idiot cops he worked with. In case they were friends. But I was thinking the same thing. There's nothing about the situation that says runaway."

"He was a senior at Culpepper," Hank said, "which means his folks had to have some money. Driving around maybe the hottest car on the road. None of his friends said he ever mentioned anything about leaving town. Looking at his picture, he wasn't bad looking. I'm sure he could get girl-friends."

"It says his parents were convinced foul play had to be involved," Joe said. "He was the kind of kid who called if he was gonna be an hour late."

"Right," Hank said.

Joe looked back at the file. "Well, at least that's one thing we can rule out now. Although, don't know what level of comfort it'll bring to his folks."

"What's that?"

"The foul play bit," Joe said. "We know why he suddenly disappeared. He missed a turn and drove off a cliff. End of story."

"Yeah," Hank said. "Guess we can take this one out of the running for our next cold case. The big mystery is solved."

"How'd things go out there with the barriers?"

"Pretty smooth. The crew had them up in about an hour-and-a-half. Minimal traffic."

"And what about the crane?"

"Confirmed they'll be out there mid-morning tomorrow. They're gonna give me a call when they're twenty minutes out, so today's crew can come back and remove the barriers. Then another city crew shows up to put up cones and guide traffic when the crane arrives and shuts down the lane closest to the fishing hole. That guy Phil and his friend Emmet are all set to show up then with their scuba gear to assist the crane operator."

"Okay," Joe said. "Good job." He closed up the McFarland file. "So, which one of us gets the job of visiting this guy's folks to tell them we know what happened to their boy? I mean after the ME confirms his ID."

ON THE OTHER side of town, Josh Hoskins was following the GPS on his phone, as it led him through one of the older neighborhoods in Culpepper. One that had seen way better days. Judging by the houses, he guessed it'd probably peaked in the 80's.

Back then, it might've been a thriving place, middle class families who mowed their lawns, trimmed their hedges, washed their cars on Saturdays. Kids playing ball in the streets. Now, not a single kid in sight. Lawns were mostly dirt and weeds. Every house in need of a paint job and new roof.

Josh fancied himself something of an entrepreneur,

made his living in a variety of ways. Never got rich, probably never would. But he liked the freedom of working his own hours and calling his own shots. One of the ways he earned extra cash was working garage and estate sales, which often brought him into neighborhoods like this all over Culpepper.

It was all about buying low and selling high. You do this long enough, you get an eye for hidden treasures. Folks don't often know the value of things. Especially with estate sales. Relatives looking to dump a bunch of junk collected by the deceased over a lifetime. They just wanted it gone and some money they didn't have to work for in their pockets.

He'd always find stuff he could then turn around and sell online—sometimes at five to ten times what he'd paid—to people looking for just that very thing in some other state.

"334 Salisbury Lane," he muttered aloud, as he turned onto the street. Third house on the right. Owned now by a Mr. Dave Schofield. He'd called to make sure Mr. Schofield would be there, said he hoped they could make some good deals.

He pulled into the driveway, the garage door already opened. It was obvious from the street, this was it. All kinds of odds and ends spread out on folding tables lining the garage. Before Josh even got out of his car, the inside door in the garage opened. Out walked a guy in his mid-fifties, balding, smoking a cigar.

"You Josh Hoskins?" the man said, smiling.

"That's me. Thanks for being willing to let me take a look at your stuff before your big sale this weekend."

"That's okay. Anything to get this stuff cleared out. Mom died two weeks ago. Wanna put the place up for sale ASAP.

Take a look around, let me know if you see anything you like. I put prices on 'em, but no good offer will be refused."

Like music to my ears. "Thank you, sir. I'll do that. Looking for some very specific things, so I shouldn't take too much of your time."

Josh walked from left to right. A smattering of the usual stuff you always see. He figured even with the general merchandise, if he could double or triple his cost, it was worth getting.

Then on the middle table in the back, his eyes fell upon something that stopped him in his tracks. He lived for moments like these. Did his best to seem only mildly amused. "Okay, if I pick this up?"

"Sure. It's pretty old. My brother used to be into cameras bigtime back in high school and college. He lived with us then but left in '86, went out to California. Left it here with most of his stuff. Don't know if it works, or not."

My goodness. A Kodak 35 Rangefinder with an original leather case. This was way older than the mid-80s. More like from WW2. Other than being dusty, looked to be in mint condition.

"I'll tell you what. I won't even dicker with you on the price," Josh said. "Seven bucks seems fair."

"Great," Mr. Schofield said. "What I like to hear."

Josh knew he could sell this—today—for at least $150 dollars, if not more. But this was such a find...he might just keep this baby for himself.

10

The Following Day
Route 40, Just Outside of Town

TOM HAZELTON LOVED HOW HIS NEW BMW HANDLED THESE hills and curves out here. By far, the nicest car he'd ever owned. Bought it complements of the big advance money he'd gotten to write that true crime book about Samuel Clemens' wrongful imprisonment, and the shocking development when a beloved high school teacher turned out to be the murderer. He was seriously thinking he might start writing books like this from now on. Sure paid better than the Gazette ever did, and people in town seemed to treat him with newfound respect.

But today, he was out here on the Gazette's dime, pursuing a call-in from someone about an hour ago, who'd driven by this way and said traffic was actually backed up on

Route 40 because of some big crane sticking out into the road at the top of one of these hills. Tom figured he'd drive out here and check it out for himself. Cranes operating on these roads outside of town were very rare, and usually only meant one thing...some poor driver ran their car or truck off the road into a deep ravine. That usually only happened in winter months or during a major rainstorm.

It wasn't the winter, and it hadn't rained for a week. So, something else was going on. Whatever it was, he'd get to the bottom of it. Based on what the caller had said, Tom was getting close. Should see the crane up ahead any minute now.

EVERYTHING WAS ALL SET. Almost. The crane was in place and properly secured. The crane operator had already lowered his cable and hookups to the pond level. The two divers, Phil and Emmett, had arrived on time, got their gear all checked out, wetsuits on, and were in the water. Hank had come out first thing to supervise the operation, called Joe about twenty minutes ago, so he could be here for the big moment.

That's when Joe thought about something and hit the pause button on the whole operation. Phil and Emmett were looking up at him, awaiting his new instructions.

"Guys, I know you've already talked with Hank and the crane guy about how to secure the vehicle, so he can haul it up safely. But Hank just confirmed something with me that you guys haven't discussed. I remembered what you said about the victim— well, the skeletal remains — how he's hanging half in and half out of the windshield. Since the car's facing straight down, once you secure these hookups to the frame and that crane starts hauling it up, what's to keep these...*skeletal remains* from falling all the way out that windshield and just dropping to the bottom of the pond?"

Joe wished he could've taken a picture of the look on their faces.

"Yeah, that wouldn't be good," Phil said.

"Never thought about that," added Emmett. "So, what you want us to do?"

"He wants us to secure the body, Emmett," Phil said, mildly scolding.

"That's right," Joe said. "Not exactly sure what to tell you about how to do that. You'd have to be careful. Wouldn't want the skeleton to start breaking apart."

"Definitely don't want that," Phil said.

"How about bungee cord?" Hank said. "I've got a bunch in my trunk. All different kinds and sizes. The cords are covered, so they're nice and soft. You can make them as loose or as tight as you want."

Joe, thinking. "Yeah, that could work. Hate to ask you to do this, but —"

"I'll be right back," Hank said. He took off along the water's edge toward the path that led back up the hill. "And Hank, let the crane operator know what's going on. Shouldn't take us more than twenty minutes or so to get this situation sorted."

"Right, Joe."

HANK HAD JUST GRABBED the bungee cords and a pair of walkie-talkies, which he'd intended to bring out earlier, and headed over to the crane operator. The guy was already watching him, waiting for instructions on what to do next.

He opened the door to his cab. "What's the holdup?"

"We were all set to give you the green light then we realized we needed to do a better job securing the victim to the car."

The man smiled. "Yeah, I could see how that'd be a problem. Doesn't bother me, waiting. You guys are paying me by the hour. How will I know what to do next? I don't even have anyone's cell number."

"Here." Hank handed him one of the walkie-talkies. "I was supposed to give you one of these before we went down. Shouldn't be much longer. Soon as I get these bungee cords to the divers, they'll get things situated, and I'll let you know when to start yanking it up."

Just then the wrecker truck pulled up, the guy under contract with the department. Hank jogged over to him. "Hey, Manny," he yelled through the open front window. "Got here right on time. Appreciate that, but ran into a little snag. As you can see, we haven't hauled up the car from the water yet. Shouldn't be more than a ten-to-fifteen-minute delay."

"Not a problem, Hank. I'll be here whenever you're ready."

Hank headed toward the big rock to make his way down when another vehicle pulled up, a shiny BMW. Who could this be? He stopped and watched to see who got out. "Oh, no. Not him." It was Tom Hazelton, from the Gazette. Joe wasn't gonna like this. Wouldn't do to just head down and ignore him. He might start interviewing the crane operator and wrecker guy, get them to share all kinds of things they wouldn't want the public to hear yet. Hank headed back to face him.

He saw Hank coming, yelled out to him as he passed the wrecker truck. "Hey, Sergeant Jensen. Fancy meeting you here. What's going on?"

Hank stood a safe distance from the road's edge, waited for Hazelton to reach him. "Well, as you can see we got a very big crane here. Just getting things going, but you know how it goes, living all these years around Culpepper. Lots of hills, lots of steep winding roads. Sometimes, bad things happen."

Hazelton came closer. "Figured as much. Car went over the edge?"

"Why we need the crane."

"Any idea who? You know, the victim? What kind of car he was driving?"

Sadly, Hank knew the answer to all these questions but couldn't say. "Well, Tom, you know how it is. We can't give that info out till we notify the next of kin."

"That the real reason you ain't telling me? You ask Joe, you can tell me stuff and ask me to hold onto it till later. I'm pretty good at that. Another thing." He looked up at the crane. "Doesn't quite add up how we got somebody going over some cliff. You're right, happens out here a good bit over the years. But mostly when the roads are icy, or we've got some serious thunderstorm dumping buckets of rain. Weather's been fine all week. Just when exactly did this car go over that cliff?"

Hank sighed. "Tell you what, Tom." He held up the bungee cords. "I got two divers down there waiting on these. Let me go down and get them these bungees, and I'll see if Joe can come up and answer your questions."

"Joe? The Lieutenant is down there? The heck is the lead homicide detective in Culpepper down some steep hillside supervising a car wreck situation?"

"Come on, Tom. I really gotta get these cords to those divers. Joe will be right up in a few minutes. Just hold tight, will ya?"

11

JOE WAS CHECKING SOME EMAILS ON HIS PHONE WHEN HANK got back with the bungee cords. But he had this look on his face. He walked carefully along the creek's edge until he reached the beaver dam. "Manny showed up with the wrecker truck."

"Good," Joe said. "I see you got the bungees."

"But he's not the only one who showed up."

"What do you mean?"

"Hazleton. He's up there asking all kinds of questions."

"You couldn't get rid of him?" Joe regretted saying it like that.

"Joe, I tried. He thinks there's something going on."

"I guess it is a story when a car goes over a cliff, but it happens around here every now and—"

"He's sure it's something fishy," Hank said. "You know, no icy roads, no big rainstorms. And I let it slip that you're down here. So, of course, *What's a homicide detective...?*"

"Okay, I get it. I'll go get rid of him. You get the cords to the divers, so we can start hauling this car up."

"Alright."

They switched places on the path. Joe remembered something else pretty important, turned and said, "Unfortunately, I just thought of something else we should've brought down. A tarp to cover the body. Especially now with Hazleton hanging around. You can go ahead and get the guys down there to secure the skeleton, but have the crane operator pause as soon as the car clears the water. Then get Phil and Emmett to attach a tarp so that the remains are completely covered when it gets up to street level."

"Yeah, should've thought of that, too," Hank said. "Not just for Hazleton's sake." He laughed, thinking about it. "A sight like that would freak Manny out, the crane operator, and anybody else driving by."

Joe smiled, imagining the sight. "Guess you'll be getting a good workout going up and down the hill."

"I'm still young."

"But my knees aren't. So, when I go up to talk to Hazleton, I won't be coming back down. You okay to handle everything down here till we're done?"

"Yeah, Joe. I got it. Go take care of Hazleton."

JOE FINALLY MADE it to the top of the hill but had to stop five minutes ago to catch his breath, and so he wouldn't look like a complete wreck when he faced Hazelton. When he got there, he saw Hazelton talking with Manny, the wrecker driver, who was still in his truck.

"I'm telling you, Mr. Hazelton. I don't know anything. Just

that they're bringing up a car that went over the cliff. I don't know when. I don't know who."

"Hey, Tom," Joe yelled, "why don't you stop bugging him and come over here?"

Hazelton turned around, acted surprised to see Joe. "I'm a reporter, Joe. Just doing my job." He came over.

Joe stopped far enough away to be out of earshot from Manny or the crane guy. "I thought you were a big author now. They send big authors out to do a story about a car going over a cliff? Isn't this kind of routine? A car takes a turn too fast out here on these hilly roads?"

"Come on, Joe. If it was just routine, why would you be out here? I can see Hank, maybe. But not you. You're like the main guy in the whole department. Everybody in town knows this."

"That almost sounded like a compliment."

"It's just a fact," Hazelton said. "The point is, you being here means it's not routine. And I noticed something else while Hank was gone. You guys took the guardrail out that used to go around this corner."

"We had to, to get the crane in here. There was no other way."

Hazelton shot him a look. "Joe, you forget how long I've worked at the Gazette. I remember writing the story about why the guardrail got put there in the first place. Some guy smashed into that big rock, and they realized if he'd driven a few feet to the right he'd have gone over the edge. Then there's something else that doesn't add up. You didn't just remove the guardrail for the crane. That guardrail's been there for years. Which means, the car you're yanking up with this crane must've gone over the edge before that. The guardrail would've kept any car from going over if they hit it. And there's one more thing, I drive by this spot pretty often. It's completely covered — usually — with bushes and shrubs," pointing toward the cliff's edge. "I'd forgotten all about the car that hit that rock. Now look, you've cleared all the brush out exposing the cliff. You guys did that. A car didn't. So, how did you know to do that? How did you know a car went over the cliff? Since it happened years ago?"

Joe had to admit, he was crazy annoying, but he was pretty observant. "Okay, Tom. You made your points. Most of them are good ones. Something is going on. But as far as we can tell right now, this isn't a big story. And I'm not just saying that. Even so, if you can just be a little patient, I will give you the entire scoop and answer all your questions. The thing is, a car did go over the cliff right here. There's a pond down there, and it's been at the bottom of that pond for years. The driver's corpse — whoever he or she is — is still down there with the car. I'm begging you to sit on this story, at least until we've notified the next of kin."

"So, you know who the victim is?"

"We think we do. In fact, we're pretty sure. But we have to wait for the ME to do an autopsy to positively identify the victim. As soon as he does, and as soon as we can talk to his folks, I will call you. I promise. After that, you can run the story and say as much as you want."

"Can you tell me, was it somebody local?"

"Yeah, it was. So, how about it? Will you be a standup guy, and do the right thing here?"

Hazelton stood there, not answering. Finally, "So, you don't think any foul play was involved?"

"Not at this time, no. Just a tragic accident that happened

years ago. Tell you what, I'll talk to the guy who figured out a car was down there, see if he'll let you interview him, too."

Hazelton held out his hand. "Okay, Joe. I'll wait. But don't forget. Call me as soon as you've notified the next of kin."

"I will." He shook his hand.

Hazelton turned back toward his car. "But Joe, this deal's off if I start reading about what happened here on social media."

"I hear you, Tom. But that's not gonna happen."

12

Joe watched as Hazelton drove off. As annoying as he was, he was good at his job. And Joe certainly didn't envy the kind of job he had, trying to navigate the news business with the myriad of changes it had gone through in recent years.

Joe was thinking he might head back to the office, start digging out and updating the contact info for Brewster McFarland, likely the deceased person they were pulling out of the pond. If this guy died in February '86, who knew if any of the relatives on the Missing Persons report were even still alive.

A lot could happen, that many years go by.

A white SUV pulled into Hazelton's spot. Reading the writing and insignia on the back door, Joe realized it was the medical examiner, Dr. Hargrave, all the way in from the county seat. Business must be slow at the morgue for Hargrave to come himself, along with one of his lab techs. These days, he didn't usually get his hands dirty unless there was a felony involved. Hargrave got out of the car, saw Joe, and waved. As he and his tech walked toward Joe, the crane started kicking into gear.

Joe looked over his shoulder. They were starting to haul the car up.

"Looks like we've come at a good time," Dr. Hargrave said.

"Yeah, thought we'd be a little further along but ran into a couple of snags. Not like we have much experience pulling cars stuck underwater for decades after driving over cliffs."

Dr. Hargrave smiled. "No, I don't imagine you would. You said on the phone you believe the body in the vehicle has been down there since 1986, correct?"

"Yeah, based on the information we have from the car. It coincides exactly with a Missing Persons report from that year. A guy's family reported he was driving the car that we're pulling up right now. And he's still in it. Did you watch the video I sent?"

"We did. That's part of the reason I'm here. Considering how old the remains are, it's going to be a delicate operation extracting the body from the vehicle. I assume your team has properly secured the remains for the...crane ride."

"We have," Joe said. The crane stopped.

Dr. Hargrave and his technician looked over but didn't see the car. "Why has he stopped?"

"That was me. I asked my guys when they got the car out of the water to stop and cover the remains with a tarp. Since you've seen the video, you can imagine—"

"Right, Lieutenant. A prudent thing to do."

"In a minute, they'll start up again. This time, they'll bring it all the way up then carefully place it on our wrecker over there. I'll get the road guys with the signs to hold up traffic for a couple of minutes, so I can get some pictures with the body still in the car. Obviously, we'll have to take the tarp off for that. It would be great if you and your tech could take the body out and get it out of sight as soon as possible, so I can get the traffic going again."

"I don't think that'll be a problem, Lieutenant," Hargrave said. "Considering what I saw on the video, and the fact that we already know the cause of death, the autopsy will be mostly about confirming the victim's identity, which we can do back in the lab. You said there was a Missing Persons report? It would greatly help to have some DNA from the closest relatives of the deceased. We can match it to the DNA we extract from the victim's bone marrow."

The crane started hauling the car up again.

"That's going to be the very next item on my list," Joe said. "When I contact any remaining family members, I'll bring that up. I can't imagine any of them will object to providing a sample."

The car finally came into view, still dripping massive amounts of pond water and covered in green scum. But Joe was happy to see the guys did a good job securing the body under the tarp. He walked over to the wrecker and yelled to Manny through the window. "If you could back the wrecker in this way maybe ten feet, think it'll make it easier for the crane to set the car down. Not to mention, it'll help the crane block the view of things from the road."

"Will do, Lieutenant. You stand back there to guide me? Help me know when to stop?"

"You got it." Joe headed to the place he wanted the wrecker truck to go. Manny started backing it in. When he reached the right spot, Joe gave a signal. He looked over and noticed the wrecked Camaro was now fully lifted to the height of the truck bed. He hurried out to the road and told the guys with the signs to stop all traffic, both ways, till he gave them the okay. Then he stood by Dr. Hargrave and the lab tech he'd brought with him.

For several moments, the crane operator hovered the car just over the wrecker, looking for the best spot to lay it down. Hank and the two divers came up from the hillside path. "Great job, guys," Joe said.

"Thanks," Hank said, "but these guys did all the work. Hardest thing I did was going back and forth on this hill. Don't think that'll be a fishing spot I'll use anytime soon."

It took the crane operator about five minutes to get the car properly situated on the wrecker. When he gave the signal, Phil and Emmett — already out of their wetsuits — climbed up and unhooked the crane from the car. Joe said to the divers. "Can you stay here a few minutes, since you did all the work with the bungee cords and tarp? Seems like you guys should be the ones to take the tarp off."

"Sure thing, Lieutenant," Phil said.

"Hank, you mind getting up there and taking a bunch of pics once they get the tarps off? It'll just be good for the record to have some photos of the victim in the car like we found him."

"Sure thing, Joe."

Joe turned to Dr. Hargrave. "Once Hank gets down, the body will be all yours. And again, if you could work quick."

"Not a problem, Lieutenant," Hargrave said. "We're all set to go."

Joe stood back and let everyone do their thing. Once Hank started taking pictures, he walked out to see how the traffic was doing. Thankfully, just a few cars backed up in either direction. Those drivers would be getting pretty mad, but it couldn't be helped. When he came back, Hank was already getting down, and the lab tech was helping Dr. Hargrave get on the wrecker.

Joe stood there watching, curious how they would do what they came to do. After a couple of minutes, Hargrave got a strange look on his face. The look changed to grave concern as he zeroed in on the victim's skull. Joe looked at Hank, who noticed the same thing.

Hargrave stood back, looked down at both of them. "Uh, gentlemen, I hate to be the bearer of bad tidings, but this situation just became a great deal more complicated."

"What's the matter, Doc?" Joe said.

"I can now say with absolute certainty that this victim did not miss that curve over there, then drive this car through the clearing and over that cliff."

"Why's that?" Joe said.

"Because this man has a bullet hole in the back of his skull. This wasn't a car accident. He was murdered, dead before the car went over the cliff into the water. To make it from that road to the cliff, it had to have been pushed there by whoever perpetrated this crime."

13

JOSH HOSKINS SAT AT HIS WORKBENCH IN THE SPARE BEDROOM ceiling, equal parts nervous and excited by what he was about to do.

Yesterday, he'd made a fascinating discovery.

The day before, he'd picked up a one-of-a-kind gem at an estate sale. A Kodak 35mm Rangefinder from the WWII era, in mint condition, including the original leather case. On his travels that day he'd picked up about a dozen other things he could easily resell online. But not this. Before he'd even gotten home, he had already decided this camera would be perfect for a new photography project he'd been planning for a while. Something he was sure would add hundreds of dollars more to his income each month.

A printed wall calendar filled with beautiful black-and-white photos from yesteryear. It would sell especially well with antique car lovers. Every picture would portray two or three classic cars parked at interesting angles in front of historic office buildings and churches. Fortunately, he didn't even have to leave town to obtain these background scenes. Culpepper dated back to the pre-Civil War era and, between the University and downtown area, they had kept many of the most attractive architectural landmarks in place.

The other exciting aspect of this calendar project were the cars themselves. There was simply no way for him to have access to antique cars like this, not in the quantity required for the calendar. It would cost a fortune. Josh looked over his shoulder at his "antique" car collection lined up on four shelves in his spare bedroom wall. Added up, Josh guessed he'd spent less than three hundred dollars for the entire collection. He purchased every single one over the years, for a fraction of its worth, on one of his many garage and/or estate sale excursions.

Josh's cars were 1:18 scale die-cast models that averaged between eight to twelve inches long. The thing is, with the cars set on a raised table at just the right height, and with the camera behind them at just the right angle, positioned in front of an old building, they looked full-sized. No one could ever tell the difference. Before finding this Kodak 35 Rangefinder, he figured he'd have to use digital cameras with special filters to artificially make the photos look like they'd been taken back in the 1940s or 50s.

But now, he had the perfect tool for the job. A camera made back in the day.

Of course, he'd have to buy some special black-and-white film, and he'd have to develop the photos himself. But that wasn't a big problem. With the innovative tools he'd picked up at Sullivan's photo, he didn't need an old-fashioned darkroom with red lights, photo trays, and wet photographs hanging up to dry. He could do the whole thing inside of a big, black canvas bag, with a small, specially-designed developing tank, and all the chemicals premixed in advance.

He'd done it a few times before. So, that part of the project was no big deal.

But then something remarkable happened yesterday that interrupted everything.

When Joshua examined the Rangefinder more closely, he was shocked to discover a roll of black-and-white film already in the camera. Wouldn't that be something, if he developed these pictures and learned they had been sitting there in the camera since the 1940s? If so, likely everyone in the photographs — unless they were small children— were already dead.

Sitting there at the bench, he'd already laid out the photo-developing gear inside the black bag. The little jugs of chemicals were just to his right. The camera in front of him. At first, he wondered if he should just bring the roll down to the Sullivan's and let the pros handle it. But then he figured, if he screwed it up, really, who'd care? It wouldn't be like he'd be ruining anything of historic value. Probably just some family photos of folks who had long since left the planet.

Very carefully, he picked up the camera and turned it over.

JOE HAD DRIVEN the whole way back from the fishing hole to the office in stunned silence. Everyone at the scene had been equally floored by the revelation discovered by Dr. Hargrave.

Brewster McFarland — a name Joe hadn't even heard of a day ago — had now become, without question, he and Hank's next cold case murder investigation. Joe had waited there at the scene trying to extract as much information from Hargrave as possible. But the good doctor was old-school and preferred not to speculate on almost anything that mattered to Joe. He and Hank obviously agreed, there was no way the kid had driven the car over the cliff. At some point, he had been shot execution-style, and placed in the front seat as though he were the driver.

For the last ten minutes, Joe had been back at his desk rereading the McFarland case, looking for any information that might stand out in light of the shocking news of his demise.

Hank walked in, looked at Joe, and just shook his head. "Definitely did not see that coming."

Joe nodded. "Everything get situated out there?" He'd asked Hank to stay long enough to watch the ME and his tech drive off.

"Yeah. Watched the crane guy get his act together. He was getting ready to leave, and the city guys were there getting ready to put the barriers back in place."

"How'd you think the talk went with Manny and the divers?" Before he left, Joe had given them all stern warning not to share the news about how the victim died.

"Won't have to worry about Manny. He knows his contract with us depends on his discretion. As far as the divers, well, I don't think you could've made it any clearer. They seem like decent guys. After you left, they both told me neither of them spend any time on social media. Doesn't mean they won't go home and tell their wives, so I brought that up and explained how bad it would be for the kid's family if this information leaked out prematurely. Just restated what you said in my own way."

"Think they bought it?"

"Think so. We'll see." He walked over and sat in his chair.

"Well," Joe said, "goes without saying that now we need to notify the next of kin ASAP. Hargrave said it would make the ID go quicker if we can get a DNA sample from a direct family member to him soon. How about this? You go through McFarland's file, dig out the family members interviewed, see if any of them are alive and in town. If so, we'll go together and have a chat with them. While you're getting that info together, I'll go update Pendleton."

WHEN JOE TOLD Pendleton's secretary, Marge, why he needed to see the captain, she agreed he'd want to hear this news right away. Joe knocked twice and opened Pendleton's door. He was writing in a notebook on his desk. Looked up, surprised.

"Sorry to interrupt you, sir, but you'll understand why in a moment."

"Take a seat, Joe. What's up? Everything go okay hauling that car up?"

"That's why I'm here. It did, as far as the task goes. No big surprises on the technical side. We got the body secured and tarped, crane got the car loaded on Manny's wrecker with no problems. Dr. Hargrave showed up, not just his lab techs."

"Hargrave came himself? Wonder why, for something like this."

"Turned out, it was a good thing he did."

"Why's that?"

"Well, that's where this gets interesting. You know how

you've been wanting Hank and I to nail down our next cold case? Looks like we have."

A puzzled look.

"As Hargrave and his assistant were extricating the remains from the car, he found something very unexpected. Turns out, this young man didn't just miss the curve and drive over the cliff thirty-five years ago. Someone put a bullet in his head first. Then the shooter, probably with help, pushed the car over the edge."

A shocked look. "This is the kid who went missing in '86, right? The college kid?"

Joe nodded.

"I remember that case. I wasn't a detective then, but I do recall his parents pitching a fit about how we handled it. Swore up and down there was no way he'd have run away from home. He was just a few months away from graduating. Wasn't anything I could do, but I do remember thinking he didn't seem a likely candidate for skipping town."

"That's the same reason Hank and I had put it at the top of our pile the last couple days. You know, as one of the cases to pursue, even though it was just a missing person situation. Didn't add up."

Pendleton leaned back in his chair. "Well, guess the parents were right. So, when you gonna tell 'em?"

"As soon as we find out they're still alive. Hank's checking that out. There's another thing. Tom Hazelton showed up."

"Oh, crap. He know about this? About the kid being killed?"

"No. He left before we found out. But I had to agree to give him first dibs on the story as soon as we ID'd the body and notified his kin. Got Manny, the crane operator, and the divers to agree not to blab about this, at least till we take care of that. Hopefully, they'll keep a lid on it."

Pendleton shook his head. "I hate social media. You guys better get on this before somebody slips."

"We will."

"Makes me miss the good old days," Pendleton said.

"Before social media?" said Joe.

"Yeah, that and...well, back then we used to be able threaten people to keep their mouths shut."

Joe nodded and headed for the door, realizing Pendleton wasn't making a joke.

14

THREE HOURS LATER, JOE AND HANK WERE JUST PULLING UP TO the front gate of a 55-plus condominium in a nice section of town, called the Whispering Hills. Hank had confirmed that Brewster McFarland's parents were still alive and had been living here for the last fifteen years. Both were in their early eighties. Joe had made the call, spoke with the mother. She could hardly believe it when she realized he was with the Culpepper PD. "*Hadn't talked with anyone there in ages.*"

Joe didn't mention he was with the cold case squad, wanted to wait on any details till he could see them in person. She'd all but insisted he at least say what this was about before she'd agree to meet with them. All Joe said was, "We have some news about your son who went missing in 1986." A long pause. Then she said yes, they could come, and they agreed upon a time.

Hank showed the guard at the gate his ID and said who they were there to see. He instantly let them through, gave them directions to the building where the McFarlands lived.

"Boy, this brings back some memories," Joe said. "You remember who used to live here?"

Hank looked around. "It's a nice place. Love all the trees. But I'm not sure I've ever been here."

"This is where Professor Thornton lived. Remember him? My first murder case in Culpepper. The guy was secretly dosing some of his students with an experimental drug. Made them have crazy dreams. Two of them died."

Hank pulled into a parking place after reaching the correct building. "Yeah, now I do. And he drugged Jack, too, as I recall. That's when you first met him and Rachel. Man, what a crazy case. Some doctor in the DC area invented the drug, right? Then blackmailed the professor into using human guinea pigs."

Joe smiled as memories flashed into his mind. "Hired a hitman to start cleaning up the loose ends, including Thornton."

Hank turned the car off. "Those were my first murders since becoming a cop. How are Jack and Rachel doing these days?"

Since that first case, Jack and Joe had become good friends, their wives too. Jack wound up taking Professor Thornton's job and was now actually a Dean at the University. "They're doing great. We still get together sometimes, though not as often since the babies came. Their youngest and our Sammy are only a few months apart." He got out of the car and stepped onto the sidewalk. He looked down at the note, reread the building number and unit where the McFarlands lived. "This was the same building Thornton lived at."

"How you want to handle this?" Hank said.

"Well, we'll just start off with the basic news. I mean, he went missing thirty-six years ago. Good chance they're not an emotional wreck after getting my call. But you never know. This'll be dredging up some pretty deep water. My hope is, they'll react mostly with relief to finally know what happened. If so, we'll be able to make some serious progress on this case, and they'll be up to answering more questions about what they remember. Maybe generate a bunch of leads right off the bat."

"And if not? If they're a mess?"

"Then we'll do the decent thing, give them some space, and come back later."

Joe rang the doorbell and took a step back. Both of them answered the door, the look on their faces, braced for bad news. Joe and Hank introduced themselves and held up their ID badges.

"Come in, Detectives," Mrs. McFarland said. "You can call me Ida, and he's Frank." They both turned and walked past the foyer into a spacious living area.

As Joe remembered, it was very similar to the layout of the professor's place.

"Care for some coffee," Frank said. "Got that Keurig machine, bunch of different flavors and styles to pick from."

No thanks both men said.

"Well, come on and sit down," he said. "Anywhere we're not sitting. At our age, you always sit in the same spot."

They waited for Ida and Frank to sit then picked seats close enough where they wouldn't have to yell.

"So, you said you had some news about our boy, Brew?"

Ida said. She pointed to a low-res 8x10 color photo centered on the mantle. A handsome young man in a suit, smiling. "That's his senior photo, taken a month before he disappeared."

Joe recognized the image from the file. "We do, I won't keep you in suspense about the news. But we both read over the file from 1986, everything the department had gathered back then. Of course, it was way before our time. There were transcripts from interviews done with you. You're both thoroughly convinced your son did not run away. That foul play had to be involved somehow."

"We were," she said. "Still think it. No way my boy would've left us like that. He just wouldn't. We had a good relationship. He was graduating in a few months. Was already looking into internship programs with a bunch of companies for the next summer."

"He had everything to live for," Frank added. "And we were close. No tension or bad blood between us. There's no way he would've run off. Not Brew."

Joe leaned forward in his seat. "Well, the news is...you were both right. Brewster didn't run away. You reported him missing the day after he disappeared. We believe he was likely murdered, probably the night before."

Both of them trembled as they absorbed the words. Ida started tearing up. "I knew it. I knew it," she said, her face angry now. "Nobody believed us, but I knew it."

Frank got up and grabbed a tissue from a box on the kitchen counter, handed it to his wife. Patted her gently on the shoulder then went back to his seat.

"So, what's happened?" Frank said. "We've heard nothing from a few months after he went missing till now."

"I'll be happy to tell you everything we know," Joe said, "but first I have to say, the ME hasn't yet positively identified the body we've found as your son."

"But you sounded so certain —" Ida began.

"We are...almost certain. The body was found in his car, a 1985 blue Camaro Z28. In his missing person's report, it says that's the car he was driving when last seen. No one else went missing from this area within several months of his disappearance. So, we have to believe it's your son's body in the car. But to make a positive ID, the Medical Examiner would like to get a sample of DNA from either or both of you. Would you be okay with that?"

"Of course we will," Frank said. "Whatever you need to make this official."

"Thank you," Joe said. "We have the kits in my briefcase. We can get to that in a few moments. But first, let me explain to you what we do know at this point."

"You said he was murdered," Ida said. "But that he was found in his car. So, where has it been all this time?"

"That's part of the story," Joe said. "When you hear it, I think you'll understand why you haven't heard anything more all these years."

"Although the Lieutenant and I both agree," Hank said, "our counterparts back in '86 could have done a whole lot more to support you two than they did. Had you come to Joe or me back then, given what we know about your son, we would've never classified this as a runaway."

"Thank you," Frank said, "for saying that. Not being believed...it was pretty painful."

"Okay," Joe said, "here's how the situation has unfolded." He spent the next fifteen minutes giving them a play-by-play account of how they came to this moment. Of course, leaving out any details about the condition of the skeletal remains hanging out of the windshield. Near the end, he was able to speculate that the nature of the gunshot likely meant their son hadn't suffered. Death would have come instantly, and it was even likely he didn't see it coming.

"Do you have any idea who did this to our boy?" Frank said.

"Not yet," Joe said. "But getting to the bottom of this is now Hank and my full-time job. One way or another, we will find out who did this to him, and if they're still alive, hold them accountable to the fullest extent of the law."

15

Joe and Hank were driving back to the station. They had hoped their interview with Frank and Ida could have turned into more, but it was clear they'd taken as much as they could stand for one day. Frank insisted they did want to be more helpful and asked if they could come back tomorrow. Of course, Joe agreed. He couldn't imagine what they'd been through. Starting years ago, when everything first went down, then the decades of not knowing a single thing, and now hearing their worst fears confirmed.

"So, where you want to go next with this?" Hank said.

"When we get back, why don't you drop me off then drive these DNA samples over to Dr. Hargrave in Dunedin? I'm sure it's just a formality. We know the remains belong to Brewster McFarland. But getting the Doc to say so will allow us to talk more publicly about this. I don't like having all of these people sworn to silence. Sooner or later, it'll show up on social media. And this way, I'll be able to let Tom Hazelton know what's going on. He's gonna love that we got a murder mystery here, instead of just some poor kid who drove off a cliff by accident."

"I guess we gotta tell him," Hank said. "But it's kind of a shame."

"Why's that?"

"Because, once this goes public, the killers will know this thing they thought they got away with all these years is suddenly alive again. That is, they'll hear if they still live in this town."

"You're right," Joe said. "Would've been nice to interview his old friends before they hear about this and have time to coordinate their stories."

"You think there's at least two perps involved?"

"Yeah, I do. I suppose it's technically possible for one person to do this. Kill McFarland, stick him in the front seat, and push the car off the cliff. But my gut tells me that's probably not how it went down. I think there's at least two people involved. Could be more, but at least two."

"Makes sense," Hank said. "Can I make a suggestion?"

"Sure."

"How about you wait on telling Hazelton for a day or two? It's possible it won't leak out by then, and if it does, at least his folks have already been notified."

It was nice how often now Hank came up with good ideas. "That's what we'll do then. You head over to Doc Hargrave's, and I'll start working on figuring out who his friends were and where they're at now."

JOSH HOSKINS SAT in his favorite chair in the living room looking over the amazing black-and-white photos he'd developed from the antique camera he recently bought. There were seven of them. He wasn't sure why the photographer stopped at seven, since there was room for twelve on the roll. But even that, it was bizarre to think there was a time when people had to limit the number of pictures they took to twelve, or even twenty-four. Then they'd have to stop and reload another roll of film.

He had seen people on Instagram take that many pictures of their own face, or doing any number of mundane, irrelevant things like...showing the world what they had for breakfast. Back then, taking a photo was a precious thing. Not only did you have so few pictures available to take, you had to wait days or weeks for them to get developed, to even see how they turned out.

Here he was holding in his hands seven photos taken sometime in the 1940s. Almost eighty years ago. The photographer and most of the people in the photos likely long since gone. None of them even got to see these pictures developed. His eyes were the first to view them.

They appeared to be pictures taken at Culpepper University. Josh recognized some of the buildings and statues in the background. He decided right then to head over to the school soon, try and locate the exact spot the photos were taken from. Then he would take the same photos from his phone, create a "then and now" montage.

Only three of the photos had people in them. Looked like three college students, all males. Perhaps, the photographer was also a friend, because they didn't look like portraits. In one, it appeared the young men didn't even know a picture was being taken. Obviously, the photographer wasn't shown in any. Back then, no one took selfies.

He wished way fewer people took them now.

He looked at each of the pictures under the lamp. None of them had any cars showing, which would have been nice to see. Because of the war, most of the cars in the early 1940s were built in the 30s. A lot of great looking cars came out of that time. He singled out the three showing the college guys. He was pretty sure they were sitting on some stone tables and benches near the Murray Building. He could just picture it in his mind. Just to the left but out of the pictures would've been the big Angel Fountain, which was featured in another picture.

All of them are still there, just like they were back then. He was surprised none of the guys were wearing hats, like fedoras. He thought all guys wore hats back then. Maybe not college guys. He wasn't sure. In the casual shot, one of the guys is reading a newspaper. The other two were talking as they looked down at the guy reading the paper. Again, nothing special in the scene. He wasn't even sure why the photo was taken. In another shot, the guy had stopped reading and the two had stopped talking, but they were all standing in the same place. They had just turned around, faced the camera, and smiled.

Josh imagined the photographer must have asked them to pose. The third one was the same guys, standing in the same positions, but closer to the camera. Since Josh knew the camera didn't have a zoom lens, he realized the photographer must have physically come closer.

In any case, even though the photos didn't capture anything significant or historic, he was still glad to have them. They really did look old-timey, and it made him realize this camera would be perfect for his calendar project.

He might even use the architectural shots for some of the background settings.

He took one last glance at each of the three smiling faces. They looked so young and alive here. He wondered what had happened to them in the days, months, and years that followed? Did they graduate? Did any of them go off to fight in WW2? It was very possible. Maybe one of them had become a POW, maybe a war hero, or maybe killed in one of the many famous battles like Iwo Jima.

And although he could recognize and even go to the places shown in the photos, he knew the world these young men faced after this picture was taken was drastically different than the world students at Culpepper—or any other college—were facing today.

He wished there was some way to find out who they were.

16

A LITTLE AFTER TEN THE NEXT MORNING, JOE AND HANK WERE
pulling back up to the front gate of the Whispering Hills
condominium. Frank McFarland had called yesterday afternoon saying he thought they'd be up to talking about their
son's case today, and they agreed to having Joe and Hank
come back at 10:15. Also yesterday afternoon, Dr. Hargrave
had thanked Hank for hand-delivering the DNA samples
and vowed to give them his highest priority. Joe was glad to
hear it. He told Hank he was able to verify that two of the
three friends who'd been interviewed about Brew's disappearance back in '86, were indeed alive and still lived in
Culpepper. The fourth, apparently, had left town a few
months after the incident, but he did have some family in
town — a younger brother — so, there was still a chance of
getting more info from him.

The guard didn't even wait to see their badges this time,
just nodded and opened the gate. As Joe hunted for a
parking space, Hank said, "I noticed when you briefed me on

what you learned so far, you kept referring to the deceased as *Brew*. Is that what we're officially calling him now?"

"Did I? Didn't even realize it. That's what both his parents called him yesterday. Guess I figured I should, too."

"I don't have a problem with it, just wanted to clarify."

Joe pulled into an open spot. "I think it's a pretty cool nickname...Brew. Bet it went over pretty good with his college friends."

"Yeah," Hank said. "I'm sure it did."

Joe turned off the car.

"So," Hank said, "what do we know about the two friends who stayed in town? They've got to be in their late fifties, I guess."

"Well, they seem to be ordinary guys, as far as I can tell. One of them might be a little shady, but he doesn't have a criminal record."

"So, what does shady mean then?" Hank said.

"His name is Victor Waters. He owned a big pawnshop downtown for a whole lot of years. There were some charges on a few occasions suggesting he might have used his business to help thieves convert their loot into quick cash. But nothing ever made it to court. Called the pawnshop and was told he retired a short while ago. His son runs it now. Got the guy's number."

"Guess that qualifies for shady," said Hank. "And the other?"

"A fairly wealthy real estate developer named Tag Harvey."

"Tag? That's the guy's first name?"

"What he goes by. His legal first name is Thomas, but I had to dig a bit to find that. Seems he prefers Tag."

"Wait a minute," Hank said. "Harvey Homes. I've heard of the guy. He's built several subdivisions in and around town."

"That's the one," Joe said. "He, Victor Waters, and another guy named Jeremiah Schofield were the ones we interviewed when McFarland disappeared. Guess they were his closest friends. Maybe his folks can tell us a little more about them. Speaking of his folks," Joe looked at his watch. "We better get in there."

TEN MINUTES LATER, they were sitting in the very same spots in the McFarland's living room they had sat in yesterday. This time, Joe and Hank had said yes to the offer of coffee but both passed on the pastries. Joe could tell right off, Frank and Ida were doing a little better, emotionally speaking.

"Thanks for coming back," Frank said. "We definitely want to do anything we can to help."

"Do you know when we're going to get Brew's body back from the coroner?" Ida said.

"It won't be long," Joe said. "The ME told Hank yesterday he'd make it his top priority."

"We'll call you as soon as we get the word," Hank added.

"Okay," she said, "so, how can we be of help?"

"Well, for starters, can you think of anyone who would have had any reason to hurt your son?" Joe took a sip of coffee. "I mean, you were convinced from the get-go foul play must've been involved."

The couple looked at each other then back at Joe. "I'm afraid we can't," Frank said. "The reason we were sure there had to be foul play had nothing to do with Brew having enemies. We can't think of a single person who didn't like him. He and his friends got along great. We never saw them together where there wasn't lots of laughter. Sometimes, it would get so loud we'd have to intervene."

"He means quiet them down a little. Back then we lived in a house and Brew and his friends would take over the family room while Frank and I would be in the living room watching TV."

"I get it," Joe said. "You remember the names of those friends?"

"Sure," Frank said. There was Brew, Vic Waters, Tag Harvey, and Jeremy Schofield. Hung around together all the time. They'd often come here after renting a movie."

"He means at our old house," Ida said. "They all went to Culpepper together and were all seniors."

"When they rode together," Frank added, "they usually drove in Brew's car."

"The blue Camaro Z28," Hank said.

"That's right," said Frank. "But see, Brew wasn't spoiled. He wanted that car so bad, he worked real hard for it. All through high school and the first two years of college. Saved every penny he had to buy that thing. He was so proud driving that around town. None of the other guys had a car near as nice."

"In all that time they spent together," Joe said, "you never heard them fight or quarrel, never got in any big arguments?"

Both Frank and Ida shook their heads no. "Not in any big or little arguments," Frank added.

"I can't imagine they had anything to do with this," Ida said.

"Me, neither."

"That was a few days after the *Challenger* blew up," she

said. "Remember? The whole country was so upset about it. Of course, after Brew went missing, that's all we could think about. Trying to find him. When I asked the boys if they'd seen him, you could tell they were more upset about him being missing than the shuttle blowing up. Just like we were."

Joe wrote down some notes.

"But I know Vic and Tag still live in town," Ida continued. "Maybe you could talk with them, see if they know whether Brew had any enemies we didn't know about."

"You see them often?" Hank asked.

Both shook their heads no. "Sadly," Frank said, "we completely lost touch with them not too long after Brew disappeared. But we bump into them every now and then in town."

"I see," Joe said. "Well, we won't take any more of your time. I think we'll do as you suggest, talk to these two men very soon. See what they have to say."

Joe and Hank stood, shook the couples' hands as they headed for the front door. "We will definitely let you know if anything solid develops," Joe said.

Once outside and well out of earshot, Hank said, "What do you think of these three friends? Definitely *not* involved?"

Joe laughed. "Yeah, right. If they're not involved, then the moon is made of bleu cheese."

As they walked down the stairs, Hank said, "Think the saying is swiss cheese, Joe."

Joe smiled. "Maybe so. I like bleu cheese better."

17

It was about midmorning the following day. Joe was in the office by himself. Hank had gotten drawn into some follow-up calls on a burglary case situated firmly in the present. Joe was still working the McFarland case, expecting a phone call very soon from Dr. Hargrave about the DNA results. The phone did ring, but not his cell. Hargrave would know to call that number. It was the desk phone, a call from upfront.

He picked up. "Hey, Eileen. What's up?"

"Hi, Joe. I've got that nice man, Trevor Burbank, on the line. You remember, the guy who brought us that car mirror. He wanted to know if he could speak with you."

Joe looked at his watch. "Maybe a quick one, expecting another call. But I'll take it." He pressed line one. "Hello, Mr. Burbank. How are you doing this morning?"

"Pretty good. Just got back from fishing on the lake. Still not quite ready to go back to that trout pond just yet. Are you folks all done with that place? Meaning, if I wanted to go back, could I?"

"Well, I don't see why you couldn't. We did everything there we needed to do. I don't think the guardrail's back up yet, but those stone barriers are. I hope what's about to happen doesn't ruin that place for you."

"Why, what's about to happen? I mean, what already has happened was rough enough."

"Well," Joe said, "expecting a call any minute from the medical examiner. He'll likely be giving me a positive ID on that body we found in the car. And, well, something very unexpected turned up when we pulled that car out of the pond. Can't get into it right now, but it'll come out soon enough. When it does, it's gonna cause even more interest in this case than usual. After the ME gives me that call, I'll be passing that info to a reporter from the Gazette, give him any of the facts I can release at this stage. I'm sure he'll be putting it all in the Gazette right away, which means it'll start making the rounds on social media."

"I don't pay too much attention to Facebook or Twitter," Trevor said. "If that's what you mean."

"You don't, but a lot of people in town do. Part of the story will obviously include the location where we found the car. Could have a whole lot of curiosity-seekers going out there to see things for themselves. I know all these years you've been able to keep that place pretty hidden."

"Oh, I see now what you're saying." He sighed. "Well, maybe I should stay away for a few weeks until the dust settles. I don't suppose the fact that I was fishing there has to be a part of the story, does it?"

"I don't know," Joe said. "Guess it depends on how he writes it. I'm sure part of the story — maybe a big part — will be how this car came to be hidden in that pond for so many years, and why we were able to finally locate it. I have to give him the facts, which means, I'll have to say something like *a man fishing there came upon it when his line snagged on part of the car.*" Joe heard him sigh again. "But you know, Trevor, I don't need to say anything more. Like how crazy-good this fishing spot is. And when you consider how hard it is to get down there, and that there isn't any good parking up on that hill, my guess is...it'll still stay pretty private once the buzz about this case passes."

"You're probably right," Trevor said. "So, when I read about it in the news, I can start talking about it to folks? Except the part about how good the fishing is."

"That's right. That'll be the signal. Do you want me to leave your name out of it? I can just say a fisherman. No one needs to know who you are, unless you'd like them to."

"Maybe that would be best. I'll just tell the few friends I have that it was me who found it."

Just then Joe's cell phone rang. It was Dr. Hargrave. "Well, Trevor. Good talking with you. I've gotta take this call. Thanks again for all your help."

They said goodbye and hung up. Joe picked up his cell and answered, "Hello, Dr. Hargrave. Is this the phone call I've been waiting for?"

"I hope so," the doctor said. "As expected, I can say with certainty now that the deceased found in the submerged car was definitely Brewster McFarland. So, no surprises there. I've forwarded all the documents to your office, but I know you wanted the info as soon as it became available."

"That's great, Doc. It'll allow me to keep moving forward

with this thing. Anything on the cause of death? Obviously, we know it's a gunshot. But anything else you can tell me?"

"Actually, I can. Speculating a little bit here, since we don't have a bullet recovered from the remains, and I don't suppose a shell casing was found."

"No, we don't have either I'm afraid. So, what do you speculate?"

"I think we can safely assume the gun used to kill the victim was a .22. Judging by the diameter of the hole in the skull, and the fact that there was no exit wound. A larger bullet, like a 9mm, would have exited through the front, pretty much destroying that part of the skull. But the skull was intact."

"I see, Doc. That's a helpful fact to have going forward. If the bullet didn't leave the brain, it still must be down there somewhere. In the pond, I mean."

"Well, you did recover the car," Hargrave said. "After the deceased's body sufficiently decomposed underwater, it could have fallen down, maybe somewhere in the front seat, or the floor."

An image of the video showing the skeleton hanging halfway out the windshield popped into Joe's mind. "I don't think that's gonna work out. Not this time." Joe explained.

"Oh, I see. Now that you mention it, I do recall seeing that when we removed the body from the car. Well, since it was in the man's brain, when the brain matter was...gone... my guess would be, the bullet would have dropped down to the floor of the pond. You had some divers out there. Perhaps they could go down with a waterproof metal detector."

"Now, that's not a bad idea, Dr. Hargrave. Believe it or not, metal detecting is kind of a hobby for me. The bottom half of mine is waterproof, so I know they make them. On mine, the electronic part can't get wet. If the divers don't already have one, maybe we could rent one for the day that's totally waterproof. If we do recover the murder weapon, or suspect we found it, we'll definitely consider your suggestion. Thanks for the help."

"Glad to be of service," he said. "Have a good day."

Joe hung up and was just about to get Tom Hazelton on the line, but decided he better first update Captain Pendleton on the case. He'd blow his stack if he thought a reporter knew more about the case than he did.

Then he remembered Hank's suggestion about waiting a day or two to inform Hazelton at the Gazette, give them a chance to interview McFarland's friends first before the news broke.

So, Hazelton could wait. He called Marge, Pendleton's secretary, asked if he could spend about ten minutes filling the Captain in on some important developments.

18

ABOUT THAT TIME, ACROSS TOWN, TREVOR BURBANK WAS OUT in the garage by the wash tub, cleaning the fish he'd caught that morning. His cell phone rang. He saw it was his old friend, Vic Waters. He really didn't want to stop what he was doing, but he went ahead and rinsed his hands off and picked up the phone.

"Hey there, Vic? How are you doing?"

"Doing just fine, Trevor. Been almost a week since you and I been out fishing on Lake Samson. We fried up and ate all the trout I brought home from the last time. Thought I'd give you a call, see when you were going out again?"

Trevor looked over at the uncleaned trout on his left, and the nice stack of fillets on his right, wondered if he should mention it. "Well, to tell you the truth, Vic, I was out this morning. Caught me quite a few nice ones. I was just out here in the garage cleaning them up."

"Oh, I see."

Did saying that hurt his feelings? Trevor couldn't tell. "If

I'm being honest, judging by how you seemed when we finished up last time, I wasn't sure you were even interested in fishing with me anymore? That's why I didn't call you." Well, Trevor knew he wasn't being totally honest. It was partly because he didn't enjoy Vic's company all that much.

"Really?" Vic said. "You didn't think I was having a good time?"

"It didn't seem so. You never once said anything like, *When can we go out again*, or anything like that. But hey, if I read you wrong, it's no big deal. I go out every few days. You want me to call you the next time, see if you could join me?"

"Yeah, let's do that."

"If you're wanting some fresh trout, you could have the ones I caught this morning. I've still got plenty in the freezer from a big haul I took in several days ago. Big ones, too. Bigger than any of the ones you and I caught at Lake Samson, and bigger than the ones I caught today."

"Is that so?" Vic said. "You get these bigger ones at some other place?"

"Yeah. As a matter fact, it's a place you know well. Or I should say, *used* to know well."

A long pause. "Where is this place, Trevor?"

"Our old fishing pond. The one we used to go to as kids. Remember when we were fishing, we talked about it? How the fish were so big there we'd never have to worry about ever catching ones too small to keep."

"I do remember you talking about it. Don't tell me you actually went down there?"

"Okay, I won't tell you."

"You really did go?"

Trevor thought he heard him release a big sigh. "Yeah, I

did. I told you I wanted to. I know you tried to talk me out of it, but I got to thinking...I've kept myself in pretty good shape through the years. Figured I could still make that hike down. I'll admit, it was steeper than I remembered, but I just took it slow and eventually made it down safely. The best part is, the fishing was as good or better than I remembered. But that wasn't all that happened. Something kinda crazy happened there at the end." Then Trevor stopped talking. He wasn't supposed to say anything about this yet.

"What?" Vic said. "What crazy thing happened?"

"Just remembered. Can't talk about it yet."

"What are you talking about, Trevor? Who said you couldn't talk about fishing at the old pond?"

"It's not about fishing there. It's about the crazy thing that happened. The detective said I needed to wait till it came out in the newspapers. He said it would be real soon. Maybe by the next time I go fishing I can tell you all about it then."

"Wait a minute, Trev. You can't do that to me. Leave me in suspense like that. What crazy thing happened?"

Trevor hesitated. "The main concern is, none of this can show up on social media. Not until the medical examiner makes a positive ID. Once he does, he'll call the detective, and then he'll be okay with word getting out."

"Medical examiner? Positive ID?" Vic said. "What in the world?"

"Yeah, crazy stuff. But seriously, this will all come out in a few days."

"Okay...but, since it will...what's the harm in giving your old friend the scoop now? I'm not even on social media. So, your secret'll be safe with me."

Trevor thought a moment. He really couldn't see the harm. "Okay, guess the place to start is with the car mirror."

"Car mirror?"

"Yeah. Like I said, I was fishing at our old spot. And Vic, I'm telling you, it was just like when we were kids. The place is just the same as it was. If anything, the trout are bigger and there's more of 'em."

"I get it. But what about the car mirror?"

"Right. Well anyway, all the fish I was catching were using shallow lures. You know, two, maybe three feet deep. Then I got an idea. I remembered how deep this pond was. How when you dove down there, you never even got to the bottom. I wondered, what the fishing might be like at the bottom, so I re-rigged my line for bottom fishing. Right off the bat, I get a hit. A big one. Well, what I thought was a big one. I'm fighting this thing and trying to haul it up, thinking it's gotta be at least a ten-pounder. Instead, it turns out to be the old rusty car mirror. You know, from a front door." Vic hadn't said anything yet. Trevor wondered if he was still on the line. "You still there, Vic?"

"Yeah, still here. Go on."

"Anyway, I got to thinking. How did a car mirror get down at the bottom of this pond? No way someone threw it. Nobody knows about this place but us. So, I look up to the top of the cliff. And it dawns on me. A car must've missed the curve up there and gone over the cliff, and it's still down there...at the bottom."

"Geez, Trev."

"I know. It's crazy. So, the short version is...I take the mirror to the police, get talking to these two detectives. One thing leads to another, and they think maybe I'm right. So, they get divers to go down there and check."

"They sent divers down?"

"Yeah, I was there. They came up with a video, showing this car right there. And here's the really crazy part...the driver is still in the car, Vic. Nothing but a skeleton now. But there he is, right on the video."

Trevor was sure he heard Vic release a big sigh. "This is probably freaking you out. I don't need to say anymore."

"Yeah, it kinda is. But probably not the way..." He stopped talking.

"Not the way, what?"

"Never mind. Not important. That really is the wildest thing I've ever heard. So, I'm guessing they pulled the car up. Were you there for that?"

"No, they wouldn't let me be. In fact, I really haven't been involved anymore. I just called the detective this morning to find out if I could start fishing at the pond again, if they were all done with it. He said he thought I could, but I might want to wait until after the news about this thing comes out. Thought there might be a whole lot of people wanting to go see this spot for themselves. Sure hope that doesn't happen."

Vic didn't answer. Trevor waited a few more moments. "Vic?"

"Yeah, Trev. I'm still here. Hey listen, something just came up. I gotta go. We'll talk again soon." He hung up.

Trevor didn't really get Vic's reaction and now wondered whether he should've said anything at all.

FOR THE FIRST FEW MINUTES, Vic sat there in stunned silence.

His heart was pounding. He couldn't believe what he'd just heard. The real reason he'd turned the pawnshop over to his son was because of his blood pressure. Apparently, his system could no longer take the stress. It wasn't just the pawn business itself, but all the side hustles they had going. The doctor had said if Vic didn't find a way to lower his stress, he'd be a serious candidate for a stroke or massive heart attack. That and he had to quit smoking.

The last thing Vic wanted was to spend his remaining years on the planet like some vegetable in a wheelchair. Since he didn't need the money, he retired. Took a few months, but he also quit smoking. That, losing a few pounds, taking his meds, it all started to help.

And now this. Why? Why this?

He got up and went to the medicine drawer, took out the aspirin bottle. He popped in a couple just to be safe. Then he got his phone back out and called somebody he hadn't talked to in maybe ten years.

"Hello?" A pleasant woman's voice on the other end. "You've reached the executive offices of Harvey Homes. This is Shawna, Mr. Harvey's personal assistant. How can I help you?"

"Hi, Shawna. You must be fairly new there."

"I've been Mr. Harvey's PA for three years. Who is this speaking?"

"Oh, well, it's an old friend. Tag and I go way back. Way, way back. Something came up. Something kinda urgent. I really need to speak with him. Now."

"I see, and your name is?"

"Just tell him it's Vic. And that we need to speak about

something right away. He knows I wouldn't call this number unless it was absolutely necessary."

"Mr. Harvey's schedule is very—"

"Just tell him, Shawna. I'll wait. I'm sure when he hears who it is, he'll want you to put me through."

19

THE BRIEFING WITH CAPTAIN PENDLETON WENT AS EXPECTED. After Joe got done explaining how their time had gone with the victim's parents, Frank and Ida, Pendleton quickly suggested Joe and Hank start off doing the very thing they were going to do anyway. That is, get interviews with McFarland's college friends ASAP. Joe didn't really mind. Made the captain feel like he was still a player.

When he got back to the office, Hank was there, so he filled him in on the few things that had happened since earlier in the morning when they last spoke. "You think you can pull yourself away from that burglary detail and go with me to talk to these guys?"

"Yeah. I'd be happy to," Hank said. "When are we going and who are we going to see first?"

"Right now. Since we both know the moon isn't made of bleu cheese, I'm banking on...these guys either were involved or know what happened. I don't want to call ahead, set up an appointment, give them any time to prepare. I figure, we just show up, show our badges, talk about this being a murder investigation, and we need to see them now."

"Works for me," Hank said.

Joe held up a sheet of paper. "Wrote the addresses of both guys down. We get in the car, punch in the first one. It's the home address of the guy who owned the pawnshop. The other address is the main office for Harvey Homes, where that guy Harvey keeps his desk."

"Okay, let's go."

Vic had to do something, find some way to relax. Tag Harvey still hadn't called him back. It had been two hours. His secretary, or assistant, or whatever she was, had gotten back on the line saying her boss was expecting a visit from a city councilman any moment, and couldn't come to the phone. But he would definitely call Vic back as soon as this appointment was over.

Vic headed over to his bar in the family room, poured himself a couple fingers of scotch. As he screwed the cap back on, the doorbell rang. It was just him in the house today. Housekeeper had the day off. He wasn't expecting visitors. Delivery guys anymore just dropped their packages by the door. He walked over and looked through the peephole. Two guys in suits. Didn't look like Jehovah's Witnesses. He opened the door, just a foot or so. "Afternoon, gentlemen."

They both took out ID badges from their coat lapels and held them up. Vic instantly started to panic. He barely heard what they said next. Their names, or something. A lieutenant and a sergeant with the Culpepper PD.

Calm down, calm down. Smile. Big smile.

"Are you Mr. Victor Waters?" the older of the two said.

"That's me. But please, everyone calls me Vic. Come on in, guys. What's this about?"

Both stepped into the foyer.

"We got your address from your son at the pawnshop. Is this a bad time?"

"No, not really. I'm retired now, don't know if my son mentioned that."

"He did," the younger one said.

"I am expecting kind of an important phone call," Vic said. "Will this take very long?"

"I don't think so," the lieutenant said.

He figured the older one had to be the higher rank. He looked familiar to Vic, but he couldn't recall why. He walked them into the spacious living area. "Feel free to sit anywhere." He sat in his favorite leather chair, set his scotch on the end table. "Get you fellas a drink?"

"We're both on duty," the lieutenant said.

"I've got iced tea, Coke, Diet Coke?"

Both men said no thanks.

"Mr. Waters, Vic, we're here on a murder investigation, believe it or not."

"A really old case," the sergeant added.

"An old murder case," Vic said, feigning surprise. "Wow. Don't hear about murders too often here in Culpepper. Lived here most of my life."

"Not too many, thankfully," the lieutenant said.

"I'm sorry," Vic said, "I didn't catch your names. Could you repeat them?"

"Sure. I'm Joe Boyd, this is my partner, Hank Jensen."

"Okay if I call you Joe and Hank, or would you prefer—"

"That'd be fine," Joe said. "As I said, we're looking into a murder that happened back in 1986, January of 1986."

Vic felt his pulse start to rise. *Calm down. You need to calm down.* "That's the year I graduated from Culpepper."

"We knew that, actually," Joe said. "Our sources say you were a close friend with the victim."

"Really? I don't know anyone who was murdered in '86." He tried to say this as credibly as he could.

"Weren't you friends with Brewster McFarland?" Hank said.

"Brewster? Yeah, I knew Brewster. He was a good friend. But he wasn't murdered, not that we know of. He just disappeared. We had no idea where he went. You're saying he was—"

"Murdered?" Joe said. "Yeah, he was. We're fairly certain he was murdered the day he disappeared. Which is why he disappeared."

Vic sat back in his chair, shook his head in mock disbelief. "Brew... murdered. I can't believe it."

"We spoke recently with his parents," Joe said. "Frank and Ida McFarland. They said you and two others, a Tag Harvey and a Jeremy Schofield, used to hang around with Brewster all the time. You were all seniors at the University."

"Mr. and Mrs. McFarland," Vic said. "Really sweet people. Felt so bad for them after Brew disappeared."

"After he was murdered," Hank said.

"Right. But we didn't know that."

"They said you used to ride around in his blue Camaro Z28, a lot."

Vic nodded, smiled. "That was a great car. We used to

take turns, you know, with each other's cars. But after Brew got that, didn't make sense to ride around in anything else."

"You were interviewed by other Culpepper detectives," Joe said, "back when he went missing. I read the interview reports. We had one for you and for Mr. Harvey, Tag. You know why we don't have any for the third friend, Jeremy Schofield?"

Vic shook his head no. Of course, he knew the real reason why. There was a long, awkward silence. "Maybe, it was because he left town shortly after Brew disappeared. Or...was murdered. That's kind of what we figured Brew did. Leave town. The only difference was, we knew Jeremy was leaving. He came to say goodbye before he left. Brew was just...gone."

"That's because somebody killed him," Hank said.

Felt kind of like a slap in the face, the way he said it. "Yeah, right. But again, we didn't know that."

"You're saying you had no idea," Joe said, "why your friend — a guy you hung around with all the time — just suddenly vanished?"

"No, we had no idea. It made no sense at the time. I wondered if maybe he took a trip out West, to California. I mean, I didn't see Brew the day he disappeared, or even a few days before. But he often talked about wanting to do that, ride his Z28 down that Pacific Coast Highway. See Hollywood, Malibu, Beverly Hills. We talked about doing that as a graduation trip."

"That's not mentioned in the original interview notes," Joe said. "Did you tell that to the detectives in '86?"

"I thought I did."

Joe wrote something down. "You didn't know anyone who had any reason to hurt or harm him?"

"No. Brew didn't have any enemies. Everybody loved him. He was a great guy. If somebody killed him, it had to be a stranger. Not somebody he knew."

Joe wrote a few more notes.

"You mentioned how sweet Brew's parents were," Hank said. "They said you guys used to hang out at their house all the time before he went missing."

"Yeah, we did."

"But then they said, after Brew went missing, they hardly ever saw you anymore. Why was that?"

Vic sighed, figured he could answer this honestly. "It was just awkward after that, you know? They were his folks. They were nice, but it wasn't like we were friends. Wasn't like we were going to go over and see if they'd let us use their family room to watch a video."

Joe wrote something else down. Then he looked Vic straight in the eye. "So, you're telling us you had absolutely nothing to do with Brew's murder or disappearance?"

"What? No. Absolutely not. I can't believe you'd even say something like that. Brew was a good friend. I miss him a lot."

The lieutenant stared at him a few moments, then smiled and said, "Okay, thanks Vic. That's all the questions we have for now. If you can think of anything else, after we leave, here's my card."

Vic took the detective's card then followed the men as they headed for the front door. After they left, Vic walked over to his chair and all but collapsed into it. He was exhausted. Still, he knew what he had to do. He picked up his phone and dialed the number for Tag Harvey.

WHEN THEY GOT BACK into the car, Hank said, "Guess we can say, the moon is definitely *not* made of bleu cheese. "That guy was sweating bullets the whole time."

"You noticed that? Did you notice this...I never told him *how* his friend was killed, and he never asked. That should've been the first question out of this mouth. You know what else he didn't ask about? How we came to know Brew was murdered now, after all these years of everyone thinking he was missing. Or where his body was found. He wasn't even a little bit curious."

"Because he already knew the how and why," Hank said.

Joe started the car. "Let's head over and pay this Tag Harvey a visit."

20

FINALLY, TAG HARVEY GOT ON THE LINE.

"Hey, Vic. Man, been a while since we chatted. How's the world treating you? How's the pawnshop business?"

"Tag, I wish I could get into some small talk with you, maybe invite you over for a beer and get caught up, but we've got big problems."

A short pause. "*We've* got big problems? What are you talking about, Vic? You and I haven't even seen each other in maybe a decade."

"I know. But this problem? Goes back over three decades?"

"What? Vic, what are you going on about?"

"I'm talking about the thing that we took care of back in our senior year. The thing that we *thought* we took care of. It's back. And it's about to hit the front pages."

A very long pause. "How? How is that possible?"

Vic realized shortly after the detectives left, he'd never asked them how this case resurfaced. He should've done that. "I'm not totally sure yet, but it has. I just had a visit from two Culpepper PD detectives. The older one, I remember seeing him on the local news for solving cold case murders in the area. Guess they're handling this like that."

"Okay, this is an old case. But why would they come talking to you about it? After all these years? What's stirred the hornets' nest?"

"Again, not sure. I was shocked by the visit, didn't have time to prepare a list of questions. Besides that, didn't want to come off as overly curious. Decided to play dumb, act like I didn't know a thing."

Tag sighed heavily on the other end. "Doesn't make any sense. You don't just dig up a thirty-plus-year-old case for no reason. And this wasn't even classified as murder. But a missing persons case. That's how it played in the news."

"I don't know. But they didn't say they were investigating a missing persons case. They led with, *We're investigating an old murder case.* They came to me, seems like for two reasons. First, because the detectives running things back then interviewed me."

"They interviewed me, too," Tag said.

"And the second reason is, Brewster's folks talked about us, since we were all such good friends back then."

"They talked to his parents?"

"Yeah, sounds like they went to them first. My guess is, they'll be coming to you next. That's why I was trying to get hold of you. So, we can sync up our stories. I know we had it all worked out back then, but it's been so long..."

"Okay, okay. I follow you. So, what did you tell them? Anything new from what we said back then?"

"I don't think so," Vic said. "Just acted like we had no idea what happened. They seemed to find that hard to believe, us being such good friends. So, I told them about Brew always wanting to go to California. See places like Hollywood and Malibu. Said we figured maybe he went there, didn't want to wait for graduation."

"Brew wanted to go to California?" Tag said. "I never heard that."

"Well, now you did. And I suggest you talk about it when they come calling. Think that's the only new thing I might've added. Oh, and I said I hadn't seen Brew the day he disappeared or a few days before that."

"Why'd you say that?"

"I don't know. It just came out. Figured it put a little distance between us. Those detectives never asked us about it back then, and these guys didn't seem to care about it. Maybe you and I could say we were studying together for a test, and Brew wasn't with us."

Tag sighed. "Okay, I'll try to remember that if it comes up. Man, I don't need this," he said. "I've got a huge property deal lined up. Last thing I need is bad publicity."

"I don't know, Tag. Whatever got this thing alive again, doesn't mean it changes anything for us. We just gotta keep on sticking to the story. They don't have anything to connect it to us. Didn't sound like it anyway. We keep our heads down, seems like this will blow over soon."

"Man, I hope so. Thanks for the heads up, Vic."

"No problem. But just in case this thing grows some legs, I won't be calling you again from this number. I'm going to go out and buy one of those burner phones, so in case we need to talk we won't leave any phone records they can trace."

"Good idea. I'll get one, too. Get me the phone number when you have it."

"I will. And expect a visit from these guys soon."

JOE AND HANK pulled into the parking lot of the plush office facility for Harvey Homes, Inc. It was about two-thirds full but they easily found a space.

Hank looked around at the other cars nearby. "Feels like we're a tad underdressed here."

Joe got out and understood what he meant. Every car in the parking lot cost three to five times the car he drove. "I looked it up. This guy built our subdivision. Kate and I are living in a Harvey Home."

"How's it feel?"

"How's what feel?"

Hank closed the door, walked toward the sidewalk. "Living in a house built by a murderer?"

Joe shook his head. "Don't ever make that joke around Kate. I could care less, but she might want to move. Besides, don't you still believe in *innocent until proven guilty*?"

"I do. In concept. Between the two of us, here and now? I have no idea how we'll make this stick, but I can't think of any other possibility. This guy had no priors, no evidence of drug use or dealing. He was well-liked by friends and family, a senior at a great university, his whole life ahead of him. I don't know why they did it, but I gotta believe they did. My money is on this guy, Tag, and the guy we just talked to, Vic."

Joe came up and stood beside him. "I'm inclined to agree with you, Hank. But let's not show all of our cards to this Harvey guy. This is gonna be a tricky situation."

"I get it. I said I was just talking between you and me." They walked up a handful of steps and headed for the glass front doors.

Once inside, they went to the reception desk and were greeted by an attractive brunette, probably mid-20s. "Welcome to Harvey Homes Executive Offices. How can I help you, gentlemen?"

Both men took out their badges and introduced themselves. Joe took the lead from there. "Hello..." Joe looked down at her name tag. "...Marlene. We need to speak with your boss, Tag Harvey. Right away."

"Do you have an appointment? Mr. Harvey is a very busy—"

"No, we don't. And we don't need one. We are here on a murder investigation. Please tell Mr. Harvey that, and that we need to speak to him immediately."

"Oh, I see. Well, I'm not sure how to handle this."

"It's not complicated, Ma'am," Hank said. "Pick up the phone and do as Lieutenant Boyd asked. This is not a routine call. Perhaps you didn't hear, this is a murder investigation."

That worked. She picked up the phone and appeared to be speaking with Harvey's personal secretary, who seemed to be explaining why he couldn't see anyone right now.

Joe was concerned, the longer they waited, the more chance Harvey would have the talk with Vic Waters. They may already be too late. "Which way to Mr. Harvey's office?" Joe said to Marlene, a stern voice. She pointed. "Let's go."

He and Hank headed toward a hallway on the left, walked past several confused office workers, headed for the door at the end. Sure enough, Tag Harvey's name was on it.

As they approached, his secretary stood and protested. "Do you gentlemen have a warrant? May I please see a warrant?"

"Ma'am, sit down," Joe said. "We don't need a warrant to question a person-of-interest in a murder investigation."

"A murder investigation?" The look on her face.

"Yes. We could either do this here in the privacy of Mr. Harvey's office, or we can escort him downtown and interview him in one of the many rooms we question suspects in. Of course, with the way social media works these days, that's likely to get a lot of attention."

Again, the look on her face. "Put that way...I suppose he would rather talk to you here. Let me just let him know." She picked up the phone.

Joe and Hank didn't wait. They opened the door and walked in.

21

As soon as Joe and Hank entered Tag Harvey's office, he closed his laptop lid like a teenager looking at something bad on the internet. He looked up, startled, stood, and pasted a fake salesman-smile on his face.

Joe instantly didn't like this guy.

"Gentlemen, good afternoon. I am Tag Harvey. How can I help you today?"

"Mr. Harvey," Joe said, "you don't seem surprised by our rude intrusion. I wonder why."

That clearly took him off guard. He quickly recovered. "I get interruptions all the time in this business. Got to roll with the punches, right?"

Both men took out their badges. "I'm Lieutenant Joe Boyd. This is my partner, Sergeant Hank Jensen."

"Considering neither of you are wearing military uniforms, I'm guessing you're with the police. Please, have a seat. Can I get you anything to drink? Coffee, something more interesting?"

"No, thanks." Joe sat in one of the chairs in front of his desk.

Hank sat in the other. "None for me either."

This was as nice an office as Joe had ever seen. Clearly, this man made lots of money and liked to show it off. He looked at Harvey, quickly guessed he spent ample time in a tanning salon and had someone who colored his hair. "We're here conducting a murder investigation. By any chance have you recently spoken to your old friend, Vic Waters?"

"What? Vic Waters? Uh, you're right. He's an old friend. Been a while since we've hung out together, though."

Joe noticed he didn't answer the question. Said something that probably wasn't a lie but meant to deflect attention away from what Joe did ask. "I didn't ask about the last time you saw him. I asked if you and he had spoken together recently? Like within the last hour?"

He looked flustered, tried to regroup his face. "Is that some kind of crime, if I did, that is?"

"No, but given the fact — as you've just said — that it's been a good while since the two of you've been together, wouldn't it be quite the coincidence for him to have called you just before we got here? Seeing that we just met with him ourselves pursuing this same investigation? If he did, in fact, call you a short while ago."

"Don't forget, Mr. Harvey," Hank added, "at some point, we might subpoena your phone records."

Harvey's face shifted quickly from alarm to anger. "Gentlemen, are you here to charge me with a crime? I don't even know why you're here. You said it's for a murder investigation. I don't even know who was murdered. Or why it has anything to do with me? I have a very good team of lawyers. Do I need to call one of them before we talk any further?"

"If you haven't done anything wrong," Joe said, "I don't know any reason why you would. We're just here to ask you some questions about an old friend of yours who disappeared back in 1986, whom we've recently learned was actually murdered. He didn't just disappear."

Harvey acted as though he was trying to remember something. "Are you referring to...Brewster McFarland? He's the only old friend that I know who disappeared. You're saying now you know he was murdered?"

Joe noticed the absence of shock on his face or any sadness in his eyes. "Yes, this is about Brewster McFarland. But I suspect by the way you've answered our questions already, you already know this. Undoubtedly updated by your old friend, Vic Waters."

Harvey didn't reply for a few moments, then said, "Brew was a good friend. I don't know why you felt the need to come barging in here treating me as though I had something to do with it. From the time Brew went missing until today, I assumed like everyone else he'd gone missing."

Joe noticed the way Harvey said *until today*. He didn't say, *until this moment*, which is what he would have said if he was just hearing it now for the first time. Joe knew now, for certain, that Vic Waters *had* called him, probably right after they'd left his house. Well, no matter. It only confirmed his and Hank's hunch that these two men were directly involved.

"So," Joe said, "you are officially saying that you had absolutely nothing to do with Brewster McFarland's disappearance or murder?"

"What? No, of course that's what I'm saying. I had nothing to do with it. How did he die, by the way?"

Oh, don't forget to ask that. "He was shot...in the back of the head, execution style."

"Execution style? So, you think it had something to do with a gang or some drug deal?"

Joe noted again, no horror at this news, no sadness in the eyes. He looked at Hank, who saw it, too.

"So," Hank said, "you guys hung around with gangs, did drugs?"

"What? No. We never did either of those things."

"Then why would you ask? According to his folks and your friend, Vic, you guys hung around together all the time."

"I just meant...you know, when you called it *execution style*. Seems like something people like that would do."

"Or," Joe said, looking him right in the eyes, "something someone would do sitting in the backseat of a car. You know, when they wouldn't want their friend to see it coming."

A direct hit. His eyes all but said it.

"Well, that's a terrible thing," Harvey said. "Poor Brew. You think maybe someone was hiding in the backseat? And they ambushed him to get his car?"

A quick thinker, Joe had to give him that.

"The only problem with that," Hank said, "he was found in his car. So, no. No thief in the backseat."

"He was found with the car? The Z28?"

As if he didn't know.

"When did this happen? Where was the car found? With Brew, I mean."

Joe really wanted to let him have it, all this fakery. But he pulled back. "It'll be coming out in the news very soon. The fact is, his body was found in the car, and all the indications are he likely died at the same time he disappeared. I looked over the interviews you and Vic gave to the detectives back in early February, 1986. Apparently, no one asked you what either of you were doing the day or night he disappeared. I need to ask you that now?"

"You're kidding, right?" Harvey said. "You expect me to remember what I did on a specific night in February thirty-something years ago?"

"I guess I am," Joe said. "See, Mr. Harvey..."

"Please, call me Tag."

So, we're good friends now. "Okay, Tag. The way the memory works for most people, we forget a lot of the mundane things in life. The day-to-day stuff that happens. I get that. But then there are certain times when very big or traumatic things happen. They have a way of imprinting those moments in our brains in a very unique way. You've probably seen interviews with World War II vets. When they think back to what happened in the heat of battle — even though the events happened seventy years ago — it's like the memories are right there, at their fingertips."

"Yeah, I get that," Tag said. "But Brew going missing wasn't as traumatic as Nazis shooting at you and bombs blowing up all around you. I guess I do remember a few more things about that week than other times, but if you want specifics, like what I was doing on a certain evening... I'm going to need a little more help."

The guy was good. Joe could see, he was fully immersed now in the facade of *innocent friend*. "This should ring a bell...it was the weekend after the *Challenger* exploded. Remember that?"

"I do remember that, yes. Brew went missing when that was still in the news, big time. But I can't recall the exact day."

"The *Challenger* blew up on a Tuesday. According to what his parents said on the missing persons report, Brew didn't come home the following Saturday night. That's five days later."

Harvey appeared to act like he was thinking hard. "I'm drawing blanks, sorry. It was a weekend. Some weekends we went out drinking and partying, other ones we were in our room studying for exams."

"And you don't remember if you were out with your friends — your usual friends, Brew, Vic, and Jeremy— the weekend after the shuttle blew up? The weekend Brew went missing?"

He shrugged. "Sorry. Wish I could be more help."

Sure you do.

"One thing I don't get," Hank said, "sounds like you guys hung around a lot. Fair to say?"

"Yeah, I guess so."

"Why would you guys all buy into the idea of your close friend just taking off — without telling any of you where or why — and you're all okay with that?"

"I wouldn't say we were all okay with it. More like, there wasn't anything we could do about it. I mean, Vic and I wondered maybe he had decided to head out to California a few months early. He always talked about going out there when he graduated. We figured, maybe that's what happened."

"Conveniently," Joe said, "neither of you mentioned this to the detectives back in '86."

"We didn't? Maybe they didn't ask." He opened his laptop lid, signifying he was done. "Is there anything else you want to ask?"

Joe stood, then Hank. "Not at the moment. But we'll need to speak with you again soon. I'm sure of it."

22

AFTER THEY'D DRIVEN A FEW MINUTES IN SILENCE, HANK SAID, "So, Joe, got a question for you. Please don't take this the wrong way, but basically...what just happened back there?"

"I'm not sure I follow. You were there. We questioned a suspect. Well, a person-of-interest using the new lingo."

"No, I get that. But you took things in a totally different direction than I expected. What happened to, *Let's not show all our cards to this Harvey guy*? Remember? You said this was going to be a tricky situation. Then we go in there guns blazing. Feels like we showed our hand right off the bat. First, to the receptionist out front, then to Harvey's secretary, then we really give it to Harvey face-first. I'm not disagreeing with the tactic. Telling them we're here investigating a murder. Made it pretty clear to anyone paying attention that we are looking at Harvey as the main guy. I mean, we both think he probably is. And it seemed to stir some good things up. But I thought you were going to start off with, you know, *good cop*."

Joe laughed. "Guess I did throw you a curveball in there. Sorry about that."

"No need to apologize. I just want to understand. You've done that a number of other times, in other cases. Do something that surprises me. Whenever you do, I just try to follow your lead and not step on your toes. But I never asked you to explain your...strategy, I guess you could call it. Is that what it is? You're thinking one thing, then you go in there, and decide a new strategy's needed? How's that work exactly? I'm trying to learn here. Because obviously, you've been doing this — solving homicides — since I was a kid playing with toys. Not just here in Culpepper, I mean, but including Pittsburgh. Since you been here, you're like a legend. A hundred percent closure and conviction rate. So, whatever you're doing, I really want to know."

Joe thought a moment. Decided to pass on pointing out he wasn't that much older than Hank. But then he thought about the real answer to Hank's question, and how much he should get into this. He had talked to Hank about faith things before. Not that much, but when it seemed right. But he never got into the nuts and bolts too much. Hank and his wife went to church, the same church he and Kate attended. But for some reason, they seemed to keep the work in a different compartment.

"If it's some kind of trade secret you don't want to share," Hank said, "just tell me, and I'll let it go."

"No, it's not that. It's just, a little hard to explain, I guess. But since you asked, I'll give it a try. Believe it or not, the reason I changed tactics back there, so abruptly as you pointed out, was because...well, like I said, it's a little hard to explain."

"Take your time," Hank said. He smiled. "Think of this as...a teachable moment. You told me about that when explaining how you talk to your kids."

"Okay, Hank. I'll just say it then. I always pray before we go in and talk with somebody. Not just when I think I need protection. But even like what we just did, interviewing a suspect. I pray about it. Mainly, I'm asking for wisdom and discernment."

A surprised look on Hank's face. Clearly, not the answer he expected.

"But I don't just pray, I keep my ears open — guess you could say — for the Lord to answer back. Not so much with words, but with a strong sense of the right thing to do, the right way to go. My pastor talked to me all about this a few years back when I went to him for counseling."

"You went to our pastor for counseling?" Hank said. "Was that like after you had to shoot somebody?"

"Yeah, probably. Think that's what it was. But it was more than that. It was just about the job in general, you know, being a cop. All the stuff we have to deal with, including... shooting bad guys sometimes. Kate suggested I do it, and turns out, the guy really helped me out. He said what I was doing — being a cop, as long as I was a good one — was a very biblical thing. Said God could actually use me to serve his purpose while we're out there doing what we do."

"Really?" Hank said. "Guess I haven't heard that sermon before. He said what we do's in the Bible?"

"Yeah. He even turned to where it was, read the verses to me out loud, then explained how they connected. Totally changed my outlook. He's the one that suggested I start praying about...well, all of it, and then to actually expect

God to help me. Because, I'm doing something he wants done."

They pulled into the station parking lot and into Joe's unofficial parking place, under a nice shady oak. Kept the car and the A/C running.

"You wouldn't happen to remember what part of the Bible he read from?" Hank said.

"I don't just remember. I memorized it. Probably read it every morning for a week. It's in the book of Romans, Chapter 13. Paul's talking about God's role for people in authority. Specifically, government authority. Like us. He's telling people how they should view them but also talks about what God's purpose is for them, why they are there in the first place. The part I remembered was when the pastor read verse four. I'm probably paraphrasing a bit, but it says, *For the one in authority is God's servant for your good. But if you do wrong, be afraid, for authorities do not bear the sword for no reason. They are God's servants, agents of wrath to bring punishment on evildoers."*

Hank looked stunned. "That's in the Bible? In the New Testament?"

"Romans is the New Testament," Joe said.

"Don't bear the sword for no reason," Hank repeated. "That would be like our guns, right?"

"That's exactly what the pastor said."

"God's servants? Agents of wrath?" Hank said.

"To bring punishment on evildoers." Joe smiled.

Then Hank smiled. "Could you text me where that is? I want to look it up when I get home."

"Sure. So, none of this freaks you out? To hear how I operate?"

"Not a bit. But I guess it takes a while to get good at this, I imagine. The hearing God part. Like, right then, we're heading for the front door to speak with Harvey. You didn't look like somebody that just got a message from God. So, how's that work exactly?"

Joe laughed out loud. "I guess it does take a while to get familiar with the concept of God helping out in a moment like that. But that's why the first part means so much. Believing you are doing something he wants done, when you're bringing justice to evildoers. I know you believe in that. So, what I look for, or listen for, I guess, is something you might call a holy nudge in the right direction."

"A holy nudge?"

"Yeah. Like while we were walking to the front door, I had planned on taking it slow, but I got a very strong impression — almost like a voice but not quite — *Harvey and Waters have just been talking on the phone.* Just like that. And I knew what it meant. They're guilty. If they weren't, there'd be no reason for Waters to call Harvey so quick."

"He was obviously trying to warn him," Hank said. "And prep him, to make sure they got their stories straight."

"Exactly," Joe said. "So, I knew we had to go in there like gangbusters and rattle his cage. And all his reactions and answers to our questions further solidified their guilt. We may not know how this thing went down yet, or why. But I do believe we know the *who*."

Hank nodded. "Gotta say, Joe. This was...I don't know. Very helpful. Thanks for explaining all this."

"God help us," Joe said. "Right? We're going to need it. Because until we know the *how* and *why*, and can prove it, we've got nothing."

23

An hour had gone by. Hank had to respond to a call to follow up on a witness on that burglary case. Joe decided he no longer had a good reason to delay informing Tom Hazelton at the Gazette about the McFarland murder. But instead of just calling, he offered to buy him a cup of coffee at a café downtown. He hoped the gesture might inspire Hazelton to be a little more cooperative in how he presented the story.

Joe got his usual coffee shop drink — a breve latte, which is just a latte made with half-and-half instead of milk. Hazelton got some mocha macchiato thing, with a half-dozen other words added at the end. One of those words was soy. Joe couldn't imagine ever enjoying coffee with soy in it.

He was waiting for Hazelton, who had taken an extra few moments to pick out one of the pastries. Joe remembered the days when he used to buy fun things with his coffee. Hazleton got to the table a few minutes later carrying his drink and a big orange scone with icing.

"That thing would probably put me in a coma," Joe said.

"You didn't get anything for yourself?" Hazelton sat down.

"On a pretty low-carb diet. Doctor's orders, and the wife's."

"Gonna bother you watching me eat it?"

"No, I'm used to this kind of torture. But don't get mad if you catch me staring at every bite."

Hazelton laughed. "So, this is kinda different. You wanting to meet face-to-face like this. Is that because I'm a big author now?"

Joe smiled, knew he was joking. "No, I just figured maybe it would get us off to the right start with this story. Sometimes, it seems we get a little...adversarial."

"I'd agree with that. But I'm a little puzzled by all this attention for such a smallish story. This is about that car you guys fished out of the pond with that crane, right?"

Joe nodded. "Well, it turned into a fairly big thing. In fact, the way this thing's shaping up, I wouldn't be surprised if you'd want to turn this into your next true-crime book."

"Really? You serious?" Hazelton took a big bite of that scone.

Joe nodded again. "Yeah, afraid I am. I want to give you the facts, and I'm willing to answer a few questions, too. But I'm hoping we can set some ground rules on this that you'll abide by, in exchange for getting an exclusive look at things... like the last time."

"Sounds very interesting, Joe. I think I'm okay with that, but can you give me a little more to go on?"

"Okay, how's this for the headline? This car in the pond has turned into a cold case murder."

"What?" Hazelton whispered, his mouth full. "A murder?"

Joe nodded. "And there's more. Lots of layers, and I think more to come. But I don't want to say more unless you agree to look at the big picture here."

"What's the big picture? I don't follow."

"The big picture is...you aiming for the book idea versus a newspaper story."

"Still don't follow."

Joe sighed. How should he explain this? "See, we have competing interests at work here, Tom. You're all about the public's right to know, and about being the first one to report new info. We're all about catching the killers, period."

"I want the killers caught."

"Not saying you don't. Just saying it's not all you want. And hope this doesn't offend, but it's not the first thing you want. Problem is, the thing you want more, often results in information getting out to the public before we want it to. Included in that group we call *the public* happen to be the killers we're trying to catch. There's stuff we don't want them to know about the case, because if they find out, it gives them an advantage. Gives them a way to get rid of evidence, for example. Or come up with a fake alibi. Or intimidate witnesses. It creates all kinds of problems for us."

"I can see that," Hazelton said.

"Good. You know things have gotten even worse with social media. It's often so hard to keep anything out of the spotlight anymore. But I'm thinking, if you get the big picture in your mind — that there may be another book deal at the end of this rainbow — you won't mind sitting on some stuff for a few days, or even longer, if I ask you to. You know, keep something off of social media. Give us more time to develop the case in the best way to catch the bad guys."

Hazelton kept eating that scone, bite after bite. Seemed like he was okay with everything Joe said.

"So, what are the facts of this...cold case murder? And what am I okay to share now versus later?"

"The facts are...we pulled a blue '85 Camaro Z28 out of that pond. The driver was still in the car. His name was Brewster McFarland. He was a senior at Culpepper, and we believe the car went into the pond the night he disappeared, which was Saturday, Feb 1st. That's five days after the *Challenger* exploded, by the way."

Talking while chewing, he said, "I think I remember something about a college kid going missing back then."

"But this was a murder, not a missing person, and not an accident," Joe said.

"What confirmed this?" Hazleton said. "When I left the scene, you guys were acting like this wasn't much of a story."

"You're right. What happened was, when we loaded the car onto the wrecker, we noticed a gunshot wound to the back of the skull. Which meant, he didn't drive the car over the cliff by himself. He was shot, then the car was likely pushed over the cliff by his killers."

"Wow."

"You can look up the original story in the archives. It was definitely in the news back in early '86. And I'll give you a copy of our reports from back then. Of course, there wasn't anything about it being a murder. He was only listed as missing. His parents, however, maintained all along that foul play had to be involved. We weren't able to confirm their suspicions until we pulled the car up and saw the bullet hole in his head."

"Do you have any idea who did this?" Hazelton said.

Joe hesitated. "See, this is where it gets tricky. Everything I just told you, you could run with now. What I'm telling you next needs to wait. The answer is, yes, we think we know who did this. But the case is very preliminary. We don't have near enough evidence to take it to the DA yet. That's why we need your cooperation. We're asking you to leave out anything to do with potential suspects right now, and for the foreseeable future."

"Until you give me the green light?"

"Right. Which will be when the information you report can no longer harm or interfere with the case. And your reward for your patience is...you'll be told everything about the case and have all your questions answered, once the case is solved and arrests have been made."

"But you're gonna give me a little advance notice before you arrest these guys, right? So, I can be there with a camera."

"Sure, if I can."

"Can you at least tell me are these *potential suspects* local guys? Do they still live in town?"

"Two of them are. But there could have been three people involved, all locals at the time. But one moved away shortly after the crime was committed. The other two have lived their whole lives here since it happened. One of them is quite well known."

Hazelton finished his scone, sipped his latte, and said, "Wow, that is a mouthful. And you want me to sit on this part of the story, for now?"

"Yes. It's essential that we don't show these guys our hand. For two reasons. First, they are very clever, and second...right now, we have very little to go on."

24

THE NEXT DAY, JOE AND HANK WERE BACK TOGETHER ON THE case as a team. Joe brought Hank up to speed on everything, and they decided their next course of action was to try and locate the missing third friend in the equation: Jeremy Schofield. He was the one who'd been part of the foursome that always hung around together. This was confirmed by McFarland's parents, as well as in the early reports.

But for some reason, Schofield had never been interviewed. Hank wondered maybe he'd left town before the case got fully underway. They were talking about it over coffee in the office. "It doesn't make sense," he said, "that they would interview Tag Harvey and Vic Waters, and leave him out."

"No, it doesn't," Joe said. "Another thing that doesn't make sense is why he'd leave at all. At least the way he did. They were all seniors, right? This case began in early February. The dates on the reports are at the end of

February. He's only got a couple of months till he graduates. Why walk away from that?"

"Maybe he transferred to a school out west," Hank said, "and finished there."

"Maybe he did. Or maybe he saw something he wasn't supposed to see, something that scared him to death, literally."

"Like his friends murdering McFarland?" Hank said.

Joe made a face, *yeah, like that.* "Didn't you say you located a brother of his that still lives in town?"

"Yes, I did. I never called him, though, but I wrote his number down somewhere. Let me get it." He thumbed through his notes. "Yeah, here it is. Dave Schofield, 334 Salisbury Lane. You want me to give him a call?"

"Yeah, see if he can meet with us now. That's less than fifteen minutes from here."

"How much you want me to tell him?"

"Just say we have some questions about a case from 1986 that we could use his help on. Something to do with a friend of his brother. Hopefully, that'll be enough to get in the door."

TWENTY MINUTES LATER, Joe pulled into the driveway. It had a realtor sign parked in the front yard. The place had that look older homes get when someone tries to make them look better than they probably are. New coat of paint, new plants across the front, driveway with fresh concrete patches.

The homes on either side looked to be in the kind of shape this one probably was before the owner decided to sell. As Joe and Hank got out of the car, the garage door slowly opened. The thing sounded like it was driven by an old steam engine. As it rose, they saw a middle-aged man standing there, smoking a cigar. Mostly bald, looked older than either Tag Harvey or Vic Waters.

Joe whispered to Hank, "Isn't this supposed to be the younger brother?"

"Yeah, by five years."

"Morning, gentlemen. You must be the detectives."

They took out their badges and said who they were, shook hands.

"I'm Dave Schofield. Didn't mean to startle you having our conversation out here instead of at the front door. But you caught me smoking my cigar. Got the place inside all painted and told my wife I wouldn't be smoking in there anymore."

"Had any offers?" Joe said.

"Had some good nibbles but nothing solid yet. But that's okay, still have some things left on my punch list. The good news is, it's paid for, so I'm not in a desperate place. It was actually my Mom's house. She died a few weeks back, left it to me. Our place is a lot nicer than this, newer neighborhood and everything. Me smoking this bother either you two guys? Cause I can put it out, and we can talk inside."

"I'm fine," Hank said.

"Me, too," Joe said. "Don't smoke them anymore, but I can tell by the aroma, you paid a little extra for that one."

Schofield took the cigar out of his mouth, stared at the inch-long ash on the tip with pride. "You know your cigars. This baby cost me twelve bucks. Be a shame to put it out early."

"No, go ahead," Joe said. "We can talk out here."

"So, I guess I spoke to you, Sergeant," he said, looking at Hank.

"Please, call me Hank."

"You can call me Joe."

"Okay, Hank and Joe. So, you want to ask me some questions about my brother, Jeremy. Something about a case in the eighties?"

"Yeah, that's right," Joe said. "This'll be coming out in the news very soon, but we're investigating what was a missing person's case from 1986, that's now turned into a cold case murder situation, based on some new evidence."

"A murder? Wow. And this has something to do with Jeremy? You think he had something to do with it?"

"Too early to tell," Hank said. "Right now, we're just exploring the idea of what he might know about the situation. At the time, he was good friends with the young man who was murdered."

"And it looks like he left town very soon after," Joe added. "Our records say you are younger by five years, is that correct?"

"Yeah, give or take."

"You remember anything about one of his good friends going missing? This would've been a few days after the *Challenger* exploded."

"Yeah," Schofield said. "You're talking about Brewster, right? What was his last name?"

"McFarland," Hank said.

"Yeah, McFarland. I remember. I was in high school. Jeremy and I didn't run in the same crowd, obviously. But I knew he and those other guys were close."

"You referring to Tag Harvey and Vic Waters?" Joe said.

"Yeah, that's them. They were always together. Then the shuttle blew up, that was a huge thing. Then a few days after, Brewster disappears. Like...he just vanished. Locally, that might've been an even bigger story. At least for a few days."

"Do you remember your brother saying anything about Brewster disappearing?" Joe said.

Schofield seemed to be trying to recall. "Not anything specific. Course, it's not like he ever confided in me...about anything. We weren't really that close."

"Did he say anything to you or your mother about why he was leaving town?" Joe said. "Wasn't that just a few weeks after McFarland disappeared?"

"If that," Schofield said. "Yeah, he did talk to us. My mom was super upset about it. I didn't really care one way or the other, except that she was so upset. I mean we didn't have very much money. He never could've gotten into a school like Culpepper, except for the scholarship he got his last year in high school. They had a School of Journalism back then. Anyway, she's yelling, *You're going to throw away your scholarship and just leave? You graduate in a few months.*"

"Yeah," Joe said, "that seemed pretty unusual to us, too."

"Did to me, too. But I guess what he said made sense. He said he got this *offer he could not refuse* from a talent agency in LA, to be a staff photographer. Said it was the job of a lifetime. And wasn't that the point of going to college, to get a good job?"

Joe looked at Hank. They both wondered if this was the real reason. Could be.

"Anyway, she was crying and continued crying about it till the day he left. The worst thing, though, was he pretty much left us in the dirt. Guess he became this big high-end celebrity photographer, had no use for us. Even changed his name."

"So, you guys haven't stayed in touch?"

Schofield shook his head no. "Not even a little. I mean, it's like, do I even have a brother? I stayed here, lived my life, looked after mom. She left the whole house to me. Not a dime to him. Not that I think he cares. Haven't been following his career, but I guess he did pretty well. Sent a nice flower arrangement to the funeral home. Biggest one there. But he didn't come, didn't call."

"Sorry to hear that," Joe said. He was sorry in more ways than one.

"So," Schofield said, "are you saying that Brewster was murdered? That he's been dead all this time?"

"Afraid so," Joe said.

"And you think maybe Jeremy left town because he had something to do with it?"

"Like I said, we just want to talk with him at this point. Know any way we can reach him?"

"Well, I know his new name is Jeremy Chevalier. Can you believe that? We're not even French. Can't imagine there are too many big photographers with that name in LA."

Joe wrote it down. "Okay, Dave. Really, thanks for taking the time to get with us. Sorry about your mom's passing."

"Thanks. If I remember anything else, who should I call?"

Hank handed him his card. They shook hands and headed for the car.

"What do you think now?" Hank said.

"Hank, I have no idea. But one way or another, we need to talk to this guy."

25

"AND SO IT BEGINS."

Real estate developer Tag Harvey was holding a copy of the Culpepper Gazette, provided for him by his personal assistant twenty minutes ago. Usually, when he read the news — like most people these days — he read it on an app on his iPad. His PA, as part of her job, had the old-fashioned print newspaper delivered to the office every day. Mainly, so she could better look over all the real estate ads Harvey Homes had put in the paper.

Body Found - Culpepper Senior Missing Since 1986— IT'S MURDER!

Along with the provocative headline, was a large picture of Brewster McFarland taken in his senior year. All smiles and full of life. Just as Tag remembered him. He quickly blocked off any sentimental feelings attempting to form in his heart and mind. No place for that. Not now, and not then.

What's done, was done. It had to happen. That's all there was to it. No sense in dwelling on the past, beyond the necessity created by reading the article.

He had to know what was said, how the story was playing out. Because it had a direct bearing on the present. He and Vic would have to — at least temporarily — renew their partnership in this matter and make sure nothing came of it from here. So, they found his body. He'd honestly thought no one ever would. Didn't even think of it anymore. Like it never happened, that's how he'd lived for decades now.

And that's how he would continue to live. It was just a sad story. Something mysterious and unexplainable that happened to an old college friend many years ago. And after a few weeks of morbid curiosity generated by this story, that's what it would remain. He opened his desk drawer and pulled out the burner phone he'd recently purchased. Vic had given him the number of his own, so he dialed it now. Only the second time using the phone. The first, a test call to Vic.

The phone rang several times. "Good morning, Tag. Figured it's you, since you're the only one I gave this number to."

"Morning, Vic. So, did you see it?"

"See what?"

"The article, in the Gazette. You haven't seen it yet?"

"I haven't read the newspaper in years. But I'm guessing — since you're a busy guy — it must be something important. Let me guess...something having to do with the reason we got these phones."

"And then some," Tag said. "You need to read it, then we'll talk."

"I need to go down to the store and buy a paper?"

"You could, or you could just look it up online. I assume you have a smart phone, or a tablet?"

"I'm a modern guy. I have both."

"Well, look it up. Just Google *Culpepper Gazette*. They got the whole paper online now. Look up the local section, probably got a tab. Click on that, you'll see it. An article just came out about them finding Brew. Call me back after you read it. But do it now."

"Sure, Tag. I'll get right back to you."

Tag hung up, decided he could use a bathroom break, refresh his coffee. By the time he got back to his desk, Vic called him back. He picked it up. "So, what do you think?"

"Could've been a lot worse. It didn't mention either one of our names. That was nice."

"Yeah, I was relieved to see that. All he said near the end was something about his friends at the time were unable to offer any explanation about his disappearance."

"I can live with that," Vic said. "If that's as far as it goes. Judging by how we left things, and how much time has passed, we should be in the clear. Don't you think?"

"I want to think that. When those two detectives met with you, did it feel like an interview or more like an interrogation?

"Not gonna lie," Vic said, "made me nervous. Felt kinda like they were fishing. Course, I didn't take the bait. How about you?"

"Felt like way more than fishing. Like I was a baby seal getting clubbed."

Vic laughed. "You always had a way of saying things. So, they were leaning on you heavy?"

"Yeah, I'd say they were. Of course, I pushed back as good as I got. Got offended, you know, like an innocent person would. That seemed to get them to back off. I mean I get why they were trying. They had just found Brew's body with a hole in his skull. Somebody had to do it. Looking at his close friends only makes sense. But I could tell, that's all they've got. No evidence. Just pushing buttons, see if anything turns on."

"That's how I'm seeing it, too," Vic said. "Because they got nothing, we keep singing from the same sheet music, that's all they'll ever have."

No one said anything for a moment. Tag wondered if Vic was thinking the same thing as him.

Finally, Vic broke the ice. "You think these detectives will wind up talking to our...California friend?"

"Is Jeremy even still alive?" Tag said. "I mean, I haven't talked to him, literally, since he left back in '86."

Vic sighed. Tag could hear it. "Oh, I think he's probably still alive. Wound up bumping into his little brother, Dave, a few years back. Came into the pawnshop. Remember him?"

"Can't say as I do."

"Well, I was a little closer to Jeremy than you. Anyway, I didn't even recognize Dave. I mean, let's just say, he hasn't aged well. But he recognized me. We talked a little bit. I asked him about Jeremy. It was pretty clear they weren't close. Like, he didn't even know that much about him. But one thing he did know, he changed his name. Forget now what it was, something French-sounding. Supposedly, he became some big name photographer in LA. But like I said, that news is a few years old."

"Well," Tag said, "I know that's the reason Jeremy gave for why he was leaving so suddenly. Maybe he was telling the truth then, about it being the photography thing. I had a feeling it had more to do with the Brew situation. Like he got spooked and took off."

"You and me both," Vic said. "At the time, don't think I bought what he was selling. But over the years, I figured, what difference does it make? I do know I didn't miss him taking pictures of us all the time. That was always annoying."

"Yeah," Tag said. "I forgot about that. It was annoying." Tag got to thinking about this some more. Decided to bring up something, just in case. "Say, Vic, you got any connections out in LA?"

"A few. What kind of connections we talking about?"

"You know, maybe from some of your...side businesses? Just in case this thing were to go south on us. Probably won't, but I didn't get this successful being sloppy. Need to plan for every contingency." He hoped Vic was getting the message.

"I think I follow you. And the answer is, that happens, you let me know. We should be okay on that score."

"Again," Tag said, "probably won't be necessary."

"Then again, if it does become so, you've probably heard...LA can be a very dangerous city."

26

JOE CAME INTO THE OFFICE TO FIND HANK READING THE Gazette article about the McFarland case. He'd just come from Pendleton's office who had read the same thing that morning and wanted an update.

Hank looked up. "So, how's the captain feeling about things? Got any concerns about how we're handling this?"

Joe sat down. "Surprisingly, no. He was actually shocked that reading Hazelton's article didn't make him mad. You know, him sharing way too much with the public. I explained to him about my coffee date with Hazelton and how that went."

"I was just finishing it," Hank said. "Judging by what I read, I can see why Pendleton didn't get upset. Looks like your little chat with Hazelton bore some fruit."

"Looks like it did. But I did fill the captain in on our suspicions about who killed the kid. He didn't care much about Vic Waters, but he didn't like it when I said Tag Harvey."

"No surprise there," Hank said. "Harvey's too well-known in town."

"Yeah, and as I was informed, too big a donor to the mayor and several other elected officials the captain doesn't want to offend."

"I can see how arresting a major financial donor could put a damper on future election campaigns."

"There's the rub," Joe said. "Not that we needed to be told, but Pendleton reminded me after hearing my update that we seem miles away from arresting anyone. So, he wants us to keep their names — especially Harvey's – out of any press updates until we really feel like we can nail this guy."

"Not that we needed to be told," Hank repeated. "To that end, I spent some time digging up what I can about Jeremy Schofield, a.k.a. Jeremy *Chevalier*."

"The photographer out in LA?"

"The very one," Hank said.

"So, is he some big deal out there? Or was he just trying to make his brother think so all these years?"

"From what I can gather — granted, I'm not done searching — but at first glance, I'd say it's a little of both. Before I go any further, how about I just call him Jeremy? I don't want to keep saying *Chevalier*."

Joe laughed. "Permission granted."

"So, it does seem like he was somebody in the LA photography scene. Gotta remember, we're talking about a span of over thirty years. From my perspective, he never made it to the A-list. When I googled *famous LA photographers*, a list did come up. With these guys and gals, there was a ton of information. Lots of websites, interviews, articles written about them. Of course, not from any publications you, or I, or anyone we'd ever talk to would ever read. But, I suppose, in the elite crowd they run with, these people made a pretty big splash."

"But not Jeremy," Joe said.

"No, not Jeremy. So, whatever level of success he attained, sounds like he probably overstated it to Dave."

"Well, who isn't at least tempted to overstate their success when talking to family, right?"

"I wouldn't know anything about that, Joe. In my family, I'm already a huge sensation. The fact that my name appeared in several newspaper articles right next to yours... I'm already a bona fide member in the Culpepper A-list."

"Geez," Joe said. "Go on."

"So, back to Jeremy. I did find some stuff on him, about his photography career. Looks like, he really did have one. He doesn't have a Wikipedia page, which seems almost entry-level if you're somebody in your field. But I did find some articles and other listings where his name was mentioned. For example, he did work for a pretty big talent agency. Looks like it was back in the 90s through about 2005. He was credited in the bio for a number of actors and actresses, but again, not the kind of big stars with names you'd recognize."

"So, he never took pics of Brad Pitt or Robert Downey Junior? Nobody like that?" Joe said.

"Nobody close to guys like that. The pictures I saw were actors I kinda recognized. Like, I knew I'd seen them in something or other. But I couldn't tell you what it was, or who they were. He took headshots for actors like that."

"Now, wait a minute," Joe said. "You said Jeremy started photographing that kind of stuff in the 90s?"

"Yeah. If he did anything before that, it didn't make the internet."

"That doesn't add up. Not unless it starts in February 1986. Because that's what he told his family. *That's* the reason he gave for needing to leave in a hurry."

Hank nodded. "I'm with you. He got an offer he couldn't refuse. The kind worth leaving your senior year for, a couple months before graduation."

They looked at each other. "Doesn't add up," Joe said.

"I imagine a guy has to have some pretty serious motivation to leave town in a hurry the way he did."

"And now we know for a fact," Joe said, "it wasn't for no top shelf photography job. Like I said, Hank, we need to talk to this guy. You figure out yet where he lives?"

"Haven't gotten that far," Hank said.

"Keep on it. I'm heading back to see Pendleton. Prep him for the idea of spending the money to send us to LA.".

ACROSS TOWN, in his makeshift studio also known as his third bedroom, Josh Hoskins was busy working on his new faux antique car calendar project. He had already decided to include the four photographs he'd recently developed from his new World War II era camera. The ones taken from the roll of film he'd found inside the camera. Of course, he couldn't use the other three because they had people in them.

A few days ago with these four pictures in hand, he'd made the drive to the Culpepper University campus and found the exact locations where the original photographer had snapped the photos. As he figured, they were taken near the big angel fountain close to the Murray Building. It felt strange standing in the exact spot, holding photos taken so long ago. He'd brought the antique Kodak camera along with his high-end digital one, and retook new photos that were identical matches to the ones taken in the forties.

While he hoped he could use those four original pictures, he'd have to make sure they matched all the other shots he needed to take for the calendar. After all, there were twelve months in a year, so at least eight of them would have to be new locations.

A knock on the door. He knew it was his Mom. She was there visiting for a few weeks. She didn't live in Culpepper anymore but in a little apartment in Dunedin, the county seat. This used to be her place. It was the house Josh grew up in, and he bought it from her a few years back.

"Come in, Ma."

She opened the door, walked in holding a copy of the Gazette. She still liked to read an actual newspaper, so he grabbed her one that morning when he'd gone out for a few things at the store.

"Have you seen this, Josh?" She held up the paper. "I remember this case, this boy who went missing back in '86. They just found his body. It was so sad. Happened the week the *Challenger* blew up. You were maybe eight years old then. You remember the *Challenger* exploding?"

"Yeah, definitely. It was a big thing at school because of that teacher. Don't remember her name."

She walked over, showed him the news story on the front page of the local section. "Brewster McFarland, it says. That was the boy's name, a senior at Culpepper. It says they just found his body in a pond just outside of town. It was still in his car. Can you imagine? His poor parents, all these years not knowing what happened. And now, it's this?"

Josh looked down at the headline, then at the big photograph of the young man, obviously a senior portrait photo. He could see the graininess in the background, typical of cameras before the digital age. "Yeah Mom, that's... awful."

Something hit him as odd as he looked again at the boy's face. It couldn't be that he knew him. As a senior in college, there was no way they'd have ever met. But why did he look so familiar?

She was about to walk away, when he stopped her.

"Could I have that for a minute?"

She handed the paper to him. "You could have it longer if you want. I'm pretty much done with that section."

He set it down on his desk, staring at the boy's face. Then it hit him. Where he'd seen that face before. But it couldn't be. It made no sense. He reached over and grabbed the three photos from the old Kodak camera, the ones with people in them. Pulled out the one where they were smiling and posing.

He zeroed in on the one who had been reading the newspaper, who was now facing the camera.

"Oh. My. Gosh."

27

WHILE HE WAITED FOR JOE TO GET BACK FROM HIS MEETING with Captain Pendleton, Hank decided to give Dave Schofield a call. He knew Dave had said he and his brother, Jeremy, weren't close, but he figured he at least knew some way to reach him out in LA. Dave picked up after a few rings.

"Hi, this is Sergeant Hank Jenkins, Culpepper PD. We spoke recently about your brother, Jeremy, in regards to this Brewster McFarland case."

"Yeah, Hank. What can I do for you?"

"Have you seen the news article about McFarland? Came out today in the Gazette?"

"Can't say as I have. But I'll check it out, now that you've mentioned it. Say anything about my brother?"

"No, thankfully, the reporter did as we asked and left out the names of McFarland's friends, at least for now. But the Lieutenant and I've agreed, we really do need to talk with Jeremy about this. See what he remembers. I recall you saying you guys aren't close."

"I'd say that's an understatement, Hank. But I'm guessing you're wondering if I have his contact info?"

"Was going to be my next question. You have any way to reach him? I'm guessing you might, since he sent flowers to your mom's funeral home."

"I sorta do. The phone number I had for him wasn't any good. So I took a shot at contacting him through his website. He's got a tab on there that says *Contact Me*. It opens a form that looks sort of like an email. That's how I told him about Mom passing away. He never really got back with me, just sent the big flower arrangement to the funeral home with a card. All it said was, *So sorry to hear about Mom, Jeremy.* Of course, he didn't write it. Probably just told someone at the florist what to say."

Hank wrote some notes while Dave talked. "By any chance, did you keep the information from the florist? Maybe I could get more direct contact info through them, if you did."

"I might have," Dave said. "I put all the cards and letters in a box. Let me look through them, and I'll get back to you on that."

"Great, thanks." They hung up.

Joe walked in.

Hank looked up. "So, when are we flying out to LA? Assuming the captain is on board with the idea."

"I think I persuaded him that it's necessary. But he wants to make sure we've done everything we can in town first. So, it got me thinking. Maybe you should call those two divers back, see if we can get them in the pond again. That won't be too expensive. We won't need the crane or any special equipment. Won't need to disturb traffic any."

"You want to go looking for the bullet?" Hank said. "The one that must've fallen out of McFarland's skull?"

"You got it. Seeing how that place has only ever been fished by Trevor and his friends when they were kids, don't think there should be too much down there. Metal stuff, I mean. Like soda cans and other crap like that. That's one of our big challenges when Jack and I go out metal detecting. More than half the things that the detector finds are just modern junk. We're usually hoping to find some Civil War relics, but we're competing with over a century of guys out there hunting, dropping all kinds of stuff that our detectors pick up on."

"Okay, Joe. I'll give them a call. Pay them the usual rate like the last time?"

"Yeah, that'd be fine."

FOR A FULL TEN MINUTES, JOSH HOSKINS' moved back-and-forth between the two photos on his desk. The grainy color picture of Brewster McFarland in the newspaper, and the black-and-white photo of what he was now convinced was the same person, taken from the Kodak WW2-era camera.

It had to be him. The resemblance was too strong for any other explanation to make sense.

He decided to do a little experiment. He'd already scanned all seven of the photos from the Kodak camera into his laptop. Opening it up, he quickly navigated to the JPEG matching the black-and-white photo in his hand. He blew it up till only the face of the young man he believed to be McFarland filled the screen, cropped it, resaved it, and sent it to his printer. He walked over and brought it back to the desk, set it next to the newspaper photo.

He didn't have the right software, but he was sure if he applied a facial recognition app to these photos they would be a match. What he did was something much more low-tech. He got up and brought both of them out to his mother in the living room. She was working on a crossword puzzle.

"Excuse me, Mom. I need your help with a little thing I'm working on."

She looked up at him, standing next to her chair. "What's that, dear?"

He handed her the newspaper, which he'd folded so that McFarland's picture was the main thing she'd see. Then he gave her the cropped, blown-up black-and-white photo he'd just printed.

Before he could even explain what he wanted, she said, "Where did you get this black-and-white photo of the boy?" She said it with certainty.

But, of course she would. Josh felt certain, if he handed these two pictures to ten people, all ten would say they were pictures of the same guy. He sat beside her in a nearby chair. "Mom, this is kind of crazy. Until a few minutes ago, I didn't know I had a black-and-white picture of Brewster McFarland. But you've made my point pretty clear." Pointing to the black-and-white one, he said, "that's him. Isn't it? It's definitely him."

"You weren't sure?" she said. "Until I pointed it out?"

He laughed. "No, I was mostly sure. But see, the problem is..." He stood. "Wait just a minute. He walked back into his studio, grabbed the original photograph that showed McFarland posing with the other two guys, and came back. "This is the photo I used to make the blown-up copy you're holding. It's from that old World War II camera I told you about, the one I bought last week at an estate sale. Remember, I found a roll of film in it, left there by the owner — what I thought was the *original* owner?"

"But how can that be?" she said. "This boy who died wasn't even alive in the 1940s."

"Exactly." The disappointment of this revelation just now set in. "I was wrong. All this time, I thought I'd found seven historical photos from the 1940s. But they couldn't be from back then. Not unless this kid somehow mastered the art of time travel. A more reasonable explanation is...the photos in the camera were taken from the 1980s. For some reason, whoever took them decided to use black-and-white film. And by some crazy coincidence, the last seven photos he took with the camera included Brewster McFarland, the dead kid in the paper."

"My goodness, Josh," his mother said. "That really is kind of crazy. I am sorry. For you, I mean. I know how excited you were thinking you found original photographs from the 1940s."

He sighed. "Yeah, it kinda stinks."

"Don't you think you should call someone about this? Maybe the police? The newspaper said he was murdered. Maybe they'll find these photographs relevant to the case somehow."

She handed him back the blown-up picture of McFarland. "Yeah," he said, "Guess I should."

28

HANK WAS OUT GRABBING A BITE TO EAT. HE'D JUST LEFT A drive-through and had found a nice big oak in the corner of the parking lot to sit under while he ate his burger and fries. He'd offered to get Joe something but, as expected, Joe turned him down. Blamed the short leash Kate had him on with his diet.

His phone rang, looked at it in the holder. It was Emmett calling back. He finished chewing and answered, using the hands-free set up. "Hey, Emmett. Thanks for calling back."

"No problem. Sorry I missed your call. Phil and me, we was out giving some diving lessons in the lake. You said something about needing us to go back down in that pond. What's up?"

"Did you read about the case in the Gazette?" Hank said.

"I did. We did. Phil and me. We were just talking about it. Appreciate you mentioning us to that reporter. Instead of just speaking about some divers going down in that pond, he actually mentioned our names."

"You guys are celebrities now."

"Not quite, but it never hurts getting your name out there. That was something finding out that poor kid had a bullet hole in his head."

"Yeah, it was. Definitely made our case more complicated. Which is why I'm calling. The ME informed us he was only shot once, likely with a .22, since it didn't go through his skull. Our CSI guys did a thorough search of that Z28, and the bullet didn't turn up. Which means...it probably fell out in the pond, which is where you and Phil come in."

"We can do that. We got waterproof metal detectors and everything else we'd need."

"Great. That was going to be my next question. We're thinking this should be a fairly simple job. We know where the car went down, and since that place has rarely ever been visited by people, hopefully, the only ping you'll hear will be that spent 22 caliber bullet."

"We like simple. When do you need us?"

"As soon as you can go down." Hank heard Emmett say something muffled.

"Phil agrees, we can do it tomorrow morning. Unless that's moving too quick for—"

"No, tomorrow works for me. We won't need to block off the road, since it'll just be us. Those stone barriers are still up, but there's room to park just off the road."

"Great," Emmett said. "How's 8:30 sound?"

"See you then," Hank said. "And Emmett?"

"Yeah, Hank?"

"Need to remind you, even though this story is out in the press, we still need you and Phil to keep a lid on anything we discuss, or anything you find."

"Okay, but...since it is out there now, why all the secrecy?"

"Because it's not *all* out there. We got the reporter covering it to agree not to share things that will mess up our investigation. Not until we're closer to an arrest. We don't want to show our hand to the guys that did this, right?"

"Oh, yeah. I can see that," Emmett said. "So, you figure those guys are still here, in Culpepper?"

"We do. At least, we're pretty sure."

"Wow, after all this time. They just been living here like everything's just fine."

"It seems so. So, are we good?" Hank said. "Can I trust you guys to help us out here and keep everything confidential."

"Sure, Hank. I'll tell Phil. You can count on us."

JOE JUST FINISHED his tuna wrap, which Kate had packed him for lunch. It wasn't bad. Joe liked tuna, ever since he was a kid. But in the kid memory, the tuna was always on white bread. It wasn't just that this was a tortilla, it was a special wrap made for people on this Keto diet. All in all, he got it down with no complaints.

The office phone rang. He picked it up. "Lieutenant Joe Boyd, how can I help you?" Sounded more like a customer service rep than a cop.

"Hello, Lieutenant. This is Dave Schofield. I spoke recently with your partner, Hank. Is he there?"

"Not at the moment. We're both working the same case, though. I can probably help you."

"I'm sure you can. He was calling about getting some

contact information for my brother, Jeremy, out in California. I didn't have anything specific, but he asked if I had the information about the florist Jeremy used to send flowers to my mom's funeral. I got that info if you want it."

"Yeah, great, Dave. Let me just grab a pen and notepad. Okay, go ahead." Joe wrote down the information. "Thanks. Hopefully, they'll have enough info to let us connect directly with him."

"Hope so. If you do wind up talking with Jeremy, I wonder if you would do me a favor. No, never mind. That's okay."

"No, Dave. What is it?"

"It's just...I don't know, it just seems kind of ridiculous that he and I don't talk. Still, after all these years. It's not like we ever had a falling out. Not that I'm aware of. And now that my Mom's gone, it's just him and me."

"I understand. I can see where that would be...confusing, if not painful."

"Yeah, it's both. I just don't get it. Why he's kept us so far out of his life. I wondered, is he gay? Is that it? Cause if you find out that he is, he's still my brother. Tell him I don't care. I just want us to talk. Hey, I'm sorry. I shouldn't get you in the middle of our family problems."

"It's okay. Doesn't bother me. At this point, don't see how I can work his sexual orientation into our line of questioning."

Dave laughed. "No, I guess not. It might not even be that. If you could just let him know, that I'd really like for him and I to talk. You could give him my number. That would be a big help. If he wants me to call, and you get his number, I'll do that."

"Okay. That might be something I could do. I'll let you know if I get anything worthwhile."

They hung up. Joe felt kind of bad for the guy. Of course, he had no idea what other reasons Jeremy Schofield — a.k.a. Chevalier — might have for breaking off ties with his family. But he was pretty sure the main reason had more to do with the Brewster McFarland murder than the amazing job offer he fabricated for his family.

29

IT WAS JUST AFTER 9:30, THE FOLLOWING MORNING. FIFTEEN minutes ago, Hank had met Emmett and Phil out by the pond area on Highway 40. They had already made the careful journey down the hillside path to the creek, made even trickier carrying all the diving gear. This time they had the added weight of the metal detectors. Right now, the two men were pulling on their wetsuits.

"Not sure why," Emmett said, "had a hard time falling asleep last night. Guess I'm just keyed up about being involved in a big murder case."

"I might've had the same trouble," said Phil, "had I not had the good sense to numb my senses with strong drink."

Hank laughed. "Hope you didn't wake up with a hangover. I don't imagine that's going to feel good when the pressure of that deep water kicks in."

"No, no hangover. I know when to stop. But I had to do something. Otherwise, scenes of that skeleton popping out of that windshield would've kept circling my brain as I lay on that pillow."

"Yeah," Emmett said, "those images stuck with me for quite a few days after that dive. I knew we were expecting to find a body down there, since you warned us it was likely to happen. But I don't think either one of us were prepared for what we saw. I know you watched the video, you and Joe. But it wasn't near the same as seeing it up close and personal."

"No, I don't imagine it was," Hank said. "But the good news is, that's not gonna happen this time around. Shouldn't see anything in that water this time but a bunch of hungry trout." He looked over at the metal detectors. "You sure those things will be able to pick up a little spent 22-caliber bullet? Even if it's sunk deep in the mud?"

Phil picked his up. "Oh, yeah. They'll do the trick. These'll pick up anything metal even buried under three feet."

"It'll even tell us how deep it is," Emmett said, "so we know how far to dig." He held up a special aluminum scoop with a mesh bottom. "This is what we use underwater instead of a shovel. We scoop down to where we're hearing the ping and lift up. All the dirt and muck will fall through this mesh screen, leaving the metal object — hopefully your little bullet — in the scoop." He made his way over to the flat stones and sat, preparing to get in the water.

Phil joined him. "Guess we better get at it."

"Will you be filming it this time, too?" Hank asked.

"I guess we can try if you need us to. Might be a little difficult with these detectors."

"No, never mind. Guess we don't need to see the moment of discovery. The main thing is getting that bullet recovered."

Both men slipped into the water. "Well," Emmett said, "here goes."

Hank watched as they disappeared into the murky depths. Moments later, all he could see was their trail of bubbles.

JOSH HOSKINS GOT out of his SUV, went around to the back, and grabbed his camera bag, feeling apprehensive about what he was there to do. He looked at the sign near the road that read, "Culpepper Police Station" then toward the glass front doors. It wasn't that he'd had any second thoughts about the contents in his bag. He guessed it was just nerves. Other than the occasional traffic ticket, he never had any dealings with police.

He slung the strap around his shoulder and headed for the front door. Once inside, he saw what looked to be a receptionist area and headed there. A young lady wearing a uniform was sitting behind the counter. She looked up from a screen and smiled. Her name tag said *Eileen*. He probably shouldn't call her that.

"Can I help you with something?"

"I think so," he said. "Or maybe, I can help you guys." He set the camera bag on the counter.

"We're always looking for people willing to help. What do you have?"

"This is about that murder case you guys are working on. The one about the college kid from 1986. My mom and I were talking about it yesterday." He instantly regretted referring to his mother. He quickly felt the need to fix it. "I don't live with her, or anything. She's just visiting for a few days."

"Okay..."

"Anyway," he continued, "I'm a photographer. I make, among other things, special calendars with antique cars and old buildings that I sell on the internet." He had to stop this. He was saying way too much. "Anyway, a short while ago I bought this antique camera made in the 1940s." He pulled the Kodak Rangefinder out of the bag and set it down. Then he spread out the seven black-and-white photos, like you would a deck of cards. "To my great surprise, it had an undeveloped role of black and white film in it. At first, I got real excited, thinking these pictures had been left there in the camera since the forties."

"I can see how you might think that," she said.

He could tell she was trying to get him to get to the point. He was never good at that, always setting up a story. "So, I developed the film."

"And these are the photos?"

"Yes."

"And...how do these have any connection to the murder case?"

"Well, at first I didn't think they did. Like you probably don't right now. I went to school at Culpepper, so I recognized the buildings in the background. Since I didn't see any cars, I still thought the pictures were taken in the 1940s. As you can see, there are some college kids in three of them. Guess I should've noticed they weren't wearing clothes from that time period. But I didn't. Anyway, yesterday my mom shows me the front page of the local section in the Gazette. It's all about the murder, and has a big picture of the kid who was killed. The one you guys found still in his car in that pond."

"Okay," she said. "I read that story, and I've seen that photo. His name is Brewster McFarland, right?"

"Yeah, that's it. So, here's the thing. I'm looking at McFarland's picture in the paper, and for some reason, he looks familiar. Then it dawns on me why. I've been looking at him for days in these black-and-white photos from my antique camera. I just didn't know it. See here?" He singled out the photo that showed McFarland and two of his friends posing and smiling, pointed to McFarland. Then he pulled out the blown up copy, showing just McFarland's face. Then he pulled the newspaper out of his bag and set it beside it. "Do you see it?"

She looked at both pictures. Her eyes said she saw it.

"It's the same guy, right?" Josh said.

She nodded her head. "Looks like it to me. That is pretty strange. I'm surprised at how clear the focus is on the black-and-white photo. It's better than the color one in the newspaper."

"Yeah, these Kodak Rangefinders have great resolution. They were way ahead of their time. See, I don't know how relevant this is to the murder case, or if it's even relevant at all. But it just struck me as strange to find these black-and-white photos with the same guy in them as the dead guy you guys are investigating. My mom thought I should bring it down, let you all decide how much it matters."

"Well, one thing seems apparent to me," Eileen said, "this has to be Brewster McFarland, in your photos. And at least to me, he looks like he's the same age as the color photo in the paper. I'm going to pass this on to the lead detective on the case, Lieutenant Boyd. Can I keep these for a little while?"

"Sure, you can have them. They're copies. And here's my contact info, if you need to reach me." Josh handed her a sheet of paper, then put the camera back in his bag.

She looked at the paper. "Thanks for coming in, Josh."

"No problem."

As he walked away, he heard her get on the phone, and say, "Hey, Joe. Could you come out here to the desk? A guy just brought in something interesting. Something I think you need to see."

30

EMMETT AND PHIL HAD BEEN UNDERWATER FOR THE LAST twenty minutes. Hank wasn't concerned. Emmett said they had an hour's worth of air in their tanks. While he waited, he was looking up Scriptures on a Bible app Joe had told him about. Something kinda triggered in him after that conversation he and Joe had about how Joe prayed about everything, even things on the job. For some reason, Hank had never considered involving the Lord in things that practical or mundane.

And he certainly never imagined the Bible actually said anything about cops. But there it was in Romans 13, just like Joe said. Of course, the Bible didn't say *cops*, but it was clearly talking about people in authority being used by God to punish evildoers. That made Hank curious about what else the Bible might have to say about the ordinary affairs of his life, so he started looking things up. Joe suggested he might enjoy reading the *Proverb of the Day*, since there were thirty-one of them and about the same number of days in a month.

He was just finishing today's proverb when the steady stream of bubbles coming from the pond got more active. He walked over to the spot where Emmett and Phil got in, just in time to see them come up to the surface. Both men swam over to the flat stones and lifted their dive masks. Both were smiling.

"So, did you find my bullet?" Hank said.

"No, but we found something," Emmett said. "Not sure what to make of it. Don't know if it came from that boy who got killed, or if it got dropped by one of those young-ins who used to fish here all the time."

"What are you talking about, Emmett?"

"Got it right here in my bag. Hold on, I'll get it out." He set the metal detector on the stones then reached into some side pouch strapped to his waist. He pulled out something that glittered in the sun and held it up.

Hank saw a chain hanging down from Emmett's palm, like from a necklace.

"Some kind of medal," Emmett said. "Don't have my glasses on, and I'm not Catholic. So, even if I could read what was on this thing, I wouldn't know what it was about."

"I was telling him it's a St. Christopher medal," Phil said. "I'm almost positive that's what it is. Or else St. Anthony. One of them saints, anyway. We were raised Catholic, but I stopped going after high school."

Hank lifted the necklace from Emmett's hand, wiped it clean, then held it close. "We used to go to church when I was a kid," he said, "but I've kinda gotten rusty on who the different saints are. I'd have to agree with Phil. That looks like one of those saint medals people wear. Let me go ahead and bag it. Somebody back at the station will know what it is. Is that the only thing you found?"

"So far, it is," Emmett said. "It's a little darker down there than last time. Wasn't even sure we were in the right spot half the time."

"So, you gonna go down again?" Hank said.

"Yeah, I know you need that bullet. We still got some air left. I wanna go down again, give it another go."

"I'd appreciate it."

"Well," Phil said, "if that medal is St. Anthony, maybe we could pray to him. I just remembered a prayer my Gramma taught me. *St. Anthony, St. Anthony. Please come around. Something is lost and must be found. If you find it, bring it to me. And oh how happy I shall be.*"

Hank laughed. "Well, should we all hold hands?"

"I can't believe you remembered something like that," Emmett said. "No way I'm gonna pray that." He picked up his metal detector. This is all we need here, and maybe ten or fifteen more minutes. Put your mask back on." He did, then dove back underwater.

Phil looked up at Hank, smiled, and followed his friend back underwater.

JOE HEADED out to the front desk after receiving Eileen's call. The last time she'd asked him to come look at something wound up being a big deal. When he got there, he saw a man in his mid-30s leaving through the front doors. He looked at Eileen, then at the pictures spread across the counter. "That guy just drop these off?"

She nodded yes.

"What's his name?"

She picked up a piece of paper. "Joshua Hoskins."

Joe took off after him. He was headed toward a black SUV. "Mr. Hoskins?"

The man turned around.

"I'm Lieutenant Joe Boyd. Could I speak with you about these photos you dropped off for a minute?"

"Am I in some kind of trouble?"

Joe laughed. If he had a dollar for every time someone asked him that. "No, not at all. I haven't even looked at them yet. Just something I want to go over with you. Could you come back inside?" Joe turned and headed back toward Eileen.

He got there and started looking over the photographs. Eileen quickly pointed to one of them and to a copy of the Gazette beside it. The picture was a large, blown-up black-and-white photo of Brewster McFarland smiling at the camera. Joe recognized the color photo from the newspaper from the McFarland's fireplace mantle. It was his senior picture. Immediately, he was curious. Just then, the front doors opened and Hoskins came in.

Eileen leaned forward and whispered, "Let me explain to you what's going on here. You can thank me later."

Hoskins came over just as Eileen began to talk. She said he had purchased an antique camera with an undeveloped roll of film inside. The camera was from the 1940s, and Josh assumed these photos were from that era too. But when this Gazette story ran showing McFarland's senior photo, Josh recognized him as the same young man in his black-and-white photos. He wasn't sure if they were relevant but thought he should bring them down.

Joe looked at the rest of the photos and singled out the three showing McFarland and two others. "First of all, Mr. Hoskins..."

"Please call me Josh."

"Okay, Josh. Thank you for taking the time to bring these down here. I would definitely agree the young man in your photos is Brewster McFarland."

"I can also confirm," Josh said, "that all seven of these photos were taken at Culpepper. I graduated from there and recently went back there and found the exact spots where these seven pictures were taken."

Joe looked at the photos he was referring to. He'd been on campus numerous times and several did look familiar to him, as well. Then he looked more closely at the three with McFarland in them. But this time, he focused on the two friends. When he saw it, he almost gasped. He couldn't believe it, and it would have to be confirmed, but he was almost sure he was looking at younger versions — college-age versions — of Tag Harvey and Vic Waters.

"Mr. Hoskins, Josh, do you mind telling me where you got this camera? The one with the black and white photos inside?"

"It was at an estate sale here in town."

"Do you remember who you bought it from, by any chance?"

"I do. His name is Dave Schofield. If I recall, his mother had passed away, and he inherited her house. He was selling everything trying to get it ready to put on the market."

Joe could hardly believe it. This could prove to be a

major find. There were three pictures of Brewster McFarland, Tag Harvey, and Vic Waters...taken at Culpepper University, likely from the camera owned by the fourth friend, Jeremy Schofield. The one who'd fled to California. He probably took the pictures himself. Joe turned them over. Didn't see any dates.

"They didn't date photos back then," Joshua said, picking up on this. "Developers, I mean. Usually, people would handwrite the dates on the back, so they'd remember. But since I'm the one who developed these, some thirty-five years later..."

"Yeah," Joe said. "That makes sense. "But McFarland here looks very much the same as he does in this color senior photo."

"I agree," Josh said. "I'd say, they were at least taken in his senior year."

"Well, Josh. Really want to thank you for bringing these down here. I'm serious. I can't explain why just yet, but these could prove very relevant to our murder investigation."

"Really?"

Joe nodded. "And for that reason, I have to ask...could you keep this confidential? The fact that you have these photos, and even that camera?"

"I guess. Yeah, sure, if you think it matters."

"It definitely could," Joe said. "Have you spoken to anyone else about this?"

"Only my mom." He looked over at Eileen for some reason. "She's visiting with me for a few weeks. But I can explain to her that it's vital that we don't tell anyone about it. If I tell her it's about the murder investigation, I'm sure she'll cooperate."

"It won't be forever," Joe said. "It just that we're gathering information, evidence really, about the possible identity of the killers. We think they still live in town."

"Oh, wow."

"Yeah, so it would really help, you guys keeping a lid on this. I'll let you know when it's okay to talk freely."

"Okay, Lieutenant. You got it. And you can have those photos indefinitely. They're copies. And if there's anything else you need, just call or email me. I gave Eileen my info."

"Great, Josh. Again, thanks for coming in." They shook hands and Josh left.

Eileen said, "You think these really could help?"

"Maybe," Joe said. "We need to confirm that these two young men on either side of McFarland are who we think they are, but yeah, they might be useful. Thanks for calling me in on this."

"You're welcome. I'll put them in a folder and drop them on your desk."

"Great, thanks." As he headed down the hall, it dawned on Joe that — as fascinating as these photos were — all they really confirmed right now were that Harvey, Waters, and McFarland were close college buddies.

An issue that wasn't being disputed by anyone.

31

FOR THE LAST TEN MINUTES, HANK HAD BEEN STARING AT THE steady trail of bubbles coming up from the bottom of the pond, wondering what was taking Emmett and Phil so long.

Finally, much bigger bubbles floated up, followed by big ripples on the surface of the water. Out of the depths emerged the arms, then heads, then the rest of the two divers. He smiled as Emmett's hand made the thumb's up gesture when it breached the water.

Had to mean he'd found the bullet.

They swam over to the flat stones and took off their masks. "Was almost about to give up," Emmett said. "Started to wonder if maybe a fish had swallowed that thing. Then we made one last pass further out from where we were looking—"

"*We* made?" Phil said. "Don't you mean *Phil made* one last pass?"

"Well, Phil, if you're gonna be that way...yes, technically, it was Phil made that last pass."

"I just figured," Phil said, "we'd looked all around the bottom where the car went down with no luck. We knew it had to be down there. So, I thought, what if when the bullet fell out — you know, from the boy's head after it sufficiently decomposed—"

"Phil," Emmett said, "for those of us who can't numb our brains with strong drink, can you leave out the gory details?"

"Oh, sorry. Anyway, point I was making was, what if when the bullet fell out it hit something and took a weird bounce? You know, in the direction of the current. So, I started detecting in that direction and, twenty feet later, I get this beautiful, strong ping. Sure enough, it was the bullet. Emmett's got it there in his bag."

The two men got out of the water, Emmett unzipped his pouch and pulled out the crunched-up bullet. Definitely looked small enough to be a 22-caliber, from Hank's perspective. He took it and put it in an evidence bag. "Great job, guys. Joe's gonna be real happy to get this."

"Will something like this do any good?" Emmett said, "if you don't have the murder weapon?"

"Well, yeah," Hank said. "Not gonna lie. Would do a lot more good if we can find the pistol, especially if we find it in the possession of one of our suspects."

"Then you can match the ballistics," Phil said, "right?"

"Right. But even without the murder weapon, it's still potentially important. If we can confirm either of the suspects owned a 22 at the time, it can help with the circumstantial side of the case. You guys need any help from me getting back up to the road? You know, with the gear?"

"No," Emmett said, "we got this, Hank. You go on get that

stuff to Joe. And don't worry, we know you don't want us talking about any of this."

"Great," Hank said. "I'll get the money moving in your direction as soon as I get back to the office."

FOR THE LAST hour or so, Joe sat at his desk looking over the seven photos Josh Hoskins had dropped off, allowing his mind to drift and wander as he pondered them, taking some notes as different thoughts began to form. He tried to imagine what could have possibly happened from the moment these pictures were taken to the moment one of them put a 22-caliber pistol to McFarland's head, pulled the trigger, and then pushed his car over that cliff.

Here they looked so happy and carefree. You'd think they were as good of friends as McFarland's parents believed, and as they claimed to be in their interviews. Joe could easily see why Josh assumed they'd been taken in the 1940s. Since they were black-and-white, he'd have thought the same thing. He wondered why Jeremy Schofield chose black-and-white film when he snapped the photos in '86.

Joe then examined again the four photos showing different university buildings. Really nice shots, like something you might see in an old Look or Life magazine. Maybe that's why Jeremy used the black-and-white film, just to be artsy.

Hank came in. Joe saw two small evidence bags in his hand. "Looks like the dive was a success. Why two bags, assuming one of them's the bullet?"

Hank dropped the bags on the table between them, closer to Joe. "One is definitely the bullet. About ninety-five percent sure ballistics will confirm it came from a twenty-two. The other was something of a surprise. Actually, the guys brought it up first. Go ahead and open it. It's the one on the right."

Joe pulled out a small medal and chain. "Looks like some kind of religious thing."

"It is," Hank said, sitting. "Phil said it's either a St. Christopher or a St. Anthony medal. Not sure if McFarland was wearing it. Guess we'll have to ask his folks if they remember him owning one. Otherwise, not sure how it got down there."

"I'll give them a call," Joe said. He reached for the other envelope, opened it. "Yeah, this is gotta be from a 22." He dropped the bullet back in the bag. "My morning was somewhat eventful, too. Had another visitor come in bearing gifts. Like Trevor with the car mirror. Only this time, it was a fellow named Josh bringing photos."

"Photos?" Hank repeated. "Of what?"

"Take a look." Joe spread the seven photos out across the table. He watched Hank's eyes scan the photos, saw them get big when he recognized McFarland.

"What am I looking at here, Joe? These look pretty old. But that definitely looks like our murder vic." He pointed to McFarland.

"Almost positive it is. We'll show his parents just to make sure. But take a look at the other two guys with him."

Hank pulled them closer. "You're thinking these guys are Tag Harvey and Vic Waters, right?"

"Looks like it to me. If we're sure that's McFarland in the middle with the newspaper. We already confirmed they all hung out together in college."

"Well," Hank said, "I could bring one of these down to the

Culpepper school library, dig up the yearbook photos of Harvey and Waters. Confirm it's them for certain."

"Might as well," Joe said. "Hopefully, McFarland's parents will confirm what we're thinking. Got something else while you were gone. Dave Schofield called looking for you, wound up giving me the florist information you'd asked for, to help locate his brother. By the way, here's another interesting little development. The guy who brought in these photos got them from an antique WWII-era camera, sold to him by...guess who?"

"No idea," Hank said.

"Dave Schofield. Remember he told us he inherited that house when his mother died? Well, this was one of the things he sold at the estate sale. We need to call him to confirm this, but I'm betting these seven photos were taken by his brother, Jeremy, sometime before he fled to California. For some reason, he left this camera here with these seven photos inside when he left, undeveloped."

"Sure sounds like he left in a hurry," Hank said.

"I know, right?" Joe said. "The question is why. You go to the library, confirm these guys are Harvey and Waters. I'll show them to McFarland's parents and call Schofield to confirm the camera was owned by his brother, Jeremy. Then we'll update Pendleton on all this. I think that should be enough to convince him...it's time for you and I to make that trip out to California."

32

JOE GOT OUT TO HIS CAR, STARTED IT, AND WAS ABOUT TO head over to the Whispering Hills condominium, where McFarland's parents lived. He decided to first call Dave Schofield about the camera. After a few rings, he picked up. "Is this Dave?"

"Yes, it is. Who's this?"

"Lieutenant Joe Boyd."

"Oh hey, Lieutenant. Were you able to locate my long-lost brother?"

"Not yet, but I'm sure we will. Haven't contacted that florist yet for their info. What I'm calling about is to confirm a detail, something I think I already know the answer to."

"What's that?"

"A few weeks back, guess you had an estate sale. You remember selling an old, antique Kodak camera to a guy?"

"As a matter of fact, I do. Don't remember the fellow's name, but I can—"

"Don't need it. We already know who he is. You probably

didn't know this, but there was an undeveloped roll of film in the camera. The guy you sold it to is something of a camera buff."

"Kinda got that impression," Dave said.

"Yeah, well, he developed the film in the camera. Turned out to be seven black-and-white photos. We're confirming their identity today, but we're pretty positive some are of Brewster McFarland, Tag Harvey, and Vic Waters. I'm guessing — since your brother was the photographer in the bunch — he probably took the photos."

"Probably accurate," Dave said. "They hung out together all the time. One of the great mysteries to me and my mom was why he left the camera here when he headed out to California."

"That was going to be my next question. Any idea why he used black-and-white film?"

"He did that sometimes. Just for the look, I think. But I didn't realize there was a roll still in the camera when I sold it to that guy. We never used it. By then, they'd come out with cameras much easier to use. So, I just put it in a box with the rest of the stuff Jeremy left in his room."

A thought just popped into Joe's head. A big one.

"So, Dave, you never used the camera after Jeremy left?"

"Nope. No interest in it."

"So, the roll of film in the camera would've been the last pictures he'd taken before he left?"

"Sounds right to me."

"And when did he leave again?" Joe said.

Dave paused. "It was just a few days after Brew McFarland disappeared. It was such a crazy time. First, the *Challenger* blows up, then Brew goes missing, then a few days later Jeremy takes off for California. Our whole world turned upside down in the span of a week."

"Okay, Dave. Thanks for taking my call. Looks like my partner and I will be heading out to California soon, hoping to connect with Jeremy."

"Really? Well, remember what I said. Just ask him to call me. If he doesn't, I'll be grateful you tried."

"I'll definitely tell him what you said. Hopefully, he'll follow through and get back with you."

"If you don't mind," Dave said, "when you get back, could you give me a ring, just to let me know how it went? I don't mean anything about the case, just about Jeremy. Like, how he reacted to you asking him to call?"

"Sure, Dave. I can do that."

After Joe hung up, he picked up his notepad and made some notes.

JOE HAD no trouble getting past the guard at the McFarland's condo. He'd called them on the way there to confirm they'd both be home. He had just rung the doorbell.

"Coming, Lieutenant." Heard Mrs. McFarland's voice on the other side of the door.

"Good to see you again," she said after opening it. "Come on in. Frank's already sitting in his chair, ready to hear whatever you have to say." She walked down the hall toward the living area.

Joe followed. "Well, it's going to be a bit of show-and-tell this time. Brought some old pictures for you to look at."

"Do you now?" She stepped into the living area, headed

for her chair. "Didn't hear from you folks for decades, and now we're hearing from you every other day."

Frank waved, sipped his coffee. Joe headed for the same spot on the couch he'd sat in before. He set the folder with the photos on the coffee table.

"Can I get you anything?" she asked.

"No, I'm fine."

"What you got there?" Frank pointed to the folder.

"That? That's the reason I'm here today. Need your help with something. But before I open this, guess I should prepare you a little first."

"Uh-oh," Frank said.

"No, it's nothing bad," Joe said. "Like crime scene photos, or anything. It's just...well, they are photos. And I just had a phone call a short while ago that confirmed they were likely taken just a few days before your son went—" he was about to say *missing* "— your son was killed. There's three of them. They're black-and-white, don't ask me why, taken by Jeremy Schofield. Do you remember him?"

"Yeah, we remember Jeremy," Frank said. "He was always taking pictures."

"Well, his younger brother confirmed they were the last photos Jeremy took before he left for California. For some reason, he left this camera behind."

"Is Brew in these pictures?" Ida said, her eyes tearing up.

"I believe so," Joe said. "That's what I need your help with, confirming Brew is definitely in them." He spun the folder around, so that the photos faced them and opened it.

Ida gasped. "Look at him, Frank." She picked up the one where he was posing, smiling, and looking right at the camera.

"Oh, my," Frank said. Tears welled up in his eyes, too. "There's my boy. Just like I remember him."

"He looks...so happy," Ida said. "Like he always did, especially hanging out with his friends."

"So," Joe said, "you do recognize the two young men with him?"

"Of course," she said. "That's Tag, and that's Vic." She pointed to each one, held the photo closer, and just stared into her son's face. Tears poured down her cheeks.

Frank got up and grabbed a box of tissues on the kitchen counter. He used one to dab his eyes and handed her the box. Still holding the photo in one hand, she wiped her cheeks with the other. She set the photo down and looked at the other two, which Jeremy had apparently taken of them while they were gathered around a newspaper, not looking into the camera.

"Is there any way...?" She looked up at Joe. "Is there any way we could get a copy of these? I'd be willing to pay whatever price the owner would think is fair."

"If I could, I'd give you those, but we need them for the investigation. But the owner of the photos is a really nice guy, and he develops his own pictures. I'd be surprised if he wouldn't make you copies of all three for nothing."

"Would you ask him for us?" Frank said.

"I'd be happy to." Joe looked around at the little tables and pictures on the walls, didn't see any evidence that the McFarlands were Catholic. He pulled out the evidence bag with the religious medal the divers had found, took it out, and held it up. "Would either of you recognize this? This isn't something your son might have been wearing when he disappeared?"

They both looked closely. "No, Brew never wore anything like that," Ida said. "Looks like something a Catholic might wear. Can I hold it?"

He handed it to her.

"Pretty sure that's a St. Christopher medal," she said. "I had a Catholic friend who wore something similar. But I'm not completely certain." She handed it back.

In any case, Joe confirmed it didn't belong to their son.

Frank then refocused on the pictures. He picked up the one where the three of them were looking at a newspaper and held it close. He adjusted his glasses, so he could see better through the lower half. "You know? I can't say a hundred percent, but almost. But I recognize that newspaper they're looking at. He held it even closer. "Yeah, I'm almost sure of it. Hon, could you get my magnifying glass?"

Ida got up. "It's on your nightstand, right?"

"Yep." He looked at Joe. "See, Brew disappeared a few days after the shuttle blew up. Every day that week the Gazette ran a big story about it, telling the latest developments. I always collected newspapers when major events happened. I'd collected one every day after the *Challenger* exploded, right up until the day Brew went ...well, missing."

Ida came back, handed Frank his magnifying glass. He used it to study the photo. "Yeah, that's definitely it. I can just pick out part of the headline. You can see most of the word, *Challenger*, and the top half of that group photo. You know, the one with the astronauts who died."

Joe asked to see it and looked at it the way Frank had. He couldn't help but smile. Frank was right, they were looking at the front page of the Gazette running a story about the *Challenger*. He couldn't make out the date, but that would be an easy thing to nail down. He'd just have to get with Tom Hazelton, see if he could go through the archives and—

Frank stood. "You know what? I'm pretty sure I have the front page for that very day. Got it in a plastic container under my bed. Along with the rest of my collection." He started heading toward the bedroom. "Give me a couple minutes, and I'll dig it out. Are you in a hurry?"

Joe laughed. "Frank, for something like that I'd be willing to wait here all day."

33

IT WAS NEAR THE END OF THE DAY.

Joe and Hank were walking through the outer offices of Captain Pendleton. His secretary, Marsha, nodded and smiled as they passed her desk. She knew he was expecting them. Hank had gotten back from the Culpepper University library with positive news about the yearbook research from 1986. Of course, Joe had some interesting things to share with him from his visit with the McFarlands.

Now it was time for both of them to brief Pendleton.

After opening the door, Joe was surprised to find the captain not busy with something.

"Glad you guys are finally checking in with me. Been wondering where things have been going with this case."

"Well," Joe said, "we didn't want to come until we had something solid. And you did say you wanted us to look into everything here in Culpepper before we hit you up for the California trip."

"I did say that. So, that mean you've got something decent to show me?"

"I think we do."

"Okay, who's going first?"

Joe looked at Hank. They discussed him leading things off, but okay. "As you know," Joe said, "we've been looking at McFarland's college friends as the likely perps for his murder, specifically the two that still live here in town, Tag Harvey and Vic Waters. Based on all the new developments we're about to share, we're still thinking along those lines."

"Really," Hank said, "they're the only ones that make sense."

Joe took the folder of photographs out of his brief bag and laid them in front of Pendleton. Just the ones with people. "We have confirmed these pictures were taken from an antique camera by Jeremy Schofield back in 1986, just a few days before he fled from here to California. And after talking with his younger brother, Dave, who still lives here in town, I'm using the word *fled* on purpose. I'll explain why in a moment. But he left this camera when he took off with the undeveloped film still in it. Fast forward to a few weeks ago, their mother dies, and Dave sells this camera to a local camera buff. He develops the film and recognizes the young man in the center of all three pics when we release the story about finding Brewster McFarland's body at the bottom of that pond. We showed these photos to McFarland's parents, and they confirmed that is definitely their son."

Pendleton leaned forward, pulled the photos closer to him. "Yeah, I see him there. Who are the two guys on either side of him?"

Joe looked again at Hank. Hank was holding just one

folder. He opened it, took out some additional pictures, and set them beside Joe's. "These photos are blown-up from the Culpepper University library yearbook collection, specifically the senior year from '86. As you can see, these are the senior pics of Tag Harvey and Vic Waters. Comparing them to the three photos with McFarland, I think it's —"

"Yeah," Pendleton said, "I think it's pretty obvious Harvey and Waters are the ones in the picture with McFarland. While these are fascinating photos, how do they help our case? How are they evidence? We already know these guys were all friends at the time. That's what I see here. Just friends being together, everyone seems to be doing fine."

"They do," Joe said, "don't they? But take a closer look at the photo on the left, the one where they're all looking at a newspaper." He took out another photograph from his bag and set it next to that one. "Here's a blow-up of that section, showing the front page of that newspaper. One good thing about this antique camera, it still took very high resolution photos. You can see it's a copy of the Gazette, and the main headline and photograph has to do with the *Challenger* explosion. That happened a few days before McFarland disappeared. Every day for several weeks it was the main story."

Pendleton studied the two photos. "Yeah, so they are looking at a newspaper about the *Challenger* disaster. But I don't see any date in this photo."

"No, but you can in this." Joe took out a copy of that front-page story, borrowed from Frank McFarland. "See the date? That happens to be the *very day* Brewster McFarland disappears. He is holding a newspaper for the very last time. Later that day or night, something will happen, that — we believe

— caused either Tag Harvey or Vic Waters to put a twenty-two caliber pistol close to his head and pull the trigger. Then both of them, possibly with Jeremy Schofield's help, shove his Camaro Z28 over the cliff and into the pond."

Pendleton looked more closely at the photo of all three of them smiling. "Poor guy. He has no idea what's about to happen." Then he looked at Joe and Hank. "Again, sensational photos. But I'm not seeing how they point to his friends as the killers."

"Well, for starters," Hank said, "both Tag Harvey and Vic Waters — even recently — told us they had no idea why McFarland disappeared and that neither one had seen him for several days. They were studying for finals, they said. But these were both lies. Lies both men told. The kind of lies guys tell when they're comparing notes, when they're making up a story. This photograph proves they were with McFarland the day he died. And while I was at Culpepper I asked someone in administration about the finals bit. They confirmed to me that they could think of no reason why any classes would ever hold finals at the end of January, since it was just the beginning of the post-holiday semester."

"And then there's this, Cap," Joe said. "We confirmed that Jeremy Schofield took these photos and were told by his younger brother, Dave, that shortly after he took them, Jeremy left town...for good. Dave says both he and his mother were shocked by the abrupt nature of his departure. They pleaded with him not to leave. He was only a few months away from receiving his four-year degree."

"Why'd he say he was leaving?" Pendleton said.

"He came up with a reason," Joe said. "He'd just been offered a job — *a dream job* — by a high-end talent agency in

LA. To be their photographer, taking photos of A-list celebrities. Dave remembered him saying, isn't that the reason why you go to college? To land a great job?"

"But that was a lie," Hank added. "He didn't get that job. I researched the guy on the internet. There was no dream job awaiting him in LA. He made it up. It would appear after a few years of struggling, he finally did get an okay job as a photographer taking pics of actors and actresses for a talent management company. But I guarantee you, you've never heard of any of these people."

"Captain," Joe said, "think about it. Why would this guy, who on this day — the day these photos were taken — seemed to be doing perfectly fine, hanging out with friends, taking black-and-white pics with his newly acquired antique camera. Why would he a few days later, quite literally, flee the state? He heads all the way out to California, leaving his family, most of his stuff, including this camera with these pictures still in it, undeveloped. And he's only a few months away from earning a four-year degree in college...an education he earned through a scholarship? It doesn't add up."

"What does add up," Hank said, "this is how somebody would act who's running scared, who saw something that frightened him enough he feels the need to flee, to leave everything behind. To this day, he's never been back to Culpepper. Not even recently to attend his own mother's funeral. Cap, we need to talk to this guy."

Pendleton sat back in his chair, released a sigh. "Okay, you convinced me. It's time for you two to head out to California. Do it soon, and don't tell anyone about your trip, except your wives."

34

THE FOLLOWING MORNING, JOE CAME DOWN THE STAIRS looking forward to the promised big breakfast sendoff Kate had talked about last night before bed. He could already smell the bacon frying and the biscuits baking in the oven. They were just Bisquick, but still. The doorbell rang. He could see Hank standing there through the glass side panels. As he opened the door, Hank's wife waved as she drove away in their car.

The idea they'd discussed last night was, she'd drop him off for breakfast, then Joe and Hank would drive to the Atlanta airport in Joe's car. They only expected to be gone two days max, so they'd just pay for extra parking at the airport, spare Kate having to drive them all the way there herself.

Hank stepped in, set his carry-on suitcase next to Joe's, already near the front door. He took a big whiff of bacon and smiled.

"No better smell in the morning," Joe said. "Come on in and get comfortable. Fresh pot of coffee over there by the fridge."

"Morning, Hank," Kate said, working on some cheesy scrambled eggs by the stove.

"Really appreciate you doing this," Hank said. "Beats the Egg McMuffin I was planning to get on the way here."

"You're welcome. The kids weren't too happy eating their cereal as they saw me getting all this stuff out."

Joe sat at his usual place at the dinette table. "They just left to catch the school bus a few minutes ago." The microwave pinged.

"Say, Joe," Kate said. "Could you —"

Joe stood. "I'm on it." He looked at Hank. "That's the sausage gravy for the biscuits, reheating from the last time Kate let me eat food this good. I love biscuits and gravy, but with this diet I'm on, biscuits are a rare treat. I don't even remember what they taste like."

Hank laughed, sat at the table with his coffee. "She's just trying to keep you alive, Joe. Means she loves you. Right, Kate?"

"I do love him, and I'd be devastated if he died. But I'm not afraid of him dying so much. He's right with God and well-insured. The thing is, I don't want him having a stroke. So, he doesn't get the good stuff very often. But I figure, hey, you guys are flying across the country on a plane, heading out to LA. I know that's a dangerous place."

Joe looked at Hank. "This is like the last meal a guy gets on death row. Just in case something happens, and we don't make it back."

"Is that right, Kate?" Hank said.

Kate laughed. "Something like that. You just never know what a day will bring." She slid all the eggs from a frying pan into a bowl.

"Well," he said, "I think I can set your mind at ease. I checked out what part of LA this guy lives at, the guy we're going out to see. It's not the fanciest part of town, but it's certainly not a high crime area. And he's just a potential witness, not a gang banger or anything. Doubt he even owns a gun."

"He's a photographer, right?" She pulled the biscuits out of the oven, then brought all the food over from the stove. "Joe filled me in on things last night."

"Yeah, works for a talent management agency. From what I gather, the most challenging part of our trip will probably be the stuff we see looking out the windows. I was reading on a travel site, sounds like the sidewalks around where this guy lives have become filled with tents and makeshift shelters."

"People doing their business out on the street," Joe said.

"Joe," Kate said, scolding. "We're about to eat this fine breakfast. Now I got that image in my head."

"I'm sorry. I'm just saying, we're not going to be in any danger, Kate. You don't have to worry."

"Okay, that's good to know. You gonna say the blessing?"

"Sure," Joe said. He did, and everyone started filling their plates with food. "Really, Kate. Thanks again for doing this. We'll be back in a couple days. Won't even be gone long enough to miss me."

"I don't know about that." She looked at Hank. "You guys

just be careful. And you keep an eye on him. Joe's managed to find plenty of trouble, even in a little town like this. Bound to be things happen you don't expect in a place like LA."

"We will, Kate," Hank said. "I won't let anything happen to him."

A FEW HOURS LATER, Vic Waters hung up his phone after receiving some unsettling news from his son, the one who now ran his pawnshop. He quickly decided he'd better call Tag. Picked up the burner phone and a few moments later, Tag answered.

"What's up, Vic? Any new developments on this case?"

"Afraid so. Nothing I can't handle, but...just talked to my son. He's got a connection who works with the Culpepper PD. I asked him to check with this guy every few days, see if anything's buzzing about the McFarland situation. Apparently, neither of the two main detectives working the case came in today. They're taking some out-of-town trip. He didn't know where to, but I gotta be thinking it has to do with our case."

A long pause. "Think they're going to see Jeremy?" Tag said.

"Don't think they're going on vacation together. This is the biggest case they're working on, so...yeah, thinking that might be what's going on."

"That's not good."

"No, it's not."

"What you thinking? There anything you can do about this?"

"Yeah. Like I said, I got folks I know out there in LA. Might be time to tie up this loose end."

"How are you—no, wait. Don't tell me," Tag said.

"Probably better I don't," said Vic. "But just letting you know...it's gonna get handled."

35

IT HAD BEEN A FAIRLY UNEVENTFUL TRIP FOR JOE AND HANK, flying from Atlanta to LAX. Wasn't too hard to secure direct flights flying to and from major airports. Of course, they flew coach. Because of their guns, they had to check in their luggage, but were still able to get a rental car and be on the road toward Santa Monica within fifty minutes. That's where Jeremy Schofield, or Chevalier as he went by now, lived. Hank did some more searching and learned Jeremy had a small photography studio near his apartment on 3rd St. in Santa Monica.

It took another forty minutes from the airport to get into Santa Monica. They had just gotten off I-10 a few minutes ago and were now driving down Wilshire Boulevard through the city toward the ocean. Joe wasn't sure they'd get to do any sightseeing on this trip. That depended on how things went with Jeremy.

Presently, he was following the GPS on Hank's phone toward a restaurant and a rendezvous with an old friend.

Also, a Lieutenant who now worked for the Santa Monica PD. His name was John Templeton. Their friendship began back in Joe's days as a younger cop in Pittsburgh. In fact, they'd graduated from the Academy at the same time.

"So," Hank said, "you and this friend we're going to meet haven't talked since you moved to Culpepper?"

"Nope. I'd heard a few years after I left Pittsburgh, he'd moved out here and joined the LAPD. I called him yesterday, seeing if he knew anybody in the Santa Monica department. Turned out, that's where he is now. He said LA got too much for him, and he made the transfer here two years ago."

It was customary when cops from one state investigated a case in another jurisdiction, to contact their counterparts and let them know their plans. Maybe see if they wanted to be involved on some level. Seeing as this was just interviewing a witness, not a likely suspect, Joe didn't figure he would. But when he realized Joe would be in Santa Monica, he quickly said yes to meeting him for lunch, even though for Joe and Hank, their bodies were saying it was 3:30 p.m., not lunchtime.

Joe had been to this area many years ago attending a homicide detectives' workshop in LA, back when he was first made detective in Pittsburgh. He and the guys who'd gone took a couple vacation days when it was over, see some of the sites nearby. Most had never been this far west, including Joe, had never seen things like the Pacific Ocean, Hollywood, or Beverly Hills. To get to the Pacific Ocean, it was decided to see it right here in Santa Monica, take in the famous Santa Monica pier. They had driven down this very road back then.

Joe couldn't believe how much things had changed. "Wow, this is kinda hard to look at."

"Tell me about it," Hank said. "I've seen this kind of stuff on the news, you know, stories about the homeless taking over places like San Francisco and here. But, seeing it up close..."

It wasn't just all the tents and tarps and homeless people walking about, Joe was also taken back by how many of the businesses had closed up. Seemed like the majority. They passed by the restaurant he and his detective friends had eaten at. It was closed, too.

"The restaurant we're meeting John at," Hank said, "should be two blocks up ahead on the left.

"Probably be easy to spot," Joe said. "It'll be the one that's actually open."

"I'd laugh if it were funny," Hank said. "This is just sad. Suddenly, I'm freshly grateful to be serving in the Culpepper PD."

Joe wondered how his friend John was making out. Guess he'd find out soon.

AN HOUR LATER, Joe and Hank had just finished the lunch with John Templeton, Joe's detective friend. It was mostly spent with Joe and John catching up while Hank listened. Joe was sad to hear John had gotten divorced two years ago, part of the reason he came here to Santa Monica. Joe remembered conversations he had with Kate back in Pittsburgh, which made him certain their marriage would've met the same fate had he not moved to Culpepper.

Right now, Joe watched as John and Hank each devoured

a hefty slice of New York-style cheesecake, while he sipped his coffee.

"You sure you don't want a bite?" John said. "Saved you the last one."

"No, I'm good. Are you watching the time?" Joe said this, because John mentioned he wouldn't be able to give them any more time after lunch, considering the crackdown on things at the department. With all the *Defunding the Police* talk and anti-police sentiment out here in California, he'd said they were shorthanded by more than thirty percent.

John glanced at his watch. "I am, but I wish I didn't have to. Really sorry about this, Joe. It really sucks being a cop out here. If you can believe it, makes me long for the way things were back in Pittsburgh."

"Even here in Santa Monica?" Hank said.

"Santa Monica, LA, all of Southern California," John said. "It's just really bad. I've only got two years left till I make my twenty, then I'm gone."

"Really, John," Joe said. "You're leaving after twenty?" That's when police officers could retire, but most worked until they had thirty years, or even more.

"Joe, if you were here, you'd be doing the same. We've lost so many guys to retirement the last couple of years. When you know the politicians don't have your back, you realize just doing your job could put you in hot water. Guys are worried about making one wrong move, just something that looks like a wrong move to somebody recording on their phone. Next thing you know, you're brought up on charges and not only lose your pension, but maybe wind up in jail. It's just not worth it."

"So sorry to hear it," Joe said.

"And then there's this homeless situation, which I'm sure you saw driving in here. It's not just destroying the local economy and hurting tourism, it's taken over our jobs. We get three to four hundred calls a week dealing with homeless issues. Which is one of the reasons I can't spend any more time with you this afternoon. I can drive you by that guy's photography studio, but then we'll have to say goodbye."

This was hard to hear. "That's all right, John. I know it's not your choice. This shouldn't be a big deal anyway. Don't know if you recall, but the guy we're needing to talk to is likely a witness in a cold case murder that happened back in '86. We don't think he participated, but we're pretty sure he may have seen it or know what really happened. In any case, we're not expecting any trouble."

"That's good. But if you do wind up needing a hand for anything, just let me know." With that, John stood, grabbed the check. "I'll get this. Probably the only upside to working out here. I'm sure they're paying me more than they're paying you guys."

Joe and Hank stood. "Thanks," Joe said. "You're probably right about that."

"I'll meet you out by the cars after I pay this. We'll just be heading one more block toward the beach then turning right on 3rd Street. That guy's place is only a few blocks from here. Oh, I almost forgot. You asked me to look into his record. Really, he's got none. Just a handful of traffic citations over the last few decades. So, this really shouldn't be a big deal."

They shook hands then Joe and Hank headed for their rental car. A few moments later, they watched John come out and get into his, then they followed him as he drove down Wilshire Boulevard.

. . .

FIFTEEN MINUTES LATER, Hector Rodriguez, sat parallel-parked on 3rd Street, like he had been the last two hours. What a crap assignment this had turned out to be. Of course, it could get better. The boss had said there was five hundred in it if he could whack the target, then leave the area without drawing any attention.

The target was some photographer guy. Hector had copied his picture from his website, to make sure there'd be no mistakes. He'd screwed on his silencer to keep things quiet. Looking across the street, didn't look like any art studio to him. Just some two-story apartments, like all the others running up and down the block. Guess the guy had converted one of them to a business. When he'd cased the place that morning, Hector did see *Chevalier's Studio* painted on a sign beneath a small window on the front door.

Hector was sitting there waiting to see two detective-looking guys who were supposed to come to the door some-time today. Apparently, they'd flown in from out-of-state to talk to this photographer about some crime that happened way before Hector was born. The details didn't matter to him. The point was, he needed to wait to hit the guy *after* these detectives came and went. He did it before, and then they showed up, it would bring all kinds of unwanted atten-tion to the situation. He waited till after, the guy would likely lay there in his studio for a day or so before anyone found him.

Patience, Hector. You got this.

At least, there were no homeless folks on this block.

They were all over the place down here. No worries about collateral damage.

Just then, two cars pulled up and stopped in front of the art studio. The guy driving in the first one got out, went back to the driver of the second car. No uniforms, but they looked like cops. They talked a bit. The driver in the first car pointed to the studio, said some things. Hector figured him to be a local guy. Even looked familiar. They shook hands through the window, and the local guy drove off.

Okay, this was probably it. The remaining car pulled into an open space, and the two guys inside got out, walked to the studio. All right then, it was going down like he'd been told. All he needed now was to wait for them to go in, come back out, and hit the road. Then he'd head in there, do the assignment, and leave quietly.

An easy five hundred bucks.

36

JOE AND HANK WALKED DOWN THE SIDEWALK AND ONTO THE walkway leading to the apartment building where Jeremy's studio was located. Judging by the address of both, his apartment must be upstairs. When they got to the front door, a sign confirmed they were at the right place. Through a glass panel in the door, they could see a small, empty waiting area, with a handful of cushioned chairs around the perimeter. A handwritten sign hung from inside: *Come on in – Doing a shoot – Have a seat – Be right with you.*

Hank opened the door, and they walked through. "Guess he's not doing well enough to hire a receptionist," Hank whispered.

"It would appear so," Joe said. "Let's take a seat, give it a few minutes. But I'm not going to wait around here all day."

"I hear you."

They had decided not to attempt to communicate with Jeremy in advance. Joe felt like a surprise attack worked best in a situation like this. Get the guy off balance right off the bat. Don't give them a chance to think through all the likely questions and come up with made-up answers. If he felt a little intimidated, all the better.

They heard some muffled voices coming from down the hall. Figured it was Jeremy taking photos of somebody. This little reception area was small, but nicely put together. Decent chairs to sit in. A nice plant in one corner, table of magazines in the other. Joe looked at them. All entertainment-oriented. The walls were covered with framed photographs of various actors and actresses, all smiling for the camera. He thought they were called headshots.

Hank got up to investigate the photos. After examining four or five, he said, "They're all addressed to Jeremy. The ones from the guys say *Thanks*, the ones from the ladies say *Love*, then their signature. Of course, I can't make out any of their names from their handwriting. But they do look familiar, don't they? Like this gal here..." He pointed to a picture of an attractive blonde. "What show was she in?"

Joe looked up. "*Matlock* maybe?"

"No, can't be that. That was before my time. And then this guy next to her. "I think he was in *West Wing*. Almost sure of it."

"No chance I'd know him then," Joe said. "Never watched that show."

"And this guy," Hank said, "pretty sure he was in *Law & Order*. Not one of the main guys, one of the side detectives."

"See anybody who ever made it to the big time? Anybody whose name you recognize?"

Hank kept looking, row after row. "Nope. Just like his website. No A-listers, but lots of actors who at least look familiar. Like this show I saw one time on Netflix, or one of those streaming channels. *That Guy...Who Was in That Thing.*"

Joe laughed. "I saw that. Bunch of actors you definitely recognized from lots of roles, but never big enough to know their names. Guess it takes all kinds to make movies and TV." He glanced down at his watch. "I think we've waited out here enough. Let's go in and introduce ourselves to...Mr. Chevalier."

Hank stood. "I'm game."

Joe walked down the hallway toward the sound of the voices. Came to a big double door. *Please let everyone have their clothes on.* He opened the right side and walked in, Hank right behind him. It was a big room. Definitely looked like some kind of professional photography set up with all kinds of lights and screens angled this way and that. In the center, a young, fairly handsome guy with dark hair was sitting on some crates. His photogenic smile froze in a look of fear.

Fully dressed.

Facing the kid, was a taller middle-aged man with long hair swept back in a ponytail. He spun around still holding his camera and pointed it at Joe and Hank. His face, grave concern. "Excuse me, gentlemen. I'm in the middle of a shoot here."

Joe and Hank had already taken out their badges, now held them up. "You *were*, Mr. Chevalier," Joe said. "Afraid you and your client will have to reschedule the rest. I'm Lieutenant Joe Boyd, and this is my partner Sergeant Hank Jensen. We've come a long way to talk with you. We're from the Culpepper PD."

His face went from concern to shock. Joe couldn't tell for

sure, but it even looked like most of the color had drained out of it.

"Culpepper," he said. "Georgia?"

"Think you know the answer to that," Hank said. "Mr. *Schofield*."

Jeremy turned around and faced the young man. He set the camera down on a table. "I'm so sorry, Anson. I have no idea what this is about, but when it's the police, you kinda have to...you know..."

The kid, Anson, stood up, looking somewhat indignant. "I get it, Jeremy. Ain't your fault. These guys act like they own the world."

Jeremy looked back at Joe. "How long do you think this will take?"

"I don't know. Depends on how straight you are with us."

"Don't worry about it," Anson said. "I'll go down to Wilshire, grab a latte. I've got some lines to memorize. You give me a call when these guys turn you loose. We'll see if there's still time to finish."

"Great, Anson. You do that. I'm sure we can get this done today."

The young man walked past Joe and Hank shooting them an angry glance on his way out. Jeremy walked behind him and followed him into the waiting area. After he'd left, Jeremy locked the door, changed the sign to *Closed*. He walked back and stood in the doorway. "Why don't you guys follow me? I've got an office. Think we'll be more comfortable talking in there." He turned and headed in the opposite direction.

Joe and Hank followed. Joe was carrying his brief bag, filled with all the things he wanted to show Jeremy.

Like the waiting area, the office looked nice. It was obvious Jeremy wasn't rolling in the dough, but he at least tried to make it look like he was the real deal. He walked behind the desk, sat down, and said, "Please officers, have a seat." He released a big sigh, sank deeper in his chair.

"Any idea why we're here?" Joe said. "Should I call you Jeremy, Mr. Chevalier, or Mr. Schofield?"

"Jeremy's fine. And no, I have no idea why you're here."

Joe looked him straight in the eyes, held his gaze, until it broke.

Yeah, he knew.

"Ever read the Gazette anymore online?" Hank said. "You know, the hometown rag?"

"Can't say I do. It's probably been decades."

"Well," Joe said, "in order to get through this as quick as possible, I should probably just cut through all the small talk and get right to why we're here. It's about the murder of Brewster McFarland."

It was like Joe just hit him across the face with an invisible 2 x 4.

Another deep sigh. Jeremy looked down, then back up.

"I noticed you're not registering any fake shock," Joe said, "when I used the word *murder*...like your friends Tag Harvey and Vic Waters did back home. They acted all dumbfounded, as if they had only ever imagined he was missing all this time. I appreciate you not doing that."

"Now, wait a minute. I had nothing to do with Brew getting murdered. Nothing. I swear it."

"But you do acknowledge he was murdered," Hank said. "In fact, that's the real reason he went missing back in '86, isn't it? He went missing because you guys killed him."

Jeremy sat straight up. "We didn't kill him. I mean, I didn't. It wasn't me. I had nothing to do with it."

Joe and Hank looked at each other. It seemed to Joe that this might go more smoothly than he had ever imagined. Maybe all Jeremy Schofield needed was a chance to finally get this terrible thing off his chest.

37

No one said anything for a few seconds. Jeremy sat back in his seat, tried to regain some composure. Like he realized, he'd reacted way too strongly just then.

Joe knew he needed to keep applying the heat before Jeremy retreated into some kind of hole. "Jeremy, let's just say upfront you didn't have anything to do with McFarland's actual murder. I'm even willing to believe that *could* be true. But Hank and I have been working this case for quite a while now, gathering some solid evidence, and uncovering some significant leads. Aren't you even a little curious what must've happened back home — after all these decades — to motivate us to fly all the way out here just to talk to you?"

"Unlike Lieutenant Boyd here," Hank said, "I've never been to LA before. I'd really like to see some of the sites, but we're really only out here for one reason." A pause. "To talk with you...about this case."

"I don't know," Jeremy said. "I'm guessing you must've found Brew's body?"

"See," Joe said, "that tells me you knew he was murdered. All this time...you've known. Maybe you didn't actually participate in his death. But I'm guessing you know who killed him and why."

"And we also know," Hank added, "that you didn't come out here in '86 because of some amazing photography job, like you told everyone before you left. I checked you out on the internet. I don't know what you did the first few years, but your big celebrity photography gigs don't show up anywhere."

"You came out here," Joe said, "because you were afraid. That's my guess. You were afraid because of what you knew, what you saw, maybe what you heard. Am I getting close?"

Jeremy looked back and forth at both men, anxiety all over his face. His eyes said Joe and Hank were on the money. "Before I say anything to either of you, I'm thinking I need to talk to an attorney."

"If you didn't have anything to do with McFarland's murder," Hank said, "why would you need an attorney? We're not here to arrest you, just get some information."

"Because, well...let's just say I did know what happened back then, at least some of it. I don't know all the various laws surrounding a situation like this. It's not like I knew you'd be coming. Didn't get a chance to look everything up, so I'd know where I stand. I could start talking and wind up incriminating myself in a whole bunch of ways. Maybe knowing what I know and not saying anything all these years is a crime. I know some serious bad things that happened back then that you guys haven't even brought up. Again, I didn't do anything bad myself, but maybe not reporting them...what if that's a felony?"

The guy's a thinker, Joe thought.

"Then there's the safety issue," Jeremy said. "Specifically, mine. As you say, if I came out here because I was afraid of what might happen if I stayed. But what will happen if I talk now? The people who did these things are still alive and well. If I was afraid of what they would do to me then, what's changed? I'm guessing you don't just want to chat, for me to give you a few good leads. You want me, at some point, to come back there and testify in court. But I don't feel safe doing that. Going back there, I mean. I came out here to make sure I'd stay out of it. And look, I have. They've left me alone all this time."

This wasn't going exactly as Joe hoped, but at least Jeremy confirmed they were on the right track. Tag Harvey and Vic Waters did kill Brewster McFarland. And Jeremy knew they did. Something they did or said afterward made him afraid to remain in town anymore. "So, what you're looking for is protection and immunity from prosecution," Joe said. "I got that right?"

"Pretty much," Jeremy said. "I don't want to get stuck in any Witness Protection Program, either. I don't believe these guys are like the Mafia, who'd send people to whack me once they were put away. But I'd want protection at least until they're safely in prison, and I could get back out here to LA."

Joe looked over at Hank, then said, "Okay, Jeremy. It's possible we could get you both of those things. Prosecutorial immunity and the kind of protection you mentioned. Those aren't unreasonable things. But I can't call my captain and ask him to get that set up unless you give me something solid, something that would make such a deal worthwhile. That's the first thing he's gonna ask."

Jeremy took a deep breath. "I guess I can see that." Spent a few moments thinking. "What if you could tell your captain I do know who killed Brew and why. I wasn't there when it happened, but I heard the plan. I tried to talk them out of it, but it didn't do any good."

"So, you heard the killers talking about doing this," Joe said. "And you know why they felt like it had to be done, even though you were all supposed to be good friends?"

"There was no *supposed to be*, we were all good friends. But something terrible happened that changed everything. Just like that. We were good friends with nothing but a bright future just up ahead for all of us, and then one night — just like that — everything changed."

"And you know what that one thing is?" Joe said.

"Oh, yeah. I definitely do. I saw what happened on that one. I didn't have anything to do with it, or what they did after...with Brew, I mean. But, yeah, I knew all about that, too, because they told me."

"Did this *other thing*—the first thing—have to do with the plot to kill McFarland?" Hank said.

"No, it didn't. Not directly. But I can say this, if this other thing hadn't happened, no way Brew would've ever been killed. There'd be no reason for it."

Joe and Hank looked at each other again. They both knew Jeremy wasn't making stuff up. "And if I could get you immunity and protection, you'd be willing to testify to all this in court?"

Jeremy nodded. "Yes, I would. And you can tell your captain when I'm done telling you what I know, you won't just solve the mystery of Brew McFarland's killing, but another killing, as well."

Joe tried to suppress the shock on his face. "Another killing? Another murder?"

"I didn't say that. I wouldn't call it a murder. But it was definitely a crime. Someone got killed who didn't deserve it, or what happened after. That's all I'm gonna say about that for now."

"Wait, just answer one more thing," Joe said. "A freebie, let's call it. Did either Tag Harvey or Vic Waters own a 22-caliber pistol?"

Jeremy looked down. "Yeah, Tag did. It was his Dad's, but he had easy access to it. We used to go out in the woods and shoot tin cans off logs."

Joe stood. "Okay, give me a few minutes. I'm going to step out into your reception area and call our boss. Run all this by him. If he agrees, I'll come back in, put the phone on speaker and have him tell you himself. Will that be enough to get you to stop sidestepping around all these things, and tell us plainly what went down?"

"Yeah," Jeremy said. "I believe that would do it. Of course, I wanna see it in writing. He can fax it to me." He wrote down his fax number, gave it to Joe.

JOE CALLED Captain Pendleton's private cell phone, the one he was only supposed to call for something urgent. After several rings, he got Pendleton's voicemail. He hung up, called Pendleton's regular number which rang out at his secretary's desk.

"Hello? This is Captain Pendleton's office, Marge speaking. How can I help you?"

"Marge, Joe here. You know we're out here in LA interviewing a key witness on this McFarland case."

"I did know that, Lieutenant."

"Well, we've had a significant break, and I need to talk to Cap right away. I got a guy willing to spill the beans on the whole situation, but he wants certain assurances first that I can't give on my own. I just called his cell phone and got voicemail. Anyway, can you get through to him?"

"Okay, Lieutenant. I hear you. Let me try. One of us will get right back with you."

Joe hung up, waited a few minutes. His phone rang. It was Pendleton.

"Okay, Joe. What's up? You're interrupting a pretty important call with a councilman. I can only talk a few minutes, or I won't be able to get him back on the line the rest of the day."

"This won't take long, sir. I need your help on something. You say yes, and I think we can start wrapping up this McFarland situation completely."

"Really? Okay, what's going on?"

Joe told him everything that mattered as quickly as he could. Pendleton understood what it all meant.

"So, you think you can get this guy immunity from the DA?" Joe said. "I know we can take care of the protection part."

"Well, if he delivers everything you just said, then yeah, I'd have no problem selling the immunity deal to the DA. Let me get this straight, he's not just talking about clearing up the McFarland murder, he's talking about some other killing that he knows about, here in Culpepper, that happened around the same time?"

"Yeah, that's what he's saying. He says this other killing is the main reason why the McFarland murder happened in the first place."

"Two for the price of one," Pendleton said. "I'll take a deal like that any day. Go ahead and bring me back into that room, put me on speaker. Let's get this thing done."

"Oh, Cap. He's gonna want this put into writing and faxed to him, before he'll talk. Can you get Marge to start typing it up?"

"Sure, soon as I get off the phone. Now, put me on with this guy, I'll tell him myself."

38

Culpepper, Georgia
Friday, January 31st, 1986
Sigma Alpha Epsilon Fraternity House

"GUYS, IT'S 11:00," JEREMY SAID, OVER THE MUSIC BLARING from inside. "We really gotta go. I gotta anyway." He walked to the edge of the front porch as a wave of dizziness suddenly hit. He grabbed the railing just before falling down the stairs.

An eruption of laughter from his friends Tag, Vic, and Brew. Of course, seeing how many red Solo cups of beer they had downed from that keg the past three hours, they'd laugh at anything.

"May I suggest you try crawling down them stairs," Vic said. "Might be a wiser move at this juncture."

Got them all laughing all over again. Jeremy played along

and did what Vic suggested, exaggerating every move on the way down. He turned around and looked up at them.

"Wish I had your camera now," Vic said.

"Seriously, guys. If I drink anymore, I'm gonna start throwing up."

"Now, there's a man," Tag said from a wicker chair, "who clearly can't hold his liquor."

This too, was somehow extremely funny.

Jeremy sat up, held his head straight till his eyes focused a little better. "Are any of you guys even fit to drive?"

Tag stood. "I sure am. Watch this." He walked about ten steps across the porch—toe to toe—turned, and walked back. He only lost his footing on one or two spots."

"How'd you do that?" Brew asked. "You drank way more than me."

"Like I said, a man who knows how to hold his liquor. I come from fine Irish stock."

"Harvey doesn't sound Irish," Vic said.

"But it 'tis, laddy." Tag in a terrible Irish brogue. "At least in my family. Guessing you must be Scottish, Brew?"

"Pretty sure we are." He tried to stand up, lost his balance, and plopped back in his chair."

"It would appear our Brew," Tag said, "has himself imbibed one too many brews."

Another volcano of laughter filled the porch.

Vic stood, a little wobbly, but made it safely to the first step. "Jeremy, it's a Friday night. We can't go home yet. The night is young, my man. Where's your sense of adventure? We're not in tenth grade, buddy. Come on."

"Guy's," Jeremy said, "you know how my mom is. She watches me like a hawk. If I don't sober up a little before I get home, she'll be in my face, giving me all kinds of grief. I gotta stop drinking and call it a night."

"Okay friends," Tag said, "we need to lighten up on our buddy here. He can't help it if his Ma's got him on a short leash." More of that butchered Irish brogue.

"Well, Jeremy you can go if you need to," Vic said. "But the three of us must soldier on. The night is young, and so are we. Someone inside told me just before we came out here, there's a big house eight blocks away with plenty of beer left in the keg...and they're giving it away for free. How can we ignore such an offer?"

Tag helped Brew to his feet then guided him to the porch rail. "What do you say, Brew? Are you with us, or agin' us? You joining Vic and me to check out this generous beer offer, or following Jeremy's example and cashing in your chips?"

Brew looked at Tag and Vic, then down at Jeremy. "Sorry, Jeremy. I don't know how much more beer this body can take, but I know I'm not ready to go home yet. Not this early on a Friday night." He looked at Tag. "But I don't think I can drive us to that big house Vic mentioned, not the way I feel right now. Might have to sit here on this porch a while, let me sober up a bit."

"Or," Tag said, "my good friend, Brew. You could hand over the keys of that beautiful Z28 to me, and I'll get us there safe and sound. You saw how I passed my little sobriety test a moment ago. What do you say? We sit here on the porch too long, and that keg might just run dry."

All three looked at Brew. Ever since he got that car, he was the only one who ever drove it. Nobody argued, because it was such a hot car. To their great shock and surprise, he pulled out the keys and handed them to Tag.

Tag reached for them, then Brew pulled them back a few inches.

"She's my baby, Tag. You better treat her right."

"You know I will, Brew. We all love her as much as you do."

He handed him the keys. "All right then. But only tonight. This isn't gonna start some new trend, okay?"

"Only for tonight, buddy. Got it." A big smile on Tag's face as he pocketed the keys.

Vic helped Brew down the steps. Jeremy got up from the grass. They all walked down the front sidewalk toward the road.

"You guys think you can drop me off at my house," Jeremy said, "before you head over to that other keg party?"

"I don't know, Jeremy," Tag said. "That's way out of our way. You're like two or three miles from here. The keg party's eight blocks."

"You're going to make me walk all the way home?" Jeremy said. "That sucks."

"Jeremy," Vic said. "He's just joshing you. Of course, we'll take you home first. You kidding? Gives him more time to drive that car."

"Oh, okay. Cause I don't think I could I could make it all the way. Probably pass out halfway there."

Brew's beautiful blue Camaro Z28 was parked just around the corner. It was a moonless night, but they could see fine with all the streetlights the University had installed in the neighborhood by the fraternity and sorority houses.

When they approached the car, Vic yelled, "I got shotgun."

"You can have it," Brew said. "The way I'm feeling, the backseat sounds just fine."

When Tag opened the driver's-side door, he just stood there a moment, taking it in. "I've wanted to do this since the first day you bought this baby." He got in.

Vic ran around to the other side, did the same. Jeremy held the back door open, helped Brew climb in, went around to the other side. As he got in, Tag turned the car on and revved it right up.

"Man, listen to that."

"Tag, take it easy," Brew said from the backseat. "Speed limit's no higher than twenty-five on all these fraternity roads."

"I hear you," he said. "But no harm in getting from zero to twenty-five in three seconds, is there?" He turned on the radio. The hit rock song, *Kyrie*, by Mr. Mister came roaring out of the speakers. "Oh, man, I love this song." He turned up the volume and pulled away from the curb.

As they drove down a block or two, it came to the chorus. Tag, Vic, and Jeremy began belting out the lyrics along with the lead singer:

KYRIE ELEISON down the road that I must travel
Kyrie eleison through the darkness of the night...

"WHAT ARE WE EVEN SAYING?" Jeremy shouted.

"I don't know," Tag said, "But I love it."

Brew groaned. "I *used* to love this song. Hearing you guys sing it makes me want to hurl."

39

SINCE HE ONLY HAD ONE CONTROLLER, FOR THE LAST THREE hours Eddie Simmons and his friend, Kyle Wilson, were taking turns playing their favorite Nintendo game, *The Legend of Zelda*. Kyle had invited Eddie over to spend the night. It was the first time Eddie had ever been to Kyle's house, even though he only lived a twenty-minute bike ride away. Kyle had been to Eddie's house maybe a half-dozen times already, even once to spend the night.

Before getting here, Eddie wasn't sure why Kyle had been so hesitant to invite him over before. It certainly wasn't his house, which was twice the size of Eddie's. And his mom sure was nice. She made Eddie feel right at home the moment he got there, then went out to get them an extra-large pepperoni pizza for dinner. But Eddie noticed they'd both get a little tense when he asked questions about Kyle's dad.

Eddie picked up that he'd been out of town and wasn't expected back until sometime tomorrow afternoon. When

Kyle told him that, without saying why, he'd suggested maybe they should leave here and head back over to Eddie's before lunch. Eddie was fine with that, but the way Kyle said it had made him think he didn't want Eddie to be there when his dad got home.

Anyway, Eddie shifted his focus back on Zelda. He could tell Kyle was just about to die, and it would be Eddie's turn again to play. But just then, they heard some loud noise coming from downstairs. Then a bunch of yelling, loud enough to hear through Kyle's closed bedroom door.

Kyle froze, then paused the game. His face, right to the door. He looked terrified, which instantly made Eddie tense up.

"What's goin' on, Kyle?"

Kyle didn't say anything. He was focused on the yelling, trying to hear what was said. He got up, went to the door, and pressed his ear against it. A few seconds later. "Oh, no. It's my Dad. He's home. I didn't hear why, but he came home a day early."

He looked like he was gonna cry. Clearly, this wasn't good.

"So, that's him? Yelling at your mom?"

Kyle nodded, his ear still against the door.

"Why's he so mad?"

"He's always mad about something. The only question is, how mad is he now?" He kept listening.

Eddie suddenly felt a strong urge to go home.

"Oh, shoot," Kyle said. "He knows you're here. He saw your bike parked next to mine in the garage. He's mad at mom for letting you stay over without asking him first."

"Your mom has to ask him permission for something like that?"

Kyle sighed. "Afraid so. She only said yes when I asked her, because she knew he'd be gone. That's why I said we should head back to your place before lunch."

Eddie stood, while Kyle continued to listen at the door. He started gathering his things together into his backpack. "Kyle, I really don't want to be here anymore. Nothing on you. Really, not your fault your Dad's that way. Is there any way you can sneak me out before he comes up here? I really don't want—"

"Yeah, we can do that. I can tell they're arguing in the living room. We go real quiet down the stairs and tiptoe towards the kitchen. The wall in front of the stairs should block him from seeing us. You can slip right out the kitchen door. If it's not on, I'll turn on the outside light. If the garage door's closed, you can get in the side door on the right. It's never locked."

"That'll work," Eddie said. "Let's do it. Like, right now."

"I'm so sorry, Eddie. This is why I haven't asked you over before. It's the only—"

"Don't worry about it, Kyle. We'll still be friends. We can just hang over my house like before."

Kyle opened the door and stepped into the hallway. The yelling instantly got louder. Eddie didn't want to listen. He just wanted out of there. Kyle hurried down the steps, with Eddie right on his tail, grateful the steps were carpeted. They got down okay and headed for the kitchen door. Kyle opened it and stood aside to let Eddie through. The outside light was already on.

Before closing the door, Kyle said, "I'll call you tomorrow when the coast is clear."

Poor Kyle. Eddie suddenly didn't envy Kyle for how big his house was. He quickly got to the garage side door and carefully maneuvered his bike out to the driveway. He hopped on and headed for the sidewalk, quick as he could. But after a few houses, he moved out to the street. The neighborhood had so many big trees, even with all the streetlights, most of the sidewalks were in the dark. He could see way better in the street. He'd never ridden his bike home this late before, or when it was this dark before.

He was glad he'd be home in twenty minutes. One nice thing about riding home now. Hardly any cars on the road.

JEREMY'S HOUSE was just five blocks away. Maybe it was the music. Maybe it was the beer. But Tag had just turned left at an intersection where he needed to turn right. Both Brew and Vic instantly yelled at him, so he pulled into the first driveway he could. Like all the others around here, it was a big one. He put the Z28 in reverse and started backing out of the driveway.

Tag was a little more sloshed than he'd realized when he first got into the car. But he was fine. So far, he'd only driven over two curbs during turns. Both times they'd rocked everyone in the car, especially Brew. "Hey, you're gonna blow my suspension," he'd said.

Tag assured him it was only because he was driving too fast, so he slowed down a little after that.

He was extra careful backing out right now. Across the

street, there was a car parked along the curb. He hadn't seen it until the last second and had to slam on the brakes.

Vic just laughed, but Brew wasn't amused. "Tag, what's going on? You said you could drive."

"I can. I'm just not used to your car. Your breaks are so touchy compared to mine." A quick recovery.

"Well," Brew said, "could you be more careful? I haven't even gotten a scratch on this paint job since I bought it."

"I will. I will. Just relax and enjoy the music. We'll drop Jeremy off and be at that keg party in no time. Brew, you feeling any more sobered up yet?"

"A little, maybe. Enough for one more beer, I think."

"Well, I am definitely ready for mo' beer, " Vic said. "Gimme some mo' beer, quick as you please." He laughed way too hard.

"Coming right up," Tag said. He shifted into first, but didn't peel out this time. Wanted Brew to see he was totally in control. "Say, guys, how about we go see that movie, *The Jewel of the Nile* tomorrow? I haven't seen it yet, and it just got moved to the drive-in."

"The drive-in," Jeremy said. "I thought that closed down."

"No, it's still ticking," Tag said. "But it's only open on weekends, and only if it's not too cold. I called before we went out tonight, and they said they'd be running it. Come on. It'll be fun. We'll do like we used to in the summer. We'll flip coins, see which two have to ride in the trunk." They had a place three blocks from the drive-in where it was nice and dark. They'd pull over and two guys would hop in the trunk until they got through the front gate. That way, they'd just split the cost for two tickets.

"I'm game," Vic said. "I heard it was a great flick, and I

didn't get to see it in the theater, either. It's the one with Michael Douglas, right?"

"Yeah," Brew said from the backseat, sitting up, "he's the star. I saw it in the theater with my folks. It *was* really good. Not as good as *Romancing the Stone*, but still good. Danny Devito's in it again, too. I wouldn't mind seeing it again at the drive-in."

"I probably can go," Jeremy said.

"I gotta turn this one up." Vic reached for the radio volume knob. The familiar intro for the hit song from *A-Ha* had just started, *Take On Me*.

"Oh yeah, Baby," Tag yelled. It was blasting at full volume now. "I can hit that note," he yelled. Holding the steering wheel with his thumbs, he started banging the dashboard like bongos.

"Not as good as me," Vic said.

"Just you watch," said Tag.

"Oh, Lord. Please, no," Brew said, covering his ears.

"Here it comes…"

Take on me (take on me)
Take me on (take on me)
I'll be gone
In a day or…two…

Tag and Vic were just screeching it out.

The car started to swerve to the right.

"Tag," Jeremy yelled. "You see that kid on the bike?"

"What?" he yelled back, still singing.

"The kid on the bike. He's right there—WATCH OUT!"

Tag saw him, just off to the right. He slammed on the brakes.

A loud bang.

Tag was too late.

They all saw the kid go flying off his bike into the shadows.

40

FOR A FEW SECONDS, NO ONE MOVED. THEY JUST LOOKED AT each other, faces terrified. Everyone instantly sober. Vic turned off the music.

From the back seat, Brew spoke first. Only this, "Oh, God – Oh, God – Oh, God."

Jeremy looked at Tag, staring blindly ahead. "Guys, we hit that kid. We can't just sit here." He got out, eyes scanning the street up ahead. They were in between streetlights, so it was pretty dark. But he could see a lump in the road over by the curb on the right. He ran to it and could instantly see even in the dim light...it was the boy they'd hit.

He wasn't moving, wasn't making a sound.

Jeremy looked around, saw a mangled bicycle about ten feet away, in the grassy area between the curb and sidewalk. As he reached for the boy's wrist, looking for a pulse, he heard two other car doors open. Glancing back, Vic and Brew had gotten out. Tag was still frozen behind the wheel. He had turned off the headlights.

When they reached Jeremy and the boy, Vic said, "How is he?"

"Not good. I can't feel his pulse. Think he might be dead."

"Oh, God, no..." Brew said. "Please, no."

"Move over," Vic said. "Let me check. Maybe you're doing it wrong."

Jeremy stood as Vic bent down. While he felt for a pulse, Jeremy noticed a dark puddle forming under the kid's head, inching its way toward the curb. "I think his head must've hit that curb."

"Don't say that," Brew said.

"It doesn't make any difference if I say it, Brew. Look at that puddle. It's blood."

"I'm not getting any pulse, either," Vic announced. "From his wrist or his neck. I think Jeremy's right. He's dead."

Brew started crying. Not hysterically, but Jeremy could see tears rolling down his cheeks. Suddenly, what Jeremy was seeing, what just happened, hit him. He felt cold inside. His brain felt numb.

Tag finally opened his door and walked over. Whispering, "Is he dead?"

"Yeah," Vic said. "He's dead."

"Okay," Tag said. "Everyone back in the car, now." Like a drill sergeant giving orders. He started walking back toward the car.

"Wait," Brew said in a loud whisper. "We can't just leave. We've got to get him some help."

"Brew, if he's dead, what kind of help can we give him? We gotta get outta here. Now. Get in the car. We'll go someplace where we can talk this out. Not far. Just not here."

Like obedient soldiers, the three of them did as they were told. Jeremy didn't want to, but the numbness had taken over, and he just followed. As soon as they got in the car, Tag drove off slowly, the headlights still off.

They drove about three blocks in total silence. One more block, and they'd hit a busy road. So, Tag turned right wanting to stay in the darkness of the neighborhood.

"Where you going?" Vic said.

"I'm not sure. Looking for a good place to stop."

"Two blocks ahead, turn left," Jeremy said, though he didn't really want to help. "There's a park there. Used to play in it all the time. Only the basketball courts are well lit. There's all kinds of spots with no streetlights."

"Okay, we go there." Tag turned the headlights back on, but still drove slowly.

They closed the short distance to the park in silence, except for Brew's quiet sobbing in the backseat. When they got to the park, it was just as Jeremy had described. Tag found a section of the parking lot on the opposite side of the basketball courts totally shrouded in darkness.

"Let's talk here," he said, turning the car off.

"This is wrong, this is wrong," Brew said. "We shouldn't have left. We shouldn't have come here. We should've called the police."

Tag whipped around in his seat and yelled. "Then where would we be at? You thought about that? The kid is dead. Nothing can change that. It was an accident. Nobody meant for it to happen. But it did."

"What was a kid that age doing out this time of night on a bike anyway?" Vic added. "All dressed in dark clothes, riding in the dark. On the street, when there's a sidewalk right there?"

"You're right," Jeremy said. "He shouldn't have been out in the street at night dressed that dark. He probably should've had a bike light and red reflectors. But Vic, he wasn't riding in the middle of the street. He was way over on the side. We hit him. He didn't hit us."

Tag turned his angry attention toward Jeremy now. "You're right, Jeremy. We hit him. But not on purpose. But the cops won't see it like that. You know how they'll see it? First thing they'll do is give us a breathalyzer test. And we'd all fail. Every one of us. They'd call what just happened vehicular manslaughter, or since we're drunk, maybe something worse. Even you guys who weren't driving, don't think you'd be spared. We'd all be hit with felonies. And because the kid died, our lives would all be ruined. It'd be in all the papers. We'd probably be expelled. Is that what you want? After all these years, being just a few months from graduating? While everyone else is walking down the aisle for their diploma, we're rotting in a prison cell?"

"It's certainly not what I want," Vic said. He looked at Jeremy then at Brew. "Guy's, come on. Think about it. We didn't mean to hurt this kid. Certainly didn't want him dead. But accidents happen. If we went and got help or called the police, nothing would be different for this kid. For his parents. He'd still be dead. They'd still be heartbroken. Knowing who did it wouldn't ease their pain, because they'd know it was an accident. They'd probably even forgive us after a while. As we get let off to prison, our whole lives destroyed. What good would that do? Think about all the good the four of us could do in the years ahead? All of it wiped out, because of that one moment back there? That one totally unintentional moment?"

"So, what are you saying?" Brew said. "We just go on, act like nothing's happened?"

"That's exactly what we do," Tag said. "If you want, I could drive a few blocks, find a gas station. Call 911, say I think I might have just driven by a body laying in the street, and tell them where. That way, they'll send folks to check it out."

"I think that's a good idea," Vic said. "Let's do that. And we'll drive Jeremy home just like we planned. If you guys want, we can skip the keg party, call it a night."

"*If we want*?" Brew repeated. "You guys — after what just happened — could just head over to that keg party, business as usual? I can't believe you'd even say that."

"Listen, Brew. Don't talk like that to me," Vic said. "I'm not the bad guy here. I said we could go home. I'm just saying, if we're going to make this work, we've got to act just like that. Like nothing's happened. Like we didn't hit that kid. And if we hear about it in the news, anyone says anything about it, we can act just as sad and sorry as everyone else. Because we are sad. Sad it happened. Nobody's got to pretend to feel any different."

"Then it's settled," Tag said and turned the car back on. "We'll take Jeremy home now."

Jeremy opened his car door. "No, that's not a good idea. I'm only a few blocks from here. I can walk. Besides, it'll give me time to calm down before I have to see my folks."

"Okay, Jeremy," Vic said. "Good idea."

He got out, said, "See you, Brew. You guys." He closed the

door, started walking away. A few steps later, he heard Tag back out of the parking space and drive off in the opposite direction. He turned to watch, saw the silhouette of Brew's head through the back window.

He didn't know it then, but that was the last time he'd see Brew alive.

41

THE NEXT MORNING, THE DEAD, NUMB FEELING JEREMY FELT last night was still there. He did his best to do as the guys suggested — act normal, just like nothing bad had happened. He barely slept, constantly being woken up by nightmares about the accident. Images of the moment before hitting the kid on the bike. Images of the kid flying into the darkness. Images of him lying all crumpled in the street.

Jeremy had no appetite for breakfast, sat there at the table drinking coffee.

"What's eating you?" his mother said standing by the sink.

"Didn't sleep well, is all."

"That because you're hungover?"

"No, I'm not hungover." Maybe he was. At least, partly.

His little brother Dave came in from outside. "You hear about that kid that got killed last night? It's all over the neighborhood."

"What kid?" his mother said. "Who got killed?"

"Some kid. He was out riding his bike last night. Somebody hit him with their car. My friend, Robby, lives down the street from where it happened. He said police cars and ambulances were lighting up the whole area. He ran down to see what was going on. By the time he got there, they already had his body covered with a sheet. He went out there this morning, and the whole section of the street is marked off with yellow tape."

"Oh, my. That's terrible. Did he know the boy's name?"

"No, Ma. He didn't. But he said whoever did it took off. The cops were asking anybody if they saw or heard anything. Robby said it seemed like no one had."

"A hit-and-run," their mother said. "That's terrible."

Jeremy stood holding his coffee cup. "I'm gonna go up to my room and study."

LATER THAT AFTERNOON, he got a phone call from Vic, asking him to meet Vic and Tag at that same park they were at last night, where they stopped to talk after the accident. "Go there now," Vic had said. "We'll be there in ten. It's urgent. You gotta come." Jeremy said he'd be there and left right away.

It was about a ten-minute walk.

When he got there, Tag and Vic were already parked in the same spot, sitting in Tag's car. He walked up and stood just outside Vic's window. The two of them got out. Tag walked around the front of the car and stood next to Vic. Both of their faces deadly serious.

"We gotta talk, man," Tag said. "You haven't told anyone, have you?"

"No. Why would I?"

"You seemed pretty upset last night."

"Uh...yeah. So did both of you. Probably the most upsetting thing I've ever been through."

"But you're not getting cold feet," Vic said. "About going to the cops."

Jeremy sighed. "No, I don't know. I don't feel right about what we did, but I don't want to go to jail, either."

"Well, we got a serious problem with Brew," Tag said. "We just got done talking with him, and he's losing it, man."

"He said he couldn't do this," Vic said. "He didn't sleep all night. He thinks it's just wrong, and we should do the right thing. Turn ourselves in and take our chances."

"What did you guys tell him?"

"We tried to talk him out of it," Tag said, "for thirty minutes. But it didn't do any good. He's dead set on us turning ourselves in. He said the front of his car is pretty scraped up. People are bound to notice."

"But," Vic added, "he also said there were no dents. The kid didn't fly up on the hood."

"So, what are we gonna do?" Jeremy said.

"What are we going to do?" Tag repeated. "We're gonna do this." He pulled his dad's 22-caliber pistol out of his waistband and held it up."

Jeremy took a step back. "Whoa, are you guys serious?"

"As a heart attack," Vic said. "We got no choice, man. We tried talking sense to him, but he won't listen."

"I'm not going to prison, because he's chickening out."

Tag put the gun back in his waistband. "So, what we need to know is...are you with us, or with him?" Tag said this, taking a step closer to Jeremy.

Jeremy was shaking inside. He had no doubt they were serious. "I'm not gonna say anything, if that's what you mean."

Tag took a step back. "Good, I was hoping you'd say that."

As if Jeremy had any other choice. "So, what are you gonna do?"

"Tag's got it all figured out," Vic said. "He asked Brew to give us a little time to think about it, like thirty minutes or so. Brew said okay. Then he and I talked and decided we'd pretend to go along with what he was saying."

"So," Tag said, "I called him back and said we'd go to the cops tomorrow morning and turn ourselves in. But I asked him if we could just have one more night out together, in case they put us in jail after hearing about what we did. He thought that'd be okay. So, we said we'd go to the drive-in tonight like we planned."

"You know," Vic said, "to see *The Jewel of the Nile*. He's gonna pick us up at seven. One more sweet ride in the Z28. We'll head to the drive-in and pull off at our usual spot. You know, to see who's going in the trunk."

"Guys," Jeremy said. "Look, I don't think I can do that. There's no way I could keep it together. Not for something like that."

"Listen, man," Vic said. "We gotta all be in this—"

"No, that's okay," Tag said. "He doesn't have to go. This can still work just fine. It's not like we're actually going to the drive-in. We'll pull over like we are. Vic, you'll be in the front seat next to Brew. I'll be in the back. It'll work." He looked at Jeremy. "So, you don't have to go. But you need to keep it together, man. You need to stay the course."

"I know, I know," Jeremy said.

"All right then," Tag said. "So, that's the plan."

42

THE PRESENT

Chevalier Studio
Santa Monica, CA

JEREMY SEEMED TO BE DONE, so Joe leaned forward and hit the pause button on the recorder.

"So, you weren't actually there when they killed Brew?" Hank said.

"No, think I was home throwing up. But I know they did it, and I knew how they did it."

"Wait a minute," Joe said. "Say that again." He turned the recorder back on and Jeremy repeated it.

"How do you know? And how can you be sure?" Hank said.

Jeremy looked down, took a deep breath. "Because both

of them paid me a little visit the next morning. They were so hyped up, you'd think they'd won some big game. My mom and brother had gone off to church, so we had the house to ourselves. They came in way too excited, considering what they just did. I'm trying not to show on my face the disgust I'm feeling inside. They just killed our close friend, in cold blood. Neither one of them showed any remorse or concern. It was all just, *We did it, man. We took him out.*"

"Who said that?" Joe said.

"Vic. But Tag was no better. Think he said something like, *Except for a little glitch, came off without a hitch.* Then he laughed when he realized it rhymed."

"What was the glitch?" Joe said.

"I wasn't sure, but apparently, right after Tag shot Brew from the backseat, it took a second or two for him to die. Guess he grabbed Vic's collar and pulled him toward him. Vic said it kind of spooked him, but then he let go and fell forward against the steering wheel. They checked, and he was dead. And it was clear to me, that they couldn't be happier. Like they'd just pulled off the perfect crime."

Joe leaned forward to make sure the recorder was still going. "They tell you what they did with his body?"

"Yeah. Not the details. But Vic said he knew of the perfect way to get rid of both Brew's body and the car. He talked about some pond they used to fish at as kids. Above it, not too far off the road was a cliff. They didn't give me a play-by-play, but I guessed they'd driven there, put Brew's body in the driver seat, then shoved it off. When they were done telling me, Vic said it was too dark to see it after it went over, but it made a monster splash."

Joe looked at Hank.

Jeremy looked at both of them. "Does that pretty much line up with the evidence you've uncovered so far?"

"Pretty much," Joe said.

Hank leaned forward, his face a little edgy. "So you knew all this, all this time, and you didn't say a thing to anyone? Did you have no feelings for McFarland's parents at all?"

"No, I didn't say anything to anyone, all this time. And I do care about Brew's parents. Guess I care more about not getting killed a little more."

"So, they threatened you?" Joe said, "to keep your mouth shut?"

"Yeah, they did. And it wasn't subtle. Before they left, Tag pulled out his pistol, put it under my chin, and said, *Don't make me have to use this. Because you know I will.* Then Vic added, *Not a word, man...to anyone. You play it smart. This whole thing blows over real soon.* Over the next few days, I'm reading about the kid on the bike getting killed and Brew going missing. It's all anyone's talking about. No one's even thinking about the shuttle blowing up anymore. And I'm losing it. I can tell, I'm not going to make it if I stay in this town. I'm just not wired that way."

"Keeping your mouth shut?" Joe said.

Jeremy nodded.

"So," Hank said, "you came up with the scheme about the great photography job out here in LA?"

He nodded again. "It was the only thing I could think of that I thought folks might believe."

"Is there anything more to tell?" Joe said.

"That's pretty much it. You think it's enough to satisfy the DA, or your captain?"

"It should be." Joe lifted his brief bag, set it on the edge of

Jeremy's desk. He opened it, pulled out the folder with the black-and-white photos, spread them out so that they faced Jeremy. He watched as his eyes quickly widened as he comprehended what they were.

"I haven't seen these in...no, I was about to say *ages*. But I don't think I've ever seen these. Think I remember taking them, a long time ago."

"With that old Kodak camera?" Hank said.

"Yeah, my Kodak Rangefinder from the 40s. I forgot all about it. I remember after getting out here that I'd left it home, even wrestled with asking my brother to send it. But I decided I just needed a clean break. So, these were the pictures in the camera?" He slid the photos closer. "Man, I think I took these just shortly before they killed Brew."

"You're right," Joe said, "you did."

He looked more closely at the one with the newspaper, then reached behind him and grabbed a magnifying glass. He pressed it down against the photo and looked. "Yeah, I thought so. The front-page story is about the shuttle exploding. You know, the *Challenger*."

"We know. And you recognize everyone in the pictures?"

"Course. Brew, Tag, and Vic. I'm behind the camera. Geez, we had no idea how much things were about to change."

Joe reached into his bag, pulled out an evidence envelope. "Say, Jeremy. Something I want you to take a look at for me." He carefully lifted out the religious medal the divers had found at the bottom of the pond. "Ever see anything like this before?"

Jeremy's eyes focused on it. "Oh, yeah. For sure. Can I hold it?"

This was encouraging. Joe handed it to Jeremy.

"Yeah, this is a St. Christopher's medal. Looks just like the one Vic wore all the time."

"Vic Waters?"

"Yeah. As a matter of fact..." He started ruffling through the different photos. "Yeah, here it is. See, right here. You can see it around Vic's neck." He pointed.

Joe and Hank stood and leaned closer. Joe saw it clearly. Why had he never noticed it before? But there it was, plain as day.

"Any way we can get this part of the photograph blown up, so you can see the medal clearer?"

"Not a problem. Fortunately, these Kodak Rangefinders took really high-res pics. Wouldn't take me long at all. Take a look at it under this magnifying glass." Jeremy centered it on the medal.

Joe couldn't believe how clear it was. He looked at the medal then back at the photograph. An obvious match.

"So, where did you guys find this?"

Hank looked at Joe. Joe gave the nod. "How about at the bottom of the pond where we found Brew's body?"

"You're kidding," Jeremy said. "It's been down there all this time?"

"Looks like it," Joe said. Everyone stopped a moment. Joe said it first. "I'll bet when Brew grabbed Vic's collar, just after being shot—"

"Must've broken away," Hank said. "Maybe it fell down between the seats."

"And then," Joe said, "It fell out through the windshield after the car hit the water. You realize what this means, Hank."

"It ties Vic to the crime scene. It's physical evidence he was there."

"Cap's gonna like this." Joe put the medal back in the evidence bag, the photos back in the folder. He stood. "This has turned out to be a very fruitful trip."

Hank stood. "Looks like we can turn the rest of this day back over to you, Jeremy. Maybe you can still finish your photo shoot with that actor."

"So, what comes next?" Jeremy said.

"You sit tight till we call you," Joe said. "Shouldn't be too long. You feel safe out here until then?"

"Don't see why not," Jeremy said. "Been safe all these years." Then he stood, and Jeremy walked them to the front door.

43

THEY GOT BACK IN THE RENTAL CAR. JOE CHECKED THE TRAFFIC then pulled out onto 3rd Street. As he approached the first intersection, about a half block a way, something pretty big dawned on him. "Hank, since I'm driving, call Eileen at the front desk back home. Something I want her to check on."

"What's that?" Hank said, reaching in his lapel for his phone. "Oh, shoot. Can't believe I did this. Can you pull over?"

"What's the matter?"

"I left my phone back at Jeremy's place."

Joe pulled into one of the open slots along the curb. "Want me to just turn around? I think these streets form a rectangle."

"No, just leave the car running and the A/C on. It's not that far. I should be back in a few." He opened the door to get out. "Oh, by the way, what did you want to call Eileen about?"

"About that kid on the bike Jeremy said they hit with Brew's car. The hit-and-run."

"I was thinking the same thing." Hank got out and stood on the sidewalk. "I bet it's the same one."

"Well, go get your phone. I'll call Eileen while I wait."

"Back in a few."

THE COAST WAS CLEAR. The cops well on their way. "Payday," Hector Rodriguez said as he got out of his car. His gun with the silencer, tucked into the pocket of his hoodie. It was way too hot to wear this thing, but you couldn't beat how effective hoodies were at blocking your face from those annoying cameras that were all over the place these days.

He walked across the street as nonchalant as he could, weaved between the two parked cars then down the sidewalk toward the photographer's place. Glad to be moving again after spending so much time sitting on his butt. He turned left down the driveway that went behind the apartments then made a quick right at the walkway that led to the studio. It ran along the front of the building, bordered by bushes that came up to his waist. Would've been nice if they were higher, but with the silencer, he wouldn't have to run back to his car.

When he got to about fifteen feet from the front door, he slid the gun out with his right hand, held it down along his side. The sign hanging on the inside of the front door said *Open*. Hector knew no one else had come in since the cops left. And he was sure that young guy who left shortly after the cops went inside was the photographer's only customer. This from sitting out there casing the place all those hours.

No, he was alone. It was the perfect time.

· · ·

HANK FELT SO stupid having to go back there like this. He remembered what happened. While Joe and Jeremy were talking at one point, his phone had vibrated, so he took it out to see who it was. Just spam. But before he put it back in his pocket, Jeremy was pointing out the St. Christopher's medal with the magnifying glass. Somehow, that distracted him from—

Wait a minute. Hank just noticed something that didn't belong, really *someone.* A guy wearing a hoodie had been walking a good ways up the sidewalk from him in the same direction. He just turned in toward Jeremy's place. Hank's instincts said something was up. He hurried his pace and took out his pistol. Maybe it was nothing, but—

No, it was something. The guy just took out a pistol from his hoodie pocket. Hank zeroed in on it, noticed it had a silencer. Shoot, this was some kind of hitman, or something. Hank reached the driveway, leveled his gun at the guy, and said loudly, "Freeze, right there. Police officer. Drop the gun! Do it now!"

The guy did freeze, but he didn't drop the gun.

"Hey, man. Just be cool," the man said. He started to turn slowly to face Hank.

"I'll be cool," Hank said, "when you drop that gun. Do it now, or I will shoot you."

Hank could see the guy's face. Hispanic, maybe mid-20s. He stopped turning but didn't drop the gun.

"I'm not playing with you," Hank said. "Drop the—"

The guy's arm started moving up. Hank fired. He hit the guy right where he planned. The guy spun slightly and flew back against the front door, then dropped to the walkway, his gun falling to the ground. For a few seconds, he didn't move.

But Hank did, came closer, still pointing his gun at the man's head.

Hank kicked the gun far out of the man's reach. "Told you I wasn't playing with you."

"THE HECK WAS THAT?"

"What's the matter, Joe?" Eileen said.

Joe had just gotten her on the phone after two tries. "Just heard a gunshot. Gotta go." He hung up, got out of the car, and started running toward the sound.

Hank. God let him be okay.

He took out his service revolver and aimed it toward Jeremy's place, as he closed the gap. In a few moments, he saw Hank standing in front of Jeremy's front door, his pistol pointing toward the ground. Joe figured someone had to be there but a row of bushes blocked his view. "Hank?" he yelled. "You okay?"

"I am, but this guy's not. You call it in? Need an ambulance here ASAP."

When Joe got to the driveway, he saw a young guy wearing a hoodie on the ground. He was moving, groaning some, but definitely alive. "I got it." Joe pulled out his phone, figured he'd call 911 first, then his friend John.

"911, what's your emergency?"

"This is Lieutenant Joe Boyd. I'm a homicide detective from Georgia. We're out here questioning a witness."

"What's your location and your emergency, Lieutenant?"

"We're on 3rd Street a short distance south of Wilshire Boulevard. My partner had to shoot a guy who pulled a gun on him. He's alive, but we need an ambulance here right away, and whoever else you need to call from the Santa Monica PD."

"Will you be remaining there till they arrive?"

"Oh, yeah, we're not going anywhere." He hung up the phone.

Hank already had the guy handcuffed and was now applying pressure to his right shoulder with a bloody handkerchief. "Do you believe this?"

"No," Joe said. "Read him his rights yet?"

"Did that first thing. After yelling some profanities at me for shooting him, he's decided to exercise his right to keep his mouth shut. But I think you and I can both figure out what's going on here."

"Yeah," Joe said. "Not like photographers carry around a lot of cash. I'm going to head back to the driveway, give my friend John a quick call."

"Good idea. Let him take the lead, since we're on his turf."

It was easy to find John's number. He was second on his Recent Calls list.

"Hey, Joe? I'm already heading your way. Guessing you're the lieutenant from Georgia who just called in to report a shooting on 3rd. Just came in over the radio."

"Actually, it was my partner, Hank. I called it in, but he did the shooting. Can't believe this, but looks like someone put a hit on the photographer we were interviewing." *Someone...* as if joe didn't know who. "We had just left the guy. Hank went back to pick up his phone and must've interrupted the perp."

"Is the photographer okay?" John said.

"I'm sure he is. Hank got to the would-be shooter before

he got inside. My guess is the photographer's probably hiding under his desk."

"Well, I'll be right there."

"See you soon." Joe heard sirens off in the distance. He walked back to Hank.

"See you went for the shoulder."

"Yeah," Hank said, "after you were able to keep from having to kill your last perp back home—you know, that teacher Dietrich—that's all I've been practicing at the range. Perfecting shoulder shots, like we discussed. As soon as I saw the gun in his hand, had my eye on his right shoulder. Worked like a charm. Dropped the gun as soon as he got hit, then he dropped to the ground half a second later."

Joe had actually shot Dietrich in the side and leg, but later decided aiming for the *gun shoulder* might be more effective. "And now," Joe said, "we got a whole lot less paperwork to deal with, you won't be struggling with guilt, and we at least got a chance to talk to the guy."

A moment later, two police cars and an ambulance pulled up.

Hank walked a few steps away from the guy on the ground. "Although, I doubt very seriously he'll say a thing about who sent him here."

"Even if he doesn't, we both know who did this," Joe said.

"Yeah, we do."

44

An hour later, the scene was much more in control.

The guy Hank shot had his ID with him. His name was Hector Rodriguez, a known felon with a lengthy rap sheet. From the time the paramedics arrived until they'd driven him to the hospital — still handcuffed — the only words he'd said was, *I wanna lawyer*. No one from the Santa Monica PD doubted Hank's version of events but, as it turned out, they didn't have to take his word for it.

A detective who reported to John Templeton, Joe's friend, had been approached by a woman who owned a hair salon across the street. She said she'd witnessed what happened through her front window. Everything she'd said lined up with Hank's story. Even better, she had a video camera that recorded the events. John had gone over to watch the video himself.

He came back and told Joe and Hank, "Yeah, the video shows exactly what you said, Hank. There's no sound, but the resolution is good. You don't always get that with these cameras. But it backs you up a hundred percent."

"So, what will you need from us?" Joe said. "We've got a flight scheduled for noon tomorrow. Will I have to cancel it?"

John thought a moment. "Don't see why you should. Not from our end anyway. We'll need Hank to come down, fill out a statement. Maybe fire his gun for our ballistics guy, to match the bullet in the perp. Though, that'll only matter if this goes to court. But Hank can do both of those things this afternoon."

"Don't guess we'll get a chance to interview the perp?" Hank said.

"Don't think so, Hank. Certainly, not before you leave. I'm sure they'll have him in surgery and recovery the rest of the day. Doubt his doctor would let you in. There's a chance you could talk to him tomorrow morning, but I don't see what good it'll do. This guy's not gonna talk. Really, he doesn't have any reason to. For starters, with the crowd he runs with he knows what happens to snitches. Back in the day, before we got soft on crime, we used to have some leverage in situations like this. We could threaten him with serious time if he didn't talk, or offer him some sweetheart deal if he did. But that's gone. And they know it. We know what he came here to do, but you stopped him. So, all we got him for is being a felon with a gun and, possibly, attempted robbery. Those used to be big things, but not these days."

"No, you're right," Joe said. "He's not gonna talk."

"I mean, we'll try," John said. "But I don't see any point you guys missing your flight for something so pointless."

"Wow," Hank said. "That really stinks, that things are so messed up here. Back home, those would still be big things.

Maybe not enough to get the guy to squeal, but it at least would be a card we could play."

"Now," John said, "this is remote, but if for some crazy reason he does make it to court over this incident, we may have to get you to come back to testify, or at least get a live-video thing set up."

"Sure, no problem," Hank said. "Just let me know."

"Well, I gotta get going," John said. "Glad you're okay." They shook hands and he left.

Joe looked at Hank. "You still doing okay? Want me to take you back to the hotel?"

"Why, what are you going to do?"

"Well, thought I would have a chat with Jeremy. He came out briefly after they drove off with the perp. Obviously, when he realized what almost happened, he got pretty shook up."

"No," Hank said, "I'd like to be there when you talk to him. I'll be fine. But first, I really need to use the bathroom."

"Well, let's go back inside his place. I'll tell him we'll go over things with him in a couple of minutes. You use the bathroom, and I'll call Eileen back. I was on the phone with her when this thing went down, had to hang up on her pretty quick. She's called me a couple of times since, but I didn't pick up."

"Yeah, you better fill her in," Hank said.

They ducked under the yellow crime tape and headed back inside Jeremy's studio.

AFTER BRIEFLY SPEAKING WITH JEREMY, who was now waiting

for them in his office, Joe sat in one of his lobby chairs, called Eileen. She picked up right away.

"Joe, are you okay? What happened? I've been dying over here. Is Hank okay?"

"We're both fine, Eileen. Although Hank just shot his first bad guy."

"Oh, no. Poor Hank. But he's okay?"

"Obviously, a little shook up, but he's handling it fine. I'm sure it helps that he didn't have to kill the guy."

"That's a relief. So, what happened?"

Joe spent about ten minutes filling her in, sharing more than he normally would, except that he'd asked her to brief Pendleton on what happened. Made sure to tell her what to tell him first, and that Joe would be calling him himself the first chance he got. He ended the call on the reason he'd called her in the first place, before the shooting.

"Eileen, could you do me a favor? Head to our office and pull out the box under our table. It's got all the cold case folder files from the 80s. Right toward the front, you should find one that talks about a kid getting killed on his bike in a hit-and-run accident. Could you pull that out and text me two things? The kid's name and the date he got hit?"

"Sure thing, Joe."

They hung up, and he called Kate. Thankfully he got her, not her voicemail. "Hey, Kate. How's your day going?"

"Not too bad. Was just ready to take the kids to the Chinese buffet we all love."

"That's right," Joe said, "forgot the time difference."

"What's the matter?"

He didn't stand a chance with Kate. She could read him like a book. He half-wondered if he didn't say anything, she might figure the rest out herself. "Well, our time with that guy Jeremy went great. Really, great. Pretty much got the case wide open for us, and he agreed to come back and testify against Harvey and Waters."

"So, he confirmed they did it."

"Oh yeah, and then some." He went on to tell her a little more and about the kid on the bike they'd killed. She was properly impressed with what she'd heard, knowing the difference this would make in the case.

"This is all good, but what's not good? Get to that part."

He decided to lead with what he'd told Eileen. "Well, shortly after our interview with Jeremy, Hank had an occasion to shoot his first bad guy."

"What? There was a shooting? What is it with you two? There's always a shooting."

Again, Joe spent about ten minutes filling her in. In the end, she was relieved how things had turned out and was grateful to God it hadn't gone so much worse. "So, Hank's really doing okay?"

"Seems to be. I'm sure once the adrenaline drops back to normal, he'll feel a little more than he does now."

"But a whole lot less than if he had killed the guy."

"Yeah, that's for sure. Listen Kate, love you much, but I gotta go. Hank's in there with our witness, Jeremy. We've got some things to sort out with him before we can go back to the hotel."

"All right, Joe. Love you, too. And so glad it wasn't you this time, if I'm being honest."

"Me, too."

"Still coming home the same time tomorrow?"

"That's the plan."

. . .

JOE WALKED BACK into Jeremy's office. He was sitting behind his desk. Hank sat in the same chair he'd used during their interview a short while ago. Looks like they'd been talking about the situation.

"As you can imagine," Hank said, "our friend Jeremy here is a little freaked out."

"A lot freaked out," Jeremy said, "but also profoundly grateful to your partner here for saving my life."

"So, you have no doubt why this guy was coming here?" Joe said.

"Obviously, to shut me up. Which is what is freaking me out. I never would've thought Tag or Vic would've done something like this. Guess I was being a little naïve."

"Don't beat up on yourself too much, Jeremy," Joe said. "We didn't see it coming, either."

"They must've heard somehow we were coming out here," Hank said.

"Yeah," Joe said, "that's a little disturbing. But they wasted no time in getting this hitman set up."

"My guess is Waters," Hank said. "Remember I said he had some shady dealings from his pawnshop days. Maybe he was into more than we knew."

"Well, in any case, my detective friend, John, doesn't think there's any chance this guy will give up whoever hired him. I agree with him. It would be great if we could use this incident in our case, but I don't think we'll need it to put them away. But we will need you, Jeremy. Alive and well. That's really what I wanted to talk to you about. How we can make sure that happens."

45

JEREMY GOT UP FROM HIS DESK. "GUYS, I'M GONNA NEED A drink. My hands are shaking." He walked over to an old-fashioned file cabinet in the corner, opened the top drawer, and pulled out a bottle of Johnnie Walker Blue Label whiskey and a glass.

Joe didn't drink whiskey anymore, but he knew that was some high-end stuff. Jeremy's photo biz must be doing pretty well to afford a brand like that.

"Either of you guys want some?" he asked. "Hank, I'm sure you could use a shot or two."

"I'm good," Hank said. "But you go right ahead. I could use a bottle of water, if you got any cold."

Jeremy walked back to his desk and sat. "If you walk back in the studio, just inside the door on the right is a fridge. Plenty of cold ones in there, and some cold beers if you'd rather." He poured himself about two inches, looked at Joe. "Sure you don't want some. This is the good stuff."

"Oh, I know. But no thanks." Hank got up to get his water. "Grab me a bottle, too."

Jeremy took a sip. Then another. "I can't believe these guys hired a hitman. It was just never a thought that it could happen. But I guess I shouldn't be so surprised, considering what they did to Brew. But still, after all these years, I just—"

"It's a pretty desperate step," Joe said. "Tells me they're running scared. My guess is, they know that apart from you, everything else in our case — all our other evidence — is circumstantial. We've got some good stuff, way more than they know. And you just added another vital piece to the equation with that St. Christopher's medal."

"That reminds me," Jeremy said, "I've got to do that blow-up shot for you guys. I'll make it so the left half will be the full-size pic showing Vic wearing it, and the right will be zeroed in on the medal. If you write down your email address, I'll send it to you this evening."

Joe pulled out his card from his lapel. "This has my e-mail and phone number, but it's the phone at my desk." He took out a pen. "I'll write my cell number on the back."

Hank came back in, gave Joe his water bottle.

"So, Jeremy," he said, "we've got to play the hand we've been dealt. These guys didn't just kill a little boy and cover it up, then kill a close friend to shut him up thirty-plus years ago."

"I know. They just tried to kill me now."

"Right, which tells us time has not improved their character. We have to assume they might try it again. At some point, they're gonna find out their guy failed. At best, we've got a day or two. I don't know if you've got somewhere safe you can go until the trial. If not, we'll need to fly you back to Culpepper, put you up in a safe house."

"Once you testify," Hank said, "you should be fine. The whole point of this was to keep that from happening."

"I know. I've seen enough crime movies. I just never thought stuff like that was real. But, I get it. Even if I decided not to testify, I'm sure at this point they'd still have me killed."

"Afraid I have to agree," Joe said. "Guilty people will do crazy things to keep from getting caught."

Jeremy sighed, took another gulp. "Well, I may have lied to my family about coming out here for a great job, and I definitely haven't hit the big time in my career. But I have done surprisingly well. I can afford to take some time off, is what I'm saying. I got an ex-girlfriend who lives in a suburb of Oakland. She's been trying to get us back together again. I'm sure she'd help me out. I could probably call her tonight and be on the road tomorrow."

Well, Joe thought, that answered the question his brother Dave had about whether or not Jeremy was gay. "Can you stay there for a couple of months? I'm hoping we'll be able to push to get this trial happening sooner, but—"

"Yeah," Jeremy said. "I've got enough set aside to last the better part of a year. I may even wind up moving up there. I'll lose most of my movie clients, but I've got other avenues I can pursue. Anything's better than getting killed or living here in fear, always having to look over my shoulder."

"That's good," Hank said, "but Jeremy, you realize, wherever you go you gotta stay off social media. And not tell any of your local connections where you've gone. At least till the trial. It's gotta be like you disappeared."

"No, I get it. That's how I'm seeing this."

"That's good, "Joe said. "And I promise you, we will get these guys arrested ASAP, and get that trial set up as quick as possible."

"I appreciate that."

Joe and Hank stood up. "Say, Jeremy. I hope you don't mind me getting a little personal, but...well, here goes...your brother Dave asked me when I saw you to please tell you how much he misses you, and wishes you guys would start connecting again. I can tell he seems kinda hurt that you two never talk."

A look of surprise. "Yeah, that's definitely something I need to fix. Dave doesn't deserve how I've treated him all these years. I think once we get this horrible business behind us, I'll definitely reach out to him, try to mend that fence."

"Well," Joe said, "this is just a thought. But I'd say you could even do that now, if you want. He certainly seems like somebody you can trust. You know, someone who can know what's really going on. I don't think you'd have to wait till after the trial. But hey, look, I'm not telling you what to do. Just a thought."

"No, Lieutenant, I appreciate that."

They shook hands and Joe and Hank headed for the door. Their next stop, the Santa Monica PD. On the way there, Joe got a text from Eileen about the file folder in the cold case box under his desk:

Joe, the little boy was 12, named Eddie Simmons. He was hit on a Friday night, Jan 31st. Let me know if you need anything more.

Joe smiled, looked at Hank. "Guess what Eileen just confirmed? Remember that cold case file we were thinking about going with, before this whole car-in-the-pond thing fell into our lap?"

"The kid that got hit on the bike?" Hank said. "That was the kid these guys hit that night?"

Joe nodded. "Cap's gonna like this little development."

An hour later, back in Culpepper, Vic Waters' burner phone began to ring. Other than Tag, there were only a handful of people who knew this number. So, he answered right away. "Hello, this is Vic."

"Vic, this is Antonio, out here in LA."

"Antonio, thanks for calling. I've been wondering when you'd call. Hoping it would be—"

"Well, don't get too excited. I ain't calling with good news."

Vic tensed up. "What's the matter?"

"I just found out, my guy, the guy I gave the hit to...he got shot. By a cop. While he was trying to do the hit. He's in the hospital now, handcuffed to his bed."

"Oh, crap."

"Yeah, tell me about it."

"What happened? What went wrong?"

"Don't got all the details yet. But from what I've heard, the cop who shot him is somebody from your neck of the woods. The word I heard is he was some detective from Georgia."

Vic's mood suddenly turned foul. "I don't understand, Antonio. Why'd your guy try to make the hit when the cops were nearby?"

"C'mon, Vic. Give me some credit here. I'm not an idiot, and I don't hire idiots to do jobs for me. Something unexpected happened. That's all I know right now. The point is, this witness fellow is still alive, and I'm out one of my best men."

"If this guy's one of your best, I hope that means he won't say anything that could come back on us."

"That's not gonna happen. I guarantee it. The point is, we're all done, you and me."

"But Antonio, I need this guy gone."

"Then you're gonna have to get somebody else. Seriously, Vic. We were never that close. I tried to do you a favor here, but now? I'm done."

"What if I paid you more—" A click. Antonio had hung up.

Vic started to panic again. He headed for the medicine cabinet, get some aspirin, maybe something stronger. This was horrible news. He dreaded calling Tag. He'd promised him he would handle this.

46

Two Days Later
Culpepper PD

AFTER MEETING WITH JEREMY SCHOFIELD, JOE AND HANK HAD driven to the Santa Monica PD, so Hank could give his statement and test-fire his gun for their ballistics tech. After a fine dinner, they'd taken in a movie at what used to be Grauman's Chinese Theatre on Hollywood Boulevard. It was the classic location for all the red-carpet Hollywood premieres back in the day. Hank loved it. Joe had been there once. Hank said he'd never seen a movie with that big of a screen, or in a place that fancy.

The next morning, before they headed to the airport, Joe had driven them both to the Santa Monica pier, Venice Beach, and then up the Pacific Coast Highway to Malibu.

Their last stop, of course, was to get to a place where Hank could see the big Hollywood sign atop Mount Lee.

Last night, they had arrived back home.

This morning, first thing, they headed down the hall from their office to meet with Captain Pendleton. Joe had already briefed him on the headlines in a phone call before they'd gone to that movie.

When they had stepped into Pendleton's outer office, Marsha said, "Go on in, gentlemen. He's expecting you."

"Hey, guys. Welcome back," Pendleton said. "Sounds like you had a fruitful trip. So, what do you think? We ready to go to the DA with this?"

"Definitely," Joe said. "We'd probably be there now just on the circumstantial stuff, but with Jeremy Schofield's willingness to testify, and the strength of what he has to say, it's pretty much a slamdunk to me."

"I agree," Hank said. "Jeremy will make a great witness."

"Great. Give me the play-by-play. Don't leave anything out."

That's what they did for the next twenty-five minutes. After, Pendleton agreed it was time to go for murder-one for both Tag Harvey and Vic Waters on the Brewster McFarland case, and vehicular manslaughter on the hit-and-run case with the boy on the bike. Although he'd added, "Given the fact they were drunk and then covered it up all these years, I wouldn't be surprised if the DA adds a whole bunch of other charges to this. Great work, guys."

"Say, Cap," Joe said, "if it's all the same to you, rather than round them up and arrest them wherever they are, think I'd like a chance for Hank and I to go at them in the interview room first. Have them come in for what they think is a talk, then hit them with the evidence, see if we can't get one or both of them shaken up enough to give us some more, maybe even get one of them to turn on the other."

Pendleton sat back, thought a few moments. "I'm okay with that, Joe, given one caveat. Seems to me this guy, Harvey, was the ringleader and the worst culprit. I'm okay if you can get Waters to turn on Harvey, but I don't want a deal going the other way around. Tag Harvey needs to pay the full price for all this."

"Got it, sir," Joe said.

NINETY MINUTES LATER, Hank informed Joe that Tag Harvey was in Interview Room 1. "Is he with his attorney?"

"No."

"Great. Let's see how far we get before he cries uncle."

When Joe had called him telling him to come down for an interview, of course he'd said no, he was too busy. Joe then said he and Hank could come there, but if they did, they'd be bringing a tech guy with them to video the interview. Might make quite a scene there at his fancy office place. Either way, they would have the interview right away. Harvey quickly relented, said he'd be right down. Then he asked if he needed to bring his attorney. Joe said he could but suggested he hear what Joe had to say first. He didn't have to say a thing if he didn't want to and could ask for his attorney to be present at any time.

Joe then did the same bit with Vic Waters, got him to agree to come down first thing after lunch.

· · ·

JOE AND HANK walked together toward the interview room. Hank opened the door. Joe walked in, sat on the opposite side of the table from Harvey. Hank came in, closed the door, and sat beside him. Harvey looked like he always did, way overdressed for the occasion. But one look in his eyes, Joe could tell he was all coiled up inside. Trying desperately to hide it.

Good.

"Thanks for coming in, Tag," Joe said. "Assuming you still want me to call you that."

"Not like you gave me much choice, about coming in. And that's fine, you want to call me Tag. I did call my attorney, by the way. He pitched a fit when I said I wanted to come in here first, without him, but he's sitting out there in his Beemer under a shady tree with the A/C turned on. So, go ahead. Take your best shot. We'll see how far this goes."

"Fair enough," Joe said. "Hank and I want to be straight with you right upfront. We think we've got enough to arrest you and your old buddy, Vic, for murder and some other very serious charges with or without your cooperation." He paused a moment to let that sink in.

Tag squirmed a bit, pursed his lips. "You do, huh? Okay, let's hear what you got. What you think you've got."

"Well, let's start with what we know you did but can't prove. We know either you or Vic, probably both, got someone out in LA to try and kill Jeremy Schofield, the only other living member of that foursome who were in the car that night. You know, when you all hit that kid on his bike back in January of '86." Tag's eyes got real wide — just for a second. "But the Almighty was looking out for Mr. Schofield, and for Hank and me, too. If you had gotten your way and your hitman succeeded in killing Jeremy, it'd make our case a good deal harder to prove. But — as I said — he failed his assignment. The good Lord had Hank here forget his cell phone, and he went back for it just in time to nail your gunner before he could do any harm."

Again, Tag's eyes reacted. "I had nothing to do with that, and...uh, I don't know what you're talking about."

"Which is it, Tag?" Hank said. "You had nothing to do with it, or you don't know what we're talking about?"

Tag didn't answer.

"So," Joe said, "We had ourselves a fine chat with Jeremy out in LA the past couple of days. I could tell you all the interesting things he had to say, but your memory seems fine to me. Bet you can already guess most, if not all of it...seeing as you were there when it all happened."

Tag looked around the room for a few seconds, even up by the ceiling. Joe realized he was trying to figure out where the cameras were. He said, "I was where? For what? You mentioned some kid got hit on a bike. I recall reading about that in the papers, I think. Happened around the time Brew went missing."

Hank looked at Joe. "Now that is some bad acting, Joe. Rates about a zero on the sincerity scale, you ask me."

Joe smiled. "It's kinda late in the show, Tag, to be playing that game. We know you hit that boy on the bike...driving Brew's Z28, because he was too drunk to drive. From the sound of it, right up until that terrible moment, you were having the best time. Singing the Mr. Mister song on the radio, remember? You were just belting it out."

Tag took a deep breath, pushed his chair back from the table.

"Someplace you need to go?" Hank said. "We got lots more to tell you. Like in that folder there under Joe's right hand. Know what's in it? A whole bunch of photos that show— among other things—that you lied to us about you guys not seeing Brew the day he disappeared. I think you said y'all were studying for finals. Funny thing, though. I talked with the folks who run the University. They said none of their teachers would ever have finals in January or the first week of February. It was just after the Christmas break. You weren't studying. You were yucking it up with your good friend, Brew. Proof positive in that folder, that you were both with him the day before he died."

Tag stood. "I think I need to speak with my attorney now. Before this goes any further."

"That's good he's here," Joe said. "But before you get him involved, you sure you don't want to confess? Might give us a little leeway with the judge if we can show him how sorry you were for all the terrible things you did. How you didn't want to put Brew's family or the family of that young boy through all the grief of a prolonged trial."

"I have nothing to be sorry about," Tag said. "So, no, I won't be making any confessions today."

Joe feigned a sigh. "That's too bad. Hank?"

"Thanks for standing," Hank said, taking out his hand-cuffs. "Now, if you'll just spin around for me."

"What? No, you can't do this."

"Oh yeah, we can," Joe said. "Tag Harvey, we're arresting you for the murder of Eddie Simmons. That's the name of the kid on the bike. See it's murder, because you were drunk.

And the pre-meditated, cold-blooded murder of Brewster McFarland. And a few other things."

"I want my attorney."

"Oh, I'll go fetch him for you," Hank said, attaching the cuffs. "He'll be in shortly."

Joe read him his Miranda rights.

47

Vic Waters was sweating bullets.

He was on his way to the Culpepper PD, supposed to be there at 1 PM, for an interview with that detective, Joe Boyd. The timing of this thing is what was eating him up inside. He knew the detectives had just gotten back from their trip out to LA to see Jeremy. Which meant, very likely, they pretty much knew everything. Jeremy was alive and well and had most certainly made a deal with these guys. His complete testimony for total immunity from any charges.

This was exactly what he'd do if he were Jeremy.

So, how should he play this? He'd called Tag on his burner phone three times since getting the call for this interview. Each time got Tag's voicemail.

Just then, his phone rang, startling him. *Please let it be Tag.*

"Hey Vic, Tag here. Saw you called."

"Tag, yeah. On my way to an interview with that detective, Boyd. Was hoping to reach you before—"

"They're probably going to arrest you, Vic. That's what this is really all about."

Vic's heart, pounding. "You calling me from jail?"

"No, but they cuffed me and fingerprinted me, took mugshots, the whole nine yards. My attorney got me off from any jail time. For now, anyways."

"What kind of evidence they got? They spell it out?"

"I'm sure they'll go over it with you. Except for what Jeremy told them, my attorney feels like they probably don't have much. All circumstantial stuff. Not like they got any DNA evidence or fingerprints, right? Not from a car and a body that's been underwater for decades. They got no murder weapon, no eyewitnesses."

"Except Jeremy," Vic said. "He pretty much knows the whole thing."

"Come on, Vic. What does he know? He didn't see anything. He only knows what we said, what we told him. You and I stick to the story we've told all along, and we'll be fine. He'll say all these things that he remembers, and we'll say we have no idea what he's talking about. His word against ours. Two against one. There's nothing to back up what he says. So, don't sweat it. Stick to the story, and we'll be fine. Oh, there is one thing. I didn't see them, but they pointed to a folder they said had pictures that prove we were with Brew the day he died."

"They do? Then that proves we lied, cause we said we hadn't seen him for a few days, cause we were studying."

"Take it easy, Vic. It doesn't prove we lied. It proves we forgot something, a small detail. It was over thirty years ago. So, what if they can prove we were with him on the day he died. They don't have pictures of us driving the car to the drive-in, or pictures of me shooting him in the head, or us pushing the car over the cliff. They did, we'd be in trouble. But they don't. We just say we forgot we saw him. No big deal. Not like that's some kinda smoking gun."

"I guess you're right. This whole thing's just got me paranoid."

"Really, Vic, there's no need to be. You just need to keep your cool."

"But if they arrest me, I don't have a lawyer who can get me off so quick like you do."

"Well," Tag said, "you do now. I'll make you a deal. You stick with the story, reject any deals they might offer you, and I'll have my attorney represent you too, even pick up the tab for it. That's no small thing. I had to put down 250G's to bond out today. I'm sure it'll be at least the same for you. What do you say?"

"Well, I guess with an offer like that, I got nothing to lose."

"Great," Tag said. "But listen, you skip town, I don't get that money back. So, don't even think—"

"I ain't going anywhere."

"Good, because that's even part of the deal with the court. We can't leave the county until after the trial. Unless we got some kind of emergency and, even then, we gotta get permission."

"Got it," Vic said.

"Oh, one more thing," Tag said, "stop at a dumpster before you get anywhere near the police station, and bury the burner phone. They had a subpoena for my phone records. Luckily, I didn't have the burner with me, just my regular cell phone. I'm back here at the office now. Soon as we hang up, I'm taking a hammer to this thing. From here on out, we can't talk to each other like we've been doing. You want to give me any messages, give them to our attorney. He'll be our go-between, like we were kids in school passing notes. Anything we say to him's attorney-client privilege. I'll make sure he's there when you get interviewed."

Vic liked hearing Tag saying *our attorney*. "Okay, Tag. I'll get rid of this thing right away. And thanks, old friend, for looking out for me."

"Well, I got to. We're in this together, right? To the end."

HANK HAD JUST TEXTED Joe to say Vic Waters was now waiting in the interview room. He'd just gotten him situated and stepped out into the hall. Joe texted back that he'd be right there. He'd already talked things over with Hank, to let him know he wanted to play this one differently than the talk they'd had with Tag.

Just before going inside, he prayed as he often did before doing anything that mattered. This time, not just for wisdom, but something that would really help them solidify the cases against both these men.

Vic smiled as he walked in, but Joe could tell he was even more nervous than Tag had been. Hank was seated where he was before. "Afternoon, Vic."

"Good afternoon, Lieutenant. Already greeted your Sergeant here." A phony smile.

Joe sat in his chair, set his file folder on the table. "Okay, Vic. I'm going to assume you've already talked with Tag before you got here. Had to be recent considering his lawyer just walked him out of here thirty minutes ago. Of course, that's plenty of time for him to have filled you in." Joe looked at his eyes. He wasn't even trying to hide his concern.

"Jeremy told us the whole thing. I mean, the whole thing. And I gotta tell you, he's gonna make an excellent witness on the stand."

"Totally convincing," Hank added. "And very likable, too. That matters to juries."

"We know you and Tag tried to have him killed," Joe said. "Don't try to defend it. We have no way to prove this. That's not my point. My point is, you failed and we will guarantee that Jeremy stays safe and healthy right up until he testifies in court. You add that to all the evidence we've already gathered, and there's no way you guys get out of this." He paused, stared at Vic a few moments. Joe could tell he wanted to say something but held back. "Listen, Vic, we know that this thing started out as a fun night that went terribly wrong. After hearing everything Jeremy said, looking at what we have in this file, I talked to my boss, and he's willing to negotiate a deal with you—if, and only if—you're willing to testify against Tag, and work with us and Jeremy, to help us convict him when this goes to trial."

"We didn't make this offer to Tag," Hank said. "We're only willing to make a deal with you."

Vic looked back and forth at both of them. "I'm sure this so-called deal doesn't include no prison time for me."

Joe shook his head no. "Vic, you're not stupid. You know that's not realistic. You were too involved in this. You helped way too much to get off scott-free. But the way Jeremy tells it, it's obvious Tag was the main push behind all this. He was the one driving the car, totally drunk, when you guys hit that kid. He's the one that came up with the idea of silencing

Brew when he insisted you guys go to the cops. And he was the one who actually pulled the trigger."

"See, Vic," Hank said, "if you cooperate with us, all these things will be emphasized in a way so that Tag properly bears the greater weight. You'll be shown as someone he manipulated into helping him pull these things off. We can almost guarantee you'll get a much lesser sentence."

Vic sat in silence a few moments. Then said, "See, I think you guys are forgetting my age. I know I look good, but not that good. The way I figure this, let's say I did cooperate with you, hypothetically speaking. Not saying I even know what y'all are talking about. But any amount of jail time you guys get for me—even reduced from what Tag'll get—still amounts to me rotting in jail the rest of my life. So, since I didn't do any of the things you men are suggesting, I will just have to take my chances with a jury—if you choose to arrest me, that is. Since it's you're word—well, Jeremy's word—against Tag's and mine."

Joe sighed. So, be it. He stood, slid the folder over toward Vic. "Is that what you think, Vic? That this is gonna just come down to which of you the jury believes?"

Vic didn't reply.

"Fact is, we've got more evidence in this folder to convict you of these crimes than we do for Tag. You walk away from this offer, and you will—without a doubt—be charged with and be found guilty of everything we've already charged Tag with. Is that really what you want?"

48

JOE COULD TELL THAT GOT TO VIC. THE QUESTION WAS, HOW much.

Vic looked down at the folder. "So, what's in there? What do you mean you have more on me than you do on Tag?"

"Well," Joe said, "for starters, you probably remember how your good friend, Jeremy, was always taking pictures of you guys."

"Yeah, it sometimes got annoying."

Joe opened the folders, spread out the black and white pictures in front of Vic, except the magnified ones, showing the newspaper headline and Vic's St. Christopher medal. "You've never seen these."

"I don't know. Let me see. Maybe I have."

"I know for a fact you haven't, because these were the last photographs Jeremy took with this old antique camera he had from the World War II era."

"I remember that camera. It was the one he was using in the weeks just before he left."

"That's right," Joe said. "But these pictures were left undeveloped in the camera. They were developed for the first time very recently by the new owner. Jeremy hadn't even seen them until we showed them to him the other day."

"Okay, so I see some pics of me, Tag, and Brew. Looks like we're at Culpepper. What's the big deal?"

"There's two big deals," Hank said. "The first one has to do with that newspaper Brew is holding. Here's a copy of that magnified, so you can see the newspaper more clearly." Hank slid that photo out from the folder. "We've confirmed that's a copy of the Gazette from the last day Brew was seen before you guys killed him. The day before he was reported missing."

"Okay," Vic said. "That's...a little freaky. But he looks fine here."

"The point is," Joe said, "you guys lied to us. You both said you hadn't seen him for several days before he disappeared. But here you're with him the very day he went missing."

Vic reacted with a moment of surprise, then quickly recovered. "We didn't lie to you. How about we forgot? We're old. It was a long time ago, over thirty years. Obviously, this picture proves we were with him on that last day. Big deal. It doesn't mean we killed him, or that we had anything to do with that kid getting hit on that bike."

"There's more, Vic," Joe said. "I'm afraid you won't be able to wiggle out of this one." Joe pulled out the pic that blew up his medal, set it beside the full-sized photograph. "Remember your St. Christopher's medal? Jeremy remembered you wore it all the time. Like in this photograph. I bet you don't even remember what happened to it, do you? It

was there around your neck—that day—and then it wasn't."
Joe looked at his eyes. Serious alarm appeared.

"Well, Vic," Hank said. "We know exactly what happened to it, and why you lost it."

Joe pulled out the evidence envelope, opened it, and pulled out the medal. He let it hang down from his index finger. "Remember this, Vic? Our divers found this at the bottom of that fishing pond, right where we found Brew's car face down in the water. There's only one way it could have gotten there. It fell from the car when it impacted the water, or maybe when Brew's body went halfway through the windshield, which is how we found him. Jeremy remembers what you and Tag said the day after you killed him. Remember? Right after Tag pulled the trigger. He didn't die immediately. First, he grabbed your collar, looked right at you, then fell forward. Obviously, that's when he grabbed hold of your medal. Must've fallen between the seats, or something. In all the excitement, you didn't realize it."

"You guys got out," Hank continued, "drove the car from where Tag shot him to the cliff above the pond, put Brew back in the driver's seat, and shoved it over the side. And your St. Christopher's medal, Vic, went sailing over the edge with the car. And there it sat all these years — along with Brew's dead body — all these years."

Vic's face went pale white. He looked at the medal, back at the blown-up photo of it, sighed, and sat back.

"Seriously, Vic," Joe said. "You know what the jury's going to think when we show them this photo, proving you were with Brew on the day he died and wearing this medal, adding that to what Jeremy will testify he heard you guys say to him personally about Brew grabbing your collar just after

Tag shot him in the head. Then we find this medal — your medal — over thirty years later at the bottom of the pond, right next to Brew's car and body? You really think in that moment it'll be just you and Tag's word over Jeremy's? Who do you think they'll believe then? Who would you believe?"

No one spoke a few moments. Joe just wanted to let that seep in. Then he got an idea. One of those holy nudges he'd talked to Hank about.

"While you're thinking about that," Joe said, "think about this. There's even more physical evidence tying both you and Tag to these crimes. Specifically thinking now what started this whole thing...you guys driving around drunk with the music blaring then smacking into that poor boy on his bike."

Vic refocused his gaze back on Joe.

"Yeah, that's right," Joe said. "Physical evidence that ties you guys to the hit-and-run death of little Eddie Simmons. Guess what we discovered on the front end of Brew's car when we pulled it out of that pond?"

Vic sat up straight, leaned forward, and blurted out, "There's no way you found any front-end damage from that kid's bike on Brew's car. That's why I came up with the cliff idea. Brew's front-end would be so smashed up from the fall that—"

He suddenly realized what he just said. His mouth, literally, hung open for several seconds.

Joe looked at Hank, who grinned. "Go on, Vic. You were saying?"

Vic blinked, shook his head, like trying to snap out of something, and sat back. "Nothing. What I meant was, Brew's car would have been so damaged by...the... never mind."

Joe leaned toward Vic. "I think you were going to say something about there'd be no way any of the front-end damage on Brew's car would have survived, you know, from when you hit Eddie Simmons. Especially after going over the cliff and smashing into the pond. Or at least, no way anyone could ever tell the difference in damage between the two. That about right?"

"No comment," Vic said.

"No comment, eh?" Hank said, smiling. "You know, Vic, if you look up in that corner of the ceiling there, you'll notice that little camera. The comment you just made a few moments ago got picked up on that. You saying what you said, loud and clear. And it's all legal. We can show this in court...along with everything else Joe just went over with you. You sure you don't want to rethink that deal we made about testifying against Tag? Seems to me you might."

Vic stood. "This interview's over. I want to speak to my lawyer."

"You do, huh?" Joe said. "Who might that be?"

"Same guy who represented Tag. I want to call him now."

"Well, you can do that in just a few minutes," Joe said. "Right after Hank puts those handcuffs on you, and we get you processed. You know, fingerprinted, mug shots, and such. Oh yeah, and I read you your rights."

JOE LET Hank handle the rest of what needed to be done to Vic. He headed back to the office to fulfill a promise he'd made to Tom Hazelton at the Culpepper Gazette.

He sat down and dialed the number from memory.

"Hey, this is Tom Hazelton at the Gazette. What you got for me today?"

"Tom, this is Joe. Joe Boyd."

"Joe. Funny you called. My editor was just asking about this situation a couple of hours ago. I was all set to call—"

"Well, I told you if you behaved, I'd give you an exclusive on this story as soon as we made an arrest."

"So...you're there?" Tom said. "You're going to tell me who now, right? And anything else you can?"

"Yes. Both men have been arrested today. One's already bonded out, the other will soon, but we're sure we got enough to make these charges stick."

"Thought you were going to give me a head's up before the arrest, so I could get the perp walks on camera."

"Sorry, Tom. Couldn't pull off that part. You want to hear the rest?"

"Yeah, definitely."

For the next fifteen minutes, Joe filled him in on everything he didn't mind getting out to the public.

When he was done, Joe said, "Listen, Tom. I need another favor. Don't put any of this out there for a couple of hours. I want to talk to the parents of our two victims in person."

"I'm okay with that. How about this? You call me as soon as you finish chatting with them. It'll be today, though, right?"

"Yeah, I'm gonna call the parents as soon as we get off the phone."

49

JOE SPENT THE LAST THIRTY MINUTES DIGGING UP THE INFO ON Eddie Simmons' parents, then calling them. Eileen had left the file on his desk. Turned out, he didn't have the option of telling them in person. Neither one of them still lived in town. Sadly, it appeared they got divorced not long after their son had been killed. He located the father in Colorado Springs, and the mother a little closer in Greenville, South Carolina.

Both of them had taken the news as well as could be expected. His mother, not surprisingly, broke down over the phone as they talked. She had all but given up hope of ever learning the truth about what happened to her son. She thanked Joe over and over again for solving the case and finally arresting those responsible. Joe had assured her, he didn't see any way either man would escape justice when it came to court.

Eddie's father, on the other hand, was mostly angry. Not

at Joe, at the men who'd killed his little boy. Just a bunch of drunken punks. Spoiled rich kids from the University. He was glad they were finally being brought to justice but didn't feel like any sentence they got could begin to balance the scales. Here they had spent the last thirty-something years living their lives, doing as they pleased, while his boy lay there dead in his grave. He was only twelve. He never even got a chance to live life or do any of the things they got to do.

The last thing he'd asked Joe was whether he could sue them in court now for Eddie's wrongful death. Joe told him he wasn't sure the statute of limitations was still in play for something that happened so long ago. He'd need to get with an attorney.

Right now, Joe was pulling up to the gate of the Whispering Hill's condominium to visit with Brew McFarland's parents. On the way here, he'd confirmed they were home. All he told them was they'd had a big break in the case and he wanted to talk to them in person, if they were up for it.

He showed his ID to the guard, who waved him forward. Found a parking place a few moments later and headed upstairs.

Frank opened the door, greeted Joe with a friendly smile. "Just tell me up front...you get the guys who killed my boy? That what this is about?"

"Yeah Frank, we got 'em."

"Good, then come on in. Ida's already waiting in the living room. Get you anything from the kitchen?"

"No, I'm good."

As they made their way into the living room, Ida was already looking their way. "They got 'em, Hon," Frank said.

"I was hoping that's the thing you needed to tell us in person," she said. "Come on in, Lieutenant. Have a seat."

Of course, Joe sat where he had the other times he'd visited the McFarland's. "Thought I'd get you guys quick as I could, before it gets out in the news. Today we arrested the two men who killed Brew."

"You say that with such certainty," Ida said. "Not alleged, or we think we got the ones who did it?"

Joe shook his head no. "I don't believe there's any doubt left, not in my mind anyway." He set the file folder down on the coffee table, looked at Frank. "And believe it or not, Frank, that newspaper headline you recognized in that pic Brew was holding turned out to be a vital clue in the case."

"Really?" A big smile.

"Yeah, it helped us prove the killers were lying about some pretty important things." He looked over at Ida. "And remember that St. Christopher's medal I showed you? Well, when I showed it to you, I wasn't sure what it was. But you were almost sure you knew what it was. And you were right. What I didn't say that day was where we had found that medal. It was at the bottom of the pond close to where we found Brew's car. That's why I asked if it was something he ever wore."

"Oh, my," she said. "You think it must've fallen out of his car somehow?"

"Oh yeah, we're sure of it. And we know how it got in his car, and who was wearing it."

"Was it one of the killers?" Frank said.

"Afraid so." He almost didn't want to tell them the rest. "Now, the next part of the story is going to be pretty painful, pretty hard for you guys to hear. But I know you want to know the truth, and it's going to come out in the news pretty soon. The main things, anyway. But I'm going to tell you guys everything we know. I think you've got a right to hear it all. Are you okay with that?"

"Definitely, Lieutenant. Don't leave anything out," Ida said.

Joe found the two pictures that showed Vic Waters wearing the St. Christopher medal. The full-size one, and the one with the medal magnified. He moved them front and center. "Do you recognize that?"

They both looked down at the photos, their eyes darting back and forth between them.

Frank looked up. "Vic was wearing that medal?"

Joe nodded.

"Then that means," Ida said, "no, it can't be." Tears welled up in her eyes. She looked up. "Vic had something to do with killing Brew?"

"I'm afraid so, Ida. We don't think he actually killed Brew himself, but knowing what we know now, there's just no other way to say this. Neither he nor Tag Harvey were the kind of friends to your son you thought they were."

"Tag, too?" Frank said, a bewildered look.

"Frank, Ida...Tag is the one who killed Brew. He and Vic planned this together, and Vic definitely helped him pull off their scheme. But Tag was the one who pulled the trigger, the one who shot your boy."

Ida began to cry pretty fully. Frank hurried over to comfort her, but Joe saw tears in his eyes, too.

"You guys want to hear the rest? I'm okay if you want me to come back another time."

Ida looked up, wiped her tears on her sleeve. Joe saw anger in her eyes. "No, we've waited too long to know what happened to our son. We want to hear it all, anything you can tell us."

Joe spent the next fifteen minutes laying out the entire scenario, everything they had so far. Including Jeremy Schofield's limited role in what happened, and his total commitment to tell everything he saw and heard under oath during the trial. "Jeremy was clearly remorseful about not telling you all what happened, leaving you with nothing but questions all these years. But he was genuinely afraid for his life."

"Sounds like he had good reason to be," Frank said. Joe had told them about the attempt on Jeremy's life recently, and who they believed was responsible.

"There's one more thing I want to add," Joe said, "before I finish up. I don't want this to get lost in all the details. Frank, Ida, you raised a fine son. I'm not sure if you picked up on this, but Brew knew all along that what Tag and Vic wanted to do was wrong. They shouldn't have been drinking and driving, and it was their fault that little boy was killed. Even though, it was really Tag's fault, not his. But Brew didn't care about what might happen to him if they told the truth. He could've been expelled from Culpepper, likely have spent some time in jail. He didn't care. He insisted they go to the police and tell them everything, and nothing Tag or Vic said could convince him otherwise. *That's* why they killed him. The only reason they killed him."

Ida dabbed away her tears from a tissue Frank had just given her. "Thank you, Lieutenant. It does help hearing this. Not a whole lot, but it does some."

"And I'm also glad to hear," Frank said, "that at least my boy didn't suffer any when he died. At least, there's that."

Yeah, Joe thought, at least there was that.

50

AFTER MAKING HIS WAY BACK UP THE HILL, TREVOR BURBANK was exhausted. But in a good way. He figured he'd better call it a day for two reasons. The sun was rapidly going down, and he'd reached the point where he'd caught so many trout he couldn't carry even one more back to the car. Not up that hill where the car was parked.

This was his first time back to the pond after all the shenanigans of late. Lieutenant Boyd had given him the green light to return a few days ago. He wanted to come that morning but had a doctor appointment. He wrestled with the idea of coming after lunch, unsure if the fish would still be biting that time of day. He came down on the side of giving it a try. Figuring there were so many trout in that pond, some of them must've missed breakfast.

His instincts had been correct. They were hitting almost as good as when he'd come in the mornings.

He got to his car and put all his gear inside and the trout

in his big cooler. He stood back and looked at the clearing where he'd parked his pickup, when it dawned on him how far back he'd been able to park from the road. It was just like it used to be when they were kids and rode here on their bikes. Then he realized why. When he'd started coming back a few weeks ago, this clearing was unreachable due to the guardrails they'd put up around the curve. He had to park off the side of the road.

Then they'd taken down those guardrails in order to get that big crane in here, put up some concrete barriers in their place when they'd got done. That's what Trevor had expected to find today. But he'd been able to put right in well off the road, just like the good old days. He figured a crew must've removed the barriers because another crew was fixing to come in and put the guardrails back up. Hopefully, typical government inefficiency would kick in, and he'd have a few more days, maybe a week, to come back before that guardrail got put back up.

As he got back in his truck, a little pang of guilt tugged on his conscience. Had to do with the fact that he'd quashed an earlier idea that he should call and invite Vic Waters to fish with him when he'd set out this afternoon. Trevor just wanted some peace and quiet today, which he definitely got plenty of, along with a big cooler full of fish.

Maybe he should swing by Vic's place on his way home, offer him half his catch. Vic had let him know he really enjoyed eating fresh trout.

Trevor turned the truck on. Yeah, that's what he should do.

. . .

Vᴵᶜ Wᴀᴛᴇʀꜱ ᴡᴀꜱ ᴀɴ ᴀʙꜱᴏʟᴜᴛᴇ ᴡʀᴇᴄᴋ, had been all afternoon.

A couple of hours ago, he'd finally got freed from the nightmare he'd experienced at the police station. Dark, ominous thoughts had dominated his mind since the moment he'd seen that St. Christopher medal and heard where they'd found it.

He was doomed, and he knew it. It didn't matter what Tag said.

Vic could just picture the scenario where — after a lengthy trial — the jury lets Tag off and finds Vic guilty. Obviously, the lawyer Tag sent to get Vic bonded out, knew who was paying his bill and who would be paying most of his fees during the trial. The bulk of his energy and talent would be applied in Tag's direction, not Vic's. As they led Vic away to spend the rest of his life in prison, Tag would just wave and smile. "Sorry, buddy. Good luck in there."

Vic toyed with calling that Lieutenant back up accepting his plea deal to get a better sentence, maybe some lesser charges, if he testified against Tag. But they'd already closed the door on total immunity. Whatever other details might be written into the plea deal, Vic would still be spending a whole lot of years in prison. The fact that he'd get a lesser sentence than Tag was irrelevant. This might be an option if Vic had been in his 20s or 30s.

But now? The best deal they'd offer him still amounted to a life sentence.

He couldn't do it. He just couldn't do it. He'd rather be dead than finish out his life like that. The way his heart had been pounding all afternoon, he wouldn't be surprised if he blew a gasket and dropped dead today.

He'd started to feel a tad better after coming up with his new master plan. Obviously, it wasn't something he could or would run by Tag. Tag would be furious. Besides, he told Vic to get rid of his burner phone—which he did—said they'd have to stop talking to each other except through the attorney. Yeah, as if he was gonna tell the attorney that he'd decided to pack his bags, transfer his funds to an offshore account, and disappear.

He did, however, call and talk to his son. After hearing him out, his son agreed. Didn't seem to him that Vic had any other choice. So, that's what he was doing now...hauling his suitcases and a few boxes out to his car. He told his son once he got far enough away from town, he'd stop somewhere and buy a new burner phone, then text him so he'd have the number.

He came back out with the last suitcase, when he heard a car pull into the driveway. It had started to get dark, and whoever it was had their lights on already. When they had driven a little further, he realized who it was.

Oh crap, it was Trevor.

As TREVOR PULLED into Vic's driveway, he was relieved to see Vic was outside by his car. He was really hoping this would be a quick stop. Just some small talk, give him the fish, and be on his way. What was that Vic was dragging behind him? Looked like a suitcase. Trevor got out of his pickup, turned out the headlights, but left it running in park.

He noticed a bunch of boxes stacked in Vic's backseat, and his trunk lid was open. "Going on a trip, Vic?"

Vic stopped, looked at Trevor, an odd expression on his face. "Uh, yeah, Trevor. Kind of a last minute thing."

"I guess so. Judging by all the stuff you're packing in the car, looks like you'll be gone for a while."

Vic looked at his backseat, put the suitcase he'd been dragging in the trunk, and slammed the lid. "A few weeks maybe. Could be longer. Visiting my...uh... my sister for a while. She, she's... been pretty sick lately. Thought I'd go out there — you know, where she lives — and take care of her for a while. Be a good brother for a change."

"Well, that's a good thing," Trevor said. "I'm sure she'll appreciate it. Where she live?"

"Uh...she lives in...Ohio, outside of Cleveland."

Trevor thought Vic was acting very strangely. He got the impression Vic was making this thing up, right there as they spoke. "That'll be a good long drive. You leaving now, when it's almost dark? I always like to go on road trips first thing in the morning."

"Yeah, well, I thought I'd get a head start, see how far I could get tonight. A lot less traffic at night."

"Well," Trevor said, "guess you won't be wanting what I came to bring you."

"What's that?"

"Half a cooler full of trout. Just caught them this afternoon. Went back to our old fishing pond. Never fished there in the afternoon before. Didn't seem to bother the fish any. Biting about as good as they did in the mornings."

"Well, thanks for thinking of me, Trevor. But can't take them in the car with me."

"No, suppose not. It was really something though, fishing

there today. Reminded me of how it used to look when we were kids. You know, they took that guardrail down when they brought that crane in. After it left, they put up these concrete barriers. You know, right there at that curve. But they weren't there today. Guess they're getting ready to reinstall those guardrails. Anyway, when I pulled in I was able to drive all the way into the clearing. Right where we used to park our bikes, remember?"

Vic came around from the trunk to the driver's side. "Yeah, I do remember, Trevor. Look, I'm kind of in a hurry. Would love to stand and chat some more about the good old days, but—"

"No, that's okay. I understand. I'll let you be on your way."

Vic stood there behind the open door. "Say, Trevor. Could you do me, like, the biggest favor? Could you not tell anyone you saw me here leaving like this? With my car all packed up? I mean like, don't tell anyone."

"Sure, Vic. I guess if that's—"

"It's just, you know, these days you can't be too careful. People find out you've left town on a big trip, word gets out, and someone breaks into your place."

"Yeah," Trevor said. "Okay, Vic. Let me just back my car out, so you can be on your way."

"Oh, I still got a few things to take care of in the house before I go. But I will be leaving very soon." He closed the front door of the car. He stuck out his hand and Trevor reached out to shake it.

That's when he noticed something odd. Vic was wearing a gun, tucked into a shoulder harness under his jacket. "Well, have a nice trip, Vic. Maybe we'll head back to that pond when you get back."

"Sure thing, Trevor. See ya later."

As Trevor drove away, back toward his place, he got a feeling something wasn't right about what he had just seen. Made him wonder if Vic even had a sister who lived in Ohio.

51

AFTER TREVOR GOT DOWN THE ROAD A WAYS, HE CLICKED HIS lights to Auto, so the headlights would come on, and turned on the radio. It was set to the local talk station. He instantly recognized the familiar voice of the gal who shared local headlines. He was startled by what she said. Took a second for it to sink in.

THE BIG STORY here in Culpepper, which just broke a short while ago on the Gazette website, is the arrest of two local men for a cold case homicide that occurred early in 1986. Many long-time residents will recall the sudden disappearance of a local college student a few days after the space shuttle Challenger exploded. Recently, the story broke that his car and body had been found underwater in a pond just outside of town. Today we learned well-known real estate developer Tag Harvey and a former college classmate, Vic Waters, were arrested for the murder of Brewster

McFarland, as well as the hit-and-run death of a 12-year-old boy, named Eddie Simmons, which happened in January 1986.

TREVOR WAS SO SHAKEN, he immediately pulled into a nearby convenience store. He flashed back to his stop at Vic's place. The packing for a surprise trip, how nervous Vic was acting, the pistol in a shoulder harness, the feeling he was making up the story about his sister. "He's getting ready to run," Trevor said to no one.

He reached for his phone in the cup holder, never figured out how to tie it into the car's electronics. Should he call 911 or the Lieutenant? Moving to the Recent Calls page, he clicked on the button for Lieutenant Boyd.

JOE HAD BEEN ENJOYING a nice quiet dinner at home with Kate, the baby still asleep from a nap, hardly ever happened at dinner time. Kristen and Joe Junior had already eaten their dinner thirty-five minutes ago. Joe had been running late. Kate wanted the kids to eat what she'd made while it was still hot. Joe had no objections, didn't mind a meal like this reheated, especially getting the extra time in with Kate. For the last few minutes, he'd been filling her in on the events of the day. Plenty of satisfying things to share with the arrest of Harvey and Waters.

His phone rang. Why'd he leave it on the table? Now he could see it, not just hear it.

"You're not gonna get that, right?" Kate said.

"Nah. Let's just ignore it." Still, he glanced over. Didn't

recognize the number. If it was Hank, maybe. He picked it up intending to shut it up. Just as he was getting ready to mash the button, he felt a big NO inside. Looked at Kate. "Sorry, feels like I'm supposed to answer it."

"Go ahead then."

"If it's nothing, I'll hang up immediately."

She smiled, nodded, took another bite.

"Hello, Lieutenant Joe Boyd here."

"Lieutenant, this is Trevor. Trevor Burbank. Remember the guy who brought you the car mirror?" His voice seemed panicked.

"Trevor, I remember you. What's up?"

"You better send somebody over to Vic Waters place right away. Think he's getting ready to take off on you guys. Just heard on the radio you arrested him today for the murder of that kid whose car we found in the pond. Could hardly believe my ears. But I was just by Vic's place, wanted to drop off some fresh trout. He was getting all packed up. Car loaded with boxes and suitcases. Acted all surprised to see me, talking real nervous like. Asked me not to tell anybody that I'd seen him, which I found odd. Said he was gonna visit a sister in Cleveland. But sounded made up to me. Then when we shook hands goodbye, I see him wearing a pistol in a shoulder harness under his jacket."

Great, just great.

"No, you were right to call me, Trevor. This isn't good. I think he is making a run for it. He was told not to leave the county until the trial. Look, don't go back there. We'll take care of it."

"Wasn't planning on it, Lieutenant. Just thought you guys ought to know."

"Thanks. I better get off the phone and get moving on this." He hung up, stood up, looked at Kate.

"You gotta go. Can't let him ruin all this great police work you were just telling me about."

He gave her a quick kiss, hurried back upstairs to get his gun and badge, called Hank.

"What's up, Joe?"

Joe told him what Trevor had just said.

"Yeah, not good," Hank said. "How you want to handle this? Want me to take care of it?"

"No, we both need to do this, and we're going to need some help. Alert everyone who's on duty. I know where Vic lives. There's really only one road leads out of town up there. Of course, once he gets to 40, he could go left or right. So, set up two roadblocks on 40, on both sides of town. I'll head to his place from here at home. That'll cut him off if he decides to come back through town."

"Probably wouldn't do that," Hank said, "if he doesn't know we're onto him."

"Agreed. Right now, don't think he is. But we gotta move on this ASAP. Give the guys his description and set up a BOLO for a blue Audi SUV."

They hung up, and Joe headed out the door.

Ten minutes later, as Joe pulled up to Vic's house, he could see him getting into his car. It was pretty dark out, but there was a streetlight right by his mailbox. Remembering what Trevor had said about him wearing a gun, Joe pulled off to the side diagonally across the street. Fortunately, there were only wooded lots on the opposite side from Vic's house. He

pulled out his gun but kept it by his side, stayed behind his
front door, and yelled out, "Hey, Vic. Lieutenant Joe Boyd
here. Where do you think you're going?"

Vic looked up, shocked. He pulled out his gun, pointed it
at Joe, and fired.

Joe ducked. Heard it hit a tree behind him. He was just
about to fire back when Vic hopped into his car. His headlights came on, and he started down the driveway. Joe got in
his car and gunned it, thinking he could block Vic's access to
the street. Vic just swerved to the left, smacked Joe's left,
front fender, and took off, headed toward 40.

Joe got on the radio. "Shots fired, shots fired. Boyd here.
I'm fine. Suspect Vic Waters has just smacked into my car
outside his residence. He's taken off east toward 40."

"Joe, Hank here. We got both roadblocks up. Your car still
run, or do I need to send someone to get you?"

Joe got in, took it out of park, and hit the pedal. His car
took off without a hitch. "Car runs, Hank. I'll do my best to
catch up to Waters. I lost sight of him, but there's nowhere
else he can go except toward one of your roadblocks."

"Well, we're ready for him. I hear you say shots fired? He
actually shot at you?"

"Yeah, he did. Couldn't believe it." Joe turned on his
siren, set his flashing light on the dash. "Don't know if he
was trying to kill me or scare me. Then he messed my front
end all up."

Joe was really moving. Thankfully, out this way and at
this time of day there were hardly any cars. And he really
knew these roads now. After a couple of minutes, he saw
Vic's SUV a few blocks ahead. They were approaching the T-

intersection for 40. Joe saw his brake lights come on, but for just a second. Vic didn't stop at the sign.

He got on the radio. "Suspect just turned left onto 40, heading north. I'm in pursuit. Get ready guys."

52

STATE ROAD 40 WAS A WINDING ROAD RUNNING THROUGH THE hills outside of town. Very few long stretches, so it was hard to keep sight of Vic's car for more than a few seconds at a time. Joe figured Hank would've set the northern roadblock on the one stretch of straight road that ran through a flat area. It was coming up in a few moments.

When Joe reached it, he saw the taillights of Vic's car up ahead and floored it, closing the distance. Not long after he saw the multiple flashing blue lights of the roadblock. He got close enough to see Vic slam on his brakes and fishtail his SUV around. One side of the car actually lifted slightly off the ground. Vic took off again heading back the way he'd come, heading right for Joe.

If the distance was shorter, Joe would have used his car to knock Vic's off the road. It was already damaged. But at this distance any such maneuver could be fatal for either one of them. Instead, he made a wide turn so that he came around just after Vic's car passed heading south. For a flash, he saw Vic's face as he drove by, full of panic, hands glued to the wheel. Joe tore off after him. "Hank, he just stopped at the northern roadblock, then turned around. He's coming your way."

"I know. The guys at the other roadblock just told us. We're ready. Are we authorized to fire?"

"If you have to. If it looks like he's trying to ram you. Don't shoot if he just turns around again. Hoping he'll see he's got no options and give up this crazy scheme."

"What are you gonna do?"

"I'm following behind him now. Assuming he doesn't turn right up ahead and head back toward town, think I'll drive past that intersection and stop somewhere between it and you. Use my car to block the road."

"You know," Hank said, "might be a good idea to stop on that tight curve above the fishing pond. He'd have to slow down there quite a bit. Might be easier to force him to stop there."

"Good idea, that's what I'll do. You let me know what he does when he reaches you."

"Will do," Hank said.

Joe gave up trying to catch Vic's car. He still drove at a high speed but decided there was no point risking his neck at night on these curvy roads. Vic really had nowhere else to go.

A couple minutes more and Joe reached the set of winding curves that led to the spot Hank had suggested. The actual curve beside the clearing that led down to the path and pond was just up ahead. Joe decided to stop here, figuring there'd be enough room for Vic to stop after rounding the curve before colliding into his car. He maneuvered it so that it blocked both lanes, kept it on, the headlights, the blue lights, even his emergency lights, then got out.

He popped the trunk, got out a big camping-sized flashlight and walked back toward the rear of his car. Needed to get far enough away in case Vic was going too fast to stop and ran right into it. Heard the radio come on, ran back to the front seat.

"Joe, Hank here. Well, don't know what he's thinking. Saw us, slammed on his brakes, and spun around. He's heading back your way."

"The guy's desperate, Hank. Maybe he thinks I won't be here, and he can catch the road heading back into town. Least he didn't try to ram you guys. I'm right here where we discussed. Car's blocking the road. Either he'll stop, or my car will stop his."

"You well out of the way?"

"Will be soon as I get off this radio."

"Should be there in less than a minute, the speed he's going. Hope he does the smart thing."

"I'll get back with you soon as I know," Joe said. "If he smashes into my car, be looking for me on your cell phone."

"Got it."

Joe waited, said a quick prayer, had his gun in one hand, the big flashlight in the other. Turned it on, pointed it toward the road up ahead but in a way that wouldn't blind Vic as he came around the curve. That's when he noticed something he hadn't seen before.

Where were the concrete barriers?

Just then he heard an engine roaring up the hills beyond the curve. Had to be Vic's car. He saw the head-lights first as they whipped around the curve, then the car. He was going way faster than Joe expected. He dove off to the right into some bushes expecting to hear the cars collide any second.

Loud, screeching brakes. Seemed to go on forever. But no crash. He got up, flashed his light. Vic's SUV missed the side of Joe's car by inches. He turned the flashlight on Vic. His face, total fear.

Joe lifted his gun, pointing it at Vic. "C'mon, Vic. It's over. Shut it off and get out of the car."

The next scene was like slow motion. Vic looked right at him. A new look on his face Joe couldn't interpret. He was sure Vic couldn't see him because of the flashlight in his face. "Vic, it's me. Lieutenant Boyd. Come on. It's time to end this."

"You're right, Lieutenant," Vic yelled. "It is."

He put the car in reverse and backed it down the way he came, heading toward the curve.

Joe followed him with the flashlight. "Vic, stop."

But he didn't stop, even when he got to the curve. Went right past it about twenty yards, then slammed on his brakes. Joe couldn't believe what he did next.

Vic hit the gas, drove forward until he reached the clear-ing, accelerating all the while. He swerved left, right into the clearing, past where the concrete barriers should have been. Then he floored it, heading right for the cliff.

Joe ran toward the scene. "Vic, no. Stop!"

But Vic drove his SUV right over the edge. Joe had the flashlight on the car, saw it disappear into the shadows.

He released a deep sigh. "Oh, Lord," he said and sighed again.

A massive crashing, splashing sound arose from the darkness beyond the cliff's edge. Joe hurried toward the sound. Nearing the edge, he got down on his hands and knees, pointed the light down. Just in time to see Vic's blue SUV disappearing into the pond's murky depths.

53

THE LAST FIFTEEN MINUTES HAD BEEN A WHIRLWIND.

Joe had hurried back to his car, knowing Hank's concern, filled him in. Hank had arrived at the scene a few minutes later. After a quick chat, they'd decided to call off the roadblocks, let traffic start flowing again. But within a hundred yards of the clearing by the curve, they'd blocked off the lane on the pond-side of the road. Not that it mattered much this time of night, and way out here. They also decided to let half the guys go home. The rest, unfortunately, would have to rotate a watch through the night.

At the moment, it was just Joe and Hank standing there about ten feet back from the cliff edge.

"Man," Hank said, "didn't see that coming."

Joe had a feeling it could end this way. Well, not exactly. "I thought he might put a gun to his head. He was pretty desperate about not going to prison. Wasn't stupid enough to imagine he'd get off at the end of a trial."

"Why didn't he take our offer to testify against Harvey?"

"Like he said this afternoon, he'd still likely spend the rest of his life in prison. You know, his age. He just wasn't having it, I guess."

"You think this will help or hurt our case against Harvey?"

"I think it'll help," Joe said. He looked toward the edge of the cliff. "An innocent guy doesn't do something like that. Pretty sure that's how a jury will see it, too. And they'll know, Tag and Vic were totally in this together. But, I don't think Tag Harvey is the kind of guy who will change his plea. You know, because of what Vic just did."

"No, he'll figure he's got the kind of money to hire the kind of lawyers who could get him off." Hank looked back toward the road. "What was the deal with the barriers? Why weren't they there?"

"Who knows? My guess? One government department got word they were putting the guardrails back in place today, so they came and took them. Another department had a different date, so they didn't come. If they had been there, Waters couldn't have driven off the edge. Don't know what he'd have done when he got to my car."

"For all we know," Hank said, "he still might've killed himself. Maybe with a gun, or maybe he might've just jumped off the cliff. If he was that desperate."

"Yeah well, you may be right. Sad thing. Will definitely save the taxpayers some money, not having to put him on trial, then all that upkeep in prison."

"Yeah," Hank said, "but then again, gonna cost taxpayers a pretty penny to get that big crane back in here, fetch Waters' SUV out of that pond."

"Yeah, guess the guys who were supposed to put up that

guardrail will catch a break. Which reminds me, I know our guys are gonna hate it, but we're gonna have to post somebody in that clearing by the road 24/7 until we get some better protection by that opening."

"I agree," said Hank. "We need to do it, and they're going to hate it. What about the CSI guys?"

"Really, considering where that car is, there's no reason to get anybody out here till the morning. I'll call the ME, but I doubt he'll come out till we have the body pulled up with the car."

"Well, I still got the contacts for the crane," Hank said. "I'll get that going first thing tomorrow."

They started walking back toward their cars. "Can't believe we're gonna have to do this all over again," Joe said.

"I know," said Hank. "Guess Phil and Emmett will be happy. They'll get another big payday, and another chance to go diving in that pond."

"Phil and Emmet," Joe said. "Yeah, though they didn't seem too enthused about that last assignment."

"Well," Hank said, "I'm sure what they'll find down there this time won't be pretty, but not the stuff that'll give them nightmares. Talk to you tomorrow?"

They parted. Joe headed to his car, while Hank gave instructions to the guys about handling the traffic situation through till morning.

After Joe got into his car, he called Kate.

She picked up right away. "Tell me two things," she said. "You're all right, and you didn't have to shoot anybody."

"I'm all right, and I didn't have to shoot anybody."

"Good," she said. "Now I can take anything else you need to tell me."

He smiled. "Maybe so, Hon. But, you're not going to believe what's happened since I left the dinner table forty minutes ago."

He told her everything...except the part about Vic shooting at him when Joe first confronted him at his house.

That could wait for another day.

EPILOGUE

4 Months Later

THE BIG DAY had finally arrived — the jury had reached a verdict in the trial of Tag Harvey.

Up until two weeks ago, Joe really wasn't sure whether Harvey would be convicted or get off. He really had put some serious money into his legal team, got as close to a Dream Team as this town had ever seen.

Not surprisingly, with Vic Waters dead and Tag Harvey on a short leash because of the trial, no further attempts on Jeremy Schofield's life had been made. He'd arrived at the courthouse, safe and sound, and from Joe's perspective couldn't have done a better job on the witness stand. The prosecutor had told Joe he'd watched the jurors' faces, and he was sure they had totally believed Jeremy was telling the truth.

The most powerful moment undoubtedly came when

Jeremy faced Brew McFarland and Eddie Simmons' parents, and spoke directly to them from the stand. He could barely get through what he'd said, choking up several times, telling them how horrible he felt for them having to live all this time not knowing the truth about what had happened to their sons. He'd only kept silent out of a genuine fear for his life. And then he said this fear was not unfounded. He went on to talk about how several months ago when Joe and Hank had come out to California to interview him, Hank had stopped a hitman who'd come to his studio — hired by Tag and Vic – to keep him from coming here to testify.

Obviously, Tag's lawyers shot to their feet screaming out their objections. The judge, of course, sustained their objections and instructed the jury to disregard the last remark made by the witness—as if anyone could.

To Joe, Jeremy seemed totally believable. In fact, he had been so persuasive, it forced Tag's legal team to abruptly change their strategy. Prior to Jeremy appearing on the stand, they had successfully argued to the jury that there was no physical evidence tying Tag to either crime, including no murder weapon. They'd admitted the St. Christopher's medal clearly proved Vic Waters' guilt. There really was no other reasonable explanation for that medal to be in the bottom of that pond next to the car.

But it was Vic's medal, not Tag's.

Of course, all the circumstantial evidence presented against Tag lined up with the eyewitness testimony Jeremy gave. But Tag's lawyers were able to offer a number of other explanations for that evidence, leaving it up to the jury to decide which of the two men they would believe. And in Tag's defense, they paraded a whole host of character witnesses who testified boldly that there was no way the Tag Harvey they knew was capable of such cold-hearted and violent crimes.

Then came the surprising turnabout when it was announced Harvey would take the stand in his own defense. Previously, his team had told the press they saw no need for him to testify. Clearly, what Jeremy had to say and the way he'd said it gave them reasonable doubt. So, the court all got to hear the ridiculous, totally fabricated fairytale from Tag Harvey, "admitting" that — like Jeremy Schofield — he, too had been a victim of Vic Waters' ruthless, criminal nature.

It was Vic, who had driven the car that night and hit young Eddie Simmons on his bike, not Tag. Vic who had then decided to kill their friend Brewster McFarland, because he refused to go along with the scheme. Tag, like Jeremy, had agreed to stay silent to avoid the same fate. He even broke down in tears at one point, talking about the terror he felt from Vic whenever they'd bump into each other in town. Vic always making sure Tag knew he'd better continue to keep his mouth shut if he didn't want to end up like Brew. He ended by saying how glad he was he could finally share the truth about what really happened, without fearing for his life.

It was utter hogwash.

Joe felt like there was no way the jury would buy this nonsense compared to the far more credible account Jeremy had given. But the prosecutor wasn't so sure, reminding Joe all they needed was to get one or two people on the jury to have reasonable doubt about Tag's guilt.

Then, two weeks ago, everything changed.

Apparently, over the many long years of their marriage,

Tag Harvey's wife had grown so weary of his constant neglect and numerous affairs that she mustered up the courage to turn on her husband. She hadn't been there every day during the trial, but she did come on the four days that Jeremy had testified. She came forward afterward to tell the prosecutor about a secret panel Tag had built in the back of their master bedroom closet that hid a special safe. She knew the officers had missed it when they'd come three months ago to conduct a search warrant, hoping to find the 22 caliber pistol used to shoot McFarland.

She knew for a fact Tag kept a pistol in there, though she didn't know what kind it was. She'd also said she had heard Tag and Vic speaking numerous times on the phone after the news broke about McFarland's body being found in that pond. She didn't hear everything they'd said, but it was plainly obvious they were friends, and that her husband had absolutely no fear of Vic Waters.

And yes, she was willing to testify to this in court. Guess she wasn't about to let this chance go by, to legally be free of him.

And yes, the judge had granted a delay, so that the state could follow up on this new development. They'd found the pistol behind the secret panel in the master bedroom closet, and yes, it was a 22 caliber pistol. And ballistics matched the gun to the bullet that Phil and Emmett — Culpepper's illustrious dive team — had found in the pond.

After this evidence had been presented, and after Tag's wife had gotten down from the stand...no one believed Tag would get away with what he had done. Not even his Dream Team, judging by the look on their faces.

. . .

JOE SAT THERE in the courtroom now, along with everyone else, fully expecting justice to be served. Sitting next to him was Kate, who had gotten completely consumed by this trial, as did most of the town. She was the one who had given Joe all the details about what happened. Since he had been a key witness for the prosecution, he couldn't attend while the evidence was being presented. A few seats down on the same row as them, sat Tom Hazelton, who hadn't missed a single day of the trial.

They'd bumped into each other coming in that morning. Tom had the biggest smile on his face, said his publisher loved the outline he'd sent about the true-crime book he was pitching about this case. "Offered to double my advance from the last one. He couldn't believe when I told him the part about Vic Waters driving his car off a cliff into the same pond he'd pushed McFarland's car into thirty-something years ago. You can't make this stuff up," Tom had said. "I might get a movie deal outta this."

Joe just smiled and said, "Great, Tom. Glad it's working out." No tragedy here for him.

One of the more pleasant things to come of out the trial was the obvious reconciliation of the Schofield brothers. Little brother Dave came every day his brother testified and, even now as they awaited the verdict, he was sitting right beside his brother, Jeremy.

In a row behind him and Kate sat Captain Pendleton and Hank. Of course, Pendleton was thrilled with the job he and Hank had done on the case, solving two mysteries out of the cold case box *for the price of one*, as he'd put it. And the positive publicity for the department was top shelf. He reached over and patted Joe on the shoulder. "This is gonna be so satisfying," he said, pointing toward Harvey.

Joe thought so too. And because Pendleton was in such a good mood, this morning he'd agreed Joe could take off the three weeks following the trial to take Kate, the kids, and their beagle named Chance on a camping trip out west.

A side door opened. The jury came out and took their places. The defendant and legal teams of both sides stood. The judge gave some instructions to the jurors and to the courtroom. The jury foreman handed the verdict info to the bailiff. She looked at it and began to read it aloud.

To no one's surprise, Tag Harvey was found guilty on every count and every charge. His head dropped as each verdict was read. But he was the only one in the courtroom not cheering this result.

After he was led away in handcuffs and all the hugs and handshakes were through, Joe and Kate, along with everyone else, began to clear the courtroom.

"Can't wait to go on this camping trip," Kate said. "We're all packed and ready to go. I just need to call Rachel, let her know we're on our way home."

Their good friends Jack and Rachel Turner would be joining them on this excursion out west. Joe had already mentally prepared himself not to be jealous of Jack's huge camper. And Kate — always the one to help him maintain perspective — had reminded him that he, too, could afford something like that if he had studied long and hard for many years, got a PhD in History, became a Dean at a prestigious university, and had written several best-selling books.

To which Joe had simply replied, "Thanks, Hon. Never thought about it that way."

WANT TO HELP THE AUTHOR?

IF YOU ENJOYED READING THIS BOOK, THE BEST THING YOU CAN do to help Dan is very simple—*tell others about it.* Word-of-mouth is the most powerful marketing tool there is. Better than expensive TV commercials or full-page ads in magazines.

Dan would greatly appreciate it if you'd rate his book and leave a brief review. Even a sentence or two will help.

You can **write a review** for *Treacherous Waters* on Amazon by going to the site and typing "Treacherous Waters by Dan Walsh" in the Search field.

Just scroll down the page a little till you see "Customer Reviews" on the Left. Below that is a button: "Write a Customer Review."

WANT TO READ MORE?

IF YOU ENJOYED, *Treacherous Water* you'll be happy to learn it's actually Book 4 of Dan's Bestselling Joe Boyd Suspense series. Have you read the other three? If not, they're available on Amazon in print, Kindle, or Kindle Unlimited.

- *If These Walls Could Talk*
- *An Inconvenient Death*
- *The Scandal of Mercy*

The Joe Boyd Suspense series is actually a "**Sequel Series**" to Dan's bestselling 4-Book *Jack Turner Suspense Series*. The events and mysteries that unfold in those 4 books take place a few years prior to the Joe Boyd series and include many of the same characters and places. These novels have received over 2,800 Amazon Reviews (4.6 Star Avg). Book 1 is called, *When Night Comes*.

WANT TO STAY CONNECTED?

If you'd like to get an email alert whenever Dan has a new book coming out or when a special deal is being offered on any of Dan's existing books, click on his website link below and sign up for his newsletter (it's right below the Welcome paragraph). Also, **every first-time visitor to his site can choose to receive one of Dan's bestselling novels for FREE** (see the Tab for the Free Book in the Menu).

From his homepage, you can also contact Dan or follow him on Facebook or Goodreads.

www.danwalshbooks.com

ACKNOWLEDGMENTS

There is really one person I absolutely must thank for helping to get *Treacherous Water* into print. That's my wife, Cindi. Her editorial advice and input on this book was indispensable. And I want to thank my friend Mark Mynheir, a great writer and officer with the Palm Bay Police Department, who helped keep me straight on police matters. He's served as a SWAT Team Member and Homicide Detective.

I also need to thank my great proofreading team. They help to catch any of the typos or other little distracting errors in the manuscript before the book goes to print: Debbie Mahle, Jann Martin, and Terri Smith.

Dan Walsh

ABOUT THE AUTHOR

Dan was born in Philadelphia in 1957. His family moved down to Daytona Beach, Florida in 1965, when his father began to work with GE on the Apollo space program. That's where Dan grew up.

He married Cindi, the love of his life in 1976. They have 2 grown children and 5 grandchildren. Dan served as a pastor for 25 years then began writing fiction full-time in 2010. His bestselling novels have won numerous awards, including 3 ACFW Carol Awards (he was a finalist 6 times) and 4 Selah Awards. Four of Dan's novels were finalists for RT Reviews' Inspirational Book of the Year. One of his novels, *The Reunion*, is being made into a major full-length feature film.